I0824520

I AM MALORY

a novel

VEVINA-ANNE SWANSON

First edition: December 2020

To those struggling with mental disorders. It's
alright to feel sad, it's alright to cry.
But try when you can, to keep your chin high.

To those that have loved ones with mental disorders.
Be patient. Be empathetic. Most importantly,
help them express their inner voice.
Help them learn to love every piece of themselves,
even if they aren't the prettiest.
That is the first step to healing.

I AM MALORY

CHAPTER ONE

MALORY

IT BEGAN WITH A SINGLE NOTE, plucking the voices out of the audience's throats. I took a slow and deep breath. Cold distilled air filled my lungs and lingered down my throat. With closed eyes, I let my ears take control. This was something I enjoyed doing while performing. Feeling the pressure of keys sinking down below my fingers and hearing the sound of spiraling notes continuing to form and disappear around me. The lights above blew a soft whisper as I finally opened my eyes, making them sting and bloom with small bubbled tears. This was what it felt like to be alive.

Gazing down, I watched my hands scatter across black and white keys. They were so mechanical, so precise. Inhuman. What was more inhumane was the audience's presence, spectating my every move. The rows of people seated from the stage were mainly composed of my competitors and their parents. Though the mass wasn't as big as usual, that didn't stop me from feeling the claws of their eyelashes pricking at my back. The scouring youthful faces, asking themselves… will she miss?

The lights tracing off my pale body and raven-colored dress urged me to sway with my music in a hypnotic trance. The deeper I got into the piece; the more things faded away. First it was those around me, then the stage below me. Finally, the lights above me blinked away into a small glimmer. My own reality had awakened, flying alongside a hill of notes coated in legato. I embraced this moment. It was something I'd been working so hard towards and didn't plan on letting it go. Never.

I'm almost done.

The surge of energy bouncing from wrist to palm grew quicker, hungry to savor the last few notes of my piece. The beating in my chest continued as adrenaline rushed through my body. The peddling grew faster, the piece's way of saying it needed to breathe. It was coming to a close, Chopin's monstrous Nocturne. How sweet and calming his pieces were to the ears of the listener. It was a dessert of pedal pumps swaying in a glass of notes for those to taste. For musicians like myself, being the one to create the sound was a whole different story. Like dangling off a cliff, seeing the stretch of how far you were from the bottom. Realizing that your hands will soon tire and make you fall. Bursting a vein in a hand from too much practice or drowning in the blurred noise of too much pedal and sweat. But I liked it. The feeling gave me a sense of how alive I was and of how far I'd come. How those hours of playing in doubt really did amount to something.

I wouldn't be hanging off any cliff today. This performance was less stressful than usual. Thank goodness. No judges were there to be skeptical of my abilities as a pianist. I did win a spot in that last round after all. This concert was to celebrate my achievement of grabbing one of the two slots available after a tiresome battle that lasted close to a month. Yes, it was very difficult. That I could admit. My competitors were no amateurs and all played exceptionally well. Hearing and seeing them mature through the years… It was almost scary how fast some improved. From what I had to do to reach these heights, I wondered what they were made to do.

Although I wanted to relax for just a beat, my guard had to remain high. Reporters could've been watching for all I knew.

One bad review and my rep—my teacher's reputation—could spiral down the drain. All his dedication towards my music had to live up to something.

My hands skimmed over the last few notes before being greeted with silence. The piece was now done. Yet, the performance was still not over. My hands, cold to the touch, yet pulsing with an internal furnace, hovered over the keys after striking that last note. The sound of a final lonesome ring jumped from wall to wall, fearing for its life as it faded away. I slipped away from the bench and Steinway, my dress dragging behind me as I stood up. Although I squinted from the lights on the ceiling, I still made out the figures in the far distance. The view in front of me was speckled with people in fancy attire. One by one, each began to emerge, and I lowered my back, head tucked between my arms. As sudden as thunder, the applause came for me.

I rose up. Maybe a hundred or so had watched my performance. The individuals that partook were mostly inner circle people from the competition; the performers that didn't make the final round, their parents, and donors towards this competition.

After observing all the watchful eyes, smiling at a face or two, I took a final bow.

"Bravo! Molto Bene!"

Voices in the distance rolled compliments at me. I grinned at the crowd one last time, taking in all the glory before it faded away. Then I took off. The echoing of my shoes followed behind me as my shadow crept off into the velvet curtains at the end of the stage. As I disappeared behind the curtains, a man came out onto the stage. Honens. I met him at a public piano near the train station. The ones colored in graffiti or marble tile. He had been sitting on it for quite some time as I waited for my father on the train. Little did I know that he was actually the founder of this branch. He was playing the first movement of Bach's Symphony No. 5. Before I knew it, I stood beside him, completing the duet with him. Honens recognized me a few times at other competitions and asked if I wanted to join his Brams and Honens Piano Competition. Little did he know, I had already applied there. One day too late. He told me that he could find a spot for me there and now here I was.

"What a lovely performance that was! Once again, that was Chopin's Nocturne Op. 27, No. 2 played by Malory Hawkins. In a few moments we'll have our last performer come out on stage!"

His voice echoed while I entered the backstage. There were barely any lights, giving me enough darkness to release the exhaustion trapped inbetween my closed lips. Plates of sweat rested under my armpits and I wiped them away with my palms. All the while, the chills of the auditorium made me search for my jacket hidden by darkness.

"Looking for this?"

A voice came closer along with something soft flying at my face. I pulled off the cloth, feeling the familiar texture in my hands. The body that appeared was my professor Andre Petrov. A man in his mid-forties. His dark purple suit faded in with the darkness around us. There was enough light to distinguish his white folded napkin tucked in his breast and something pink peeking from behind his back. Judging by his pencil-like stance, my professor desperately tried to hide them from my sight.

"Congratulations on your performance!" His grin brought light into the room.

"Thank you." Moving closer to him, I stretched my head to the side. "I know it's dark, but I can see what's behind your back."

Defeated, my professor let out a sigh and surrendered the bouquet to me. He sometimes brought me flowers after performing, along with a smile slowly aging with time. Other musicians got flowers from their family members, so I remember finding it odd when he first got them for me. But over the years, it became something to look forward to. He was family to me, being my teacher since I could remember. Professor saw something in me that others didn't. Some type of talent I'd never been able to see in myself. Over the years of studying under him, he helped my talent flourish. Now I hoped it was something everyone could see too.

"I heard that passage you'd been struggling with last week. You really got it down this time." Professor revealed the pink baby's breath that smelled like peaches. I took the bouquet, leaving my torso completely smothered by them. My face hid in its embrace as I breathed in the soft fragrance.

"Thank you for always bringing these for me."

His laughter teased his thick black curls. Small creases pinched the sides of his closed eyes.

"Malory, Chopin would have been very proud if he heard you today." Professor paused, looking at the room's closed door. "But I can see it in your eyes, you're tired. Are you sure you still have enough energy to face that reporter today? You can still cancel before he comes knocking."

I nodded. "Of course! He's been waiting for me all this time and scheduled an interview with me months ago… It would be rude if I suddenly said no."

"Just… Don't over work yourself. You need rest."

"Don't worry, I got plenty of sleep last night."

The lowering of his eyebrows gave hint that he knew more. Or maybe he caught a glimpse of the plums growing underneath my eyes. I rubbed an eye, thinking it would wipe the sleepiness away. Because of how long professor had known me, he also knew that I sometimes overworked. A pounding headache and dizzy brain was something I hated, yet grew accustomed to. Staring at those black railroads of notes for hours on end did a lot to a body that barely left teenhood. Although, the thought of a single mistake while performing always outweighed my well-being. Music was, and always would be alive. Things with life weren't always predictable. So, every day, I practiced a familiar piece as if I had never seen it in my life.

Our conversation was disrupted by a soft knock on the wooden door that sealed away the backstage from the rest of the building.

"Speak of the devil." Professor brought a finger to his brow. "Hopefully, this thing won't be as long as last time."

"Don't worry, it's only his job. And I'm glad he's interested in my playing."

I went over to open the door, viewing a lone reporter and two camera men. They wore tan suits and slicked back hair to the point of it looking like wax. The reporter held a clipboard in his hand and spun a pen with the other.

"Hello, Miss Hawkins! Your performance was stunning as always." Even his voice sounded forced. A pitch too high for his looks and the eagerness of wanting to interview me revealed by the protruding veins in his neck.

"Do you feel prepared for the finale? Or do you think this will be another tie?"

"Can we bring this to a quieter area? If you don't mind? The other performer is about to start, it would be rude of us." Andre came forward, his face shadowed with disappointment.

"O-oh of course! I'm so sorry miss for my rude behavior."

We left the backstage and walked past a hall flooded with people pacing back and forth. Most of them were other performers I had competed with. Each one of them usually participated in the same competition as I. Although we didn't make any type of eye contact, I felt their glares scraping at my back. If I were to come face to face with one, they'd greet me with hugs and act as if we'd been friends forever. It was one reason why father didn't like me talking to them. He'd say they were toxic. I guess in a few ways, he was right.

As we scuffled through the madness of rushed feet heading towards a room brimming with complimentary food, one musician grazed my shoulder. Small specks of pollen from my bouquet sprinkled to the ground. The contact was light, I knew it was intentional. Seeing his dark swooped hair and bronzed skin with that tense look in each step he took, told me it was Oliver Walker. The pianist I'd always tied with. Never in our musical careers had we ever been able to beat one another. Maybe it was how similar our hands moved, how I often mistook his playing for my own. Each battle was the same with us being in first place if we happened to be in the same competition. It had happened three times already. The first time the judges heard us head on with each other, they made us tie with no problem. It was something that never happened too often in competitions anyway. Another time, we'd ended up having the same piece. We played as the composer had written. Down to every accent mark and crescendo. Small competitions were agreeing to water down the first prize. Others happened to have two slots for their winners. That was three years ago, and we haven't battled since then. Now that I was twenty, I hoped this competition would've settled things. The judges made sure that if we were somehow tied, then the chairman would sever it.

I glanced at him while following the man with his plastic-looking hair. Sure enough, Oliver's face scoured at me, filled with a dead expression as he stood in place and watched me walk away.

We entered a small room filled with antique green-cushioned chairs, vanilla coffee walls, and a lone window. The reporter sat across from me, our bodies separated by a wooden table, the ends rounded like a bear's claw. The two camera men followed us and prepared their equipment, ready to record my every action. I knew how these interviews went down. This was customary for finalists during competitions and made into a disk later for purchasing. Other times, reporters were given permission to enter the competitions in hopes of getting a few words from the next greatest performer. I'd been to many before, so this was nothing but a walk in the park. Multiple questions would've been thrown at me. These reporters never hesitated for a second to feed me with a silver spoon. Looking past their giddy personalities and enthusiastic questions, I knew they only cared about what I was, not who I was.

"Hello, Miss Hawkins! It's so wonderful to be able to have this interview with you today. I know you're a busy young lady! So thank you for taking the time to have this interview with us! You were stunning as always up there!" Crossing his legs, he skimmed through his clipboard.

"Thank you, sir." I smiled, still keeping the bouquet close to my lap.

"You know..." He began again and leaned. "Ever since you started getting a bigger name in the music world, you never ceased to surprise people like myself. But that does take so much energy and time! Not to mention the dedication! As you've said in the past, you've been homeschooled. Correct?"

"Yes, that's right." I held onto the flowers tighter, feeling an internal fog starting to reel in.

"Alrighty. So now that you're past your teenage years, do you feel like you'll have more time to finally socialize and do other things besides music?"

I looked down at the bouquet, studying the reporter's words.

"My mind hasn't changed since I was younger. It is and has been hard for me to go out and meet people since it's something I never really do. At the same time, music has given me the opportunity to meet many other musicians like myself."

"Would Oliver be one of those musicians?" The man's back curved forward so much, as if hoping to roll any stones of gossip across it.

Oliver's glare was printed on my back again, hot and intensified. I looked behind, ready to meet his cold eyes. The moment I did, his ghostly presence dissipated. Only the camera men stood behind me and my professor with his arms crossed loosely in the back of the room.

"Something like that."

"It's been what…? Three or four times now… No? That you two have been tied. Do you feel as if this one will be different?"

"I do. The judges have known about our predicament of being tied. When they found out that we were the last two for the final round, they told us personally that only one of us will make it."

"You two butting heads for all these years. Has it made you two sour towards one another?"

"I can't really say." I felt Oliver's shoulder bounce off of me again. "I've never been that close with him."

This back and forth paddle to ball conversation continued for a while longer. I was actually surprised at how short it had been compared to other interviews. Maybe he wasn't hearing what he wanted from me, my answers being short and vague. Before I knew it, the camera men already packed up all their things and I shook the reporter's hand one last time before watching him leave.

"I swear. Guys like him don't have a filter. But he really seems to know his stuff about you." Andre stretched out of the corner, massaging the palms of his hands. "You ready to win first place?"

"I sure hope so…" I held the bouquet in a single hand, zipping up my jacket and adjusting the brown fuzzy collar with the other.

"Heading out already? You know there's free food in the other room. And I'm sure there are still a lot of people that want to talk with you."

I pulled out my phone and slipped it back into my pocket. Three new messages. Four missed calls. Five fast heart beats.

"I know, I know… But my father has been waiting in the car for a while now. It's already late."

"I really never get him." Andre let out a heavy sigh. "He should come here, instead of waiting out there."

"He's quiet, that's all."

"Quiet?" His pitch cranked higher and was filled with a sarcastic tone. "Well, I don't know about that. I myself am going to eat." He took a step out of the open door leading back into the bustling hallway. "I'll see you on the stage tomorrow. Work hard, okay? Remember to take care of yourself too."

I skimmed past a few people, shaking hands with a few losing contestants and guests that came due to the fact that this was a free open performance. Some struck up a conversation with me. I made sure it was short. When I got to the exit, a blast of pins scattered across my face. Within seconds, snow dusted over my shoulders as I walked out onto the bustling street. Wind whipped my black hair in a hungry manner. It was everywhere. White particles blanketed anything within its icy grip. Darkness was something that didn't exist in New York. In the distance were bold lights of cars constantly hitting on their brakes due to the heavy traffic. Behind me were the lights of Carnegie Hall. It danced in intricate patterns past my body, coloring my hair with strands of bright gold. The calling of numbness in my knees didn't bother me much. I was born and raised here after all.

As I waited on the pavement for my father's car to arrive, I thought back to the conversation with that reporter. Not just him, but all the past ones as well that always tried to tickle answers out of me.

Was this something other people experienced too?

I thought it was at first. Living in the present with a void for the past. Father never explained it completely to me. In fact, he never would've if I didn't ask. One story was that I hit my head hard when I was younger. Another was that I got a bad fever, making me forget huge chunks of memory by the time it finally broke. Each story was always different. Eventually, I stopped asking because he got really mad. Was I really homeschooled? I only had his answers to believe. I was glad it never brought harm to my playing. That was all that really mattered.

Past the drifting snow, I saw the lone figure of a man. His familiar jade eyes hadn't caught sight of me as his brown coat tussled in the wind with soft snaps. All his attention was on an empty brown bottle. When he heard me coming closer, a glance was all I was given.

"You took your damn time," Father began as he walked off. "I circled so many times around this building thinking you'd get out soon. All the while needing to take a piss. I had no choice but to park in the back and let it all out."

"I'm sorry. That reporter had an appointment with me after the performance. I don't remember his name but I'm sure you must remember. I didn't realize how long things took." I hurried behind him while feeling each step in the snow moisten the rim of my heels.

"Well, you did. And now I have to walk all the way back in this cold."

It took us under ten minutes to reach the parking structure. He had stopped speaking. Only the sound of fresh liquid glugging down his throat, the crunching of his shoes, and the sound of his thick coat scrubbing against his skin. I rubbed the back of my hand across my nose which had gone raw. The cold did seem to stop the dripping. The chipping paint of his black car gave me a sigh of relief. The corners of my feet were throbbing, making the earth wobble back and forth below me. Father turned the key in the ignition and backed out of the parking lot. Once he did, the silence broke. Not from his voice, but from the clanking of bottles swaying drunkenly under my feet.

"Get changed as soon as we get home and start reviewing your piece for tomorrow. Dinner is in the freezer, but no eating until you finish that passage."

I stretched the seat belt and clicked myself in. "Of course, father."

CHAPTER TWO

MALORY

Tick. Tick. Tick.

The mechanical clink of a metal hand continued to move slowly in a circular motion. Time seemed to not exist within that room. The clock was the only confirmation that this was in fact reality. It felt like it could've been minutes, or perhaps hours that passed by since I sat down. The chewing of nails and the patterning of fingertips on a music book's surface echoed throughout my years. I turned to look around for the worried students. It was only him and I sitting a few chairs away from each other. Any closer and my jugular might have been ripped out. His silent breathing heated the room, leaving a stale taste in my mouth from how long I hadn't been talking.

Two heavy weights hung over my eyes as I stared at the boy. Wrong choice of words, he was far from one. Though being a year younger than myself, everything about him seemed aged. Maybe it was the rounded shadows of sleepless nights under his eyes. Oliver's posture was of a wooden board, as if already on stage. He stared off into nothing, not bothering to break contact with whatever he was looking at on the wall. As time passed, he rocked back and forth in small intervals. Only then was I able to realize that he must've been nervous. His hands clasped together to the point of them pigmenting brown and red. Maybe that was why I spoke to him. I'd never seen hands shake that much in my entire life.

"Good luck... with your playing today." My voice barely louder than a whisper, continued to prance back and forth in the room. I felt the sleeplessness drying out my throat. I shouldn't have played so much last night...

No reply. His stature remained the same, his head not bothering to acknowledge my existence. I expected no less. He and I were never really on good terms. In fact, we were never on any terms at all. A cold shoulder or quick glance was usually all he shared with me. Like oil and water.

"Good luck today." Maybe he hadn't heard me the first time. If he ignored me this time, I knew to give up.

Of course, his reply back was nothing more than a puff of air, his eyes moving farther away from the blank space he fixated on—distancing his eyes away from me as much as possible. Oliver's fingers continued to tap in sync with the clock's consistent moan. His fingers were those of a hard working pianist. His mother and father might deny that he was anything but. Though, the veins stringed from each finger to the wrist told a different story. Each moved independently from one another, revealing the wear and tear of hours and hours spent on the Black Beast. The room was quiet enough to hear the crackle of each bone grind and pop against one another.

"Oliver Walker, pianist number twenty-eight! Please prepare for the stage! You're on in five!"

The shout of a man's voice came from the speakers on each corner of the walls. The arrival of its presence made Oliver's skin look like it would've jumped off. His knees buckled against one another like a timid goat. My gaze was still stuck on those chestnut hands, their meticulous tapping now evolving into a pair of curled balls. Oliver was often called names such as 'robot' or other lifeless nicknames due to his permanent poker face and uncaring nature. No one ever said it to his face, but they'd be surprised at how loud whispers can be. During this moment—a split moment—I saw a human. He must've seen me watch him, or maybe he knew the entire time. Perhaps, it was what made him more nervous. But I really meant no harm. Oliver never acknowledged me, talked to me… What more could I have done but continue to watch?

"It's alright to be nervous. We all get like that sometimes."

As quickly as it came, the nervousness, fidgeting legs, and clenched fists disappeared. My smile did too. There it was again, the robot everyone always spoke about. It got up slowly, turning its gears to face me with those cold fisheyes. My rear itched to the back of the wooden chair.

"I won't let you win." Oliver's words were black and white. Plain, yet managed to wedge a dagger in the ball of my throat.

I tried to swallow but his gaze sucked my tongue dry. Then he was gone. Black suit and slicked-back hair, growing smaller and smaller into the hallway. His disappearing presence was engulfed by the swing of the wooden door that led backstage. My lungs unclenched. With a hand wedged in the middle of my chest, I looked at the television propped high above me. The small screen revealed Oliver coming onto the stage and three shadows that I suspected were judges, sitting right below. The grainy quality of the screen zoomed in closer on him and I still squinted to see.

While waiting for his piece to begin, I kneaded my thumb into my palm, hoping the stimulation would keep me awake. It'd been quite a while since I really got on my rear with realizing how far ahead my expectations were of myself. It started with playing an extra hour before sleep. Then two, three. I'd have to force myself to bed sometimes as the sun crept through my window.

I leaned my head against the wall, still hearing the pattering of the sweat-slicked notes from last night. The yells of my father as he downed another bottle. Twelve turned to two, and two turned into four. Even if I had enough sleep, it wouldn't have helped. I had another episode while in bed. They were always random; sometimes happening once or twice a week. The only thing that was consistent was them happening at night. Recently they had been increasing in number, sometimes occurring every night. At least I had the privilege of knowing when one was coming close. It usually started at my fingertips and toes. A static feeling that would numb my entire body till I couldn't move. A few moments later would come the blackness, followed by morning and a booming in my brain that made me question if I really slept at all.

Oliver's piece rolled in. The first notes of Rhapsody in Blue plucked my eyes awake. It was surprising that the judges allowed him to play such a large piece. But how long it was didn't scare me. Quality over quantity.

My phone chimed in harmony with the ticking clock and I took it from my side.

Good luck today! I'll be a little late because of traffic but I will be there. Stay focused.

Seeing the text from my professor helped spark some energy in me. It quickly died out when the weights began to pull down on my lids again. Round and round the notes in my head went. Their pitch was so piercing that they almost sounded like violin strings. Oliver's piece made its way past the middle, rolling over hills of notes both precise and to the composer's liking. It was nothing short of perfect. I guess the judges knew that too, judging by their shadowy heads nodding on the tiny screen like dandelions.

Seven minutes later and my body aching for rest, his piece came to a close. I must have dozed off for most of it. My body slouched to the side of the chair. When I looked back up, he was gone. I got up too, shaking my hands, trying to wake them up. I heard the sound of the backstage door slamming shut and his feet treading closer. Grabbing for my music book, Oliver came back in, dropping his textbook onto a chair with a loud slap and slumping onto another with a glazed face. My mouth widened before closing tightly again. There was no need to try and make small talk. I already knew he wouldn't respond.

"Malory Hawkins! Number eighteen, be ready in five!" The voice called for me.

Before, leaving I simply mouthed a quiet, "You played really well."

Making my way into the hallway, the floor yawned under me. Each step I took became heavier than the last. An unknown symphony of strings started playing in the distance. That was impossible. Oliver and I were the only ones playing today. I ignored the sound and kept going. At moments while walking, I was barely able to see at all. It was only when I felt the smack of a door that my mind snapped back into reality. A moaning throb planted its kiss in the middle of my head as I pushed the door open. The backstage was close to being nothing but darkness, just like yesterday. It wouldn't be surprising if a lot of accidents happened back here. Ropes from large curtains were spiraled in a jumbled mess. Wires which lead to nowhere were hanging vines against the walls. It was the lights from the stage that helped guide me from slipping.

When I came into the light, no clapping was heard. This was normal for a final round. Usually, guests came to listen during concerts of the winning performers. On days like these, it was only the judges and pianist. One had climbed up the small stairs at the side of the stage and greeted me. Her white hair was tucked neatly behind her ears.

"Goodluck," she said as I gave her the music score. Clarice was always the kindest to us, always greeting performers to help alleviate their nerves. The other two judges didn't seem to care, doing nothing but scribbling on their notepads and constantly adjusting their thin-rimmed glasses.

I sat on the bench, hoping the feeling of exhaustion might've gone away a little. My vision began to warp, and hairs poked outward from the bumps on my spine.

"Alright, whenever you are ready," one of the judges said, his head finally looking up from a piece of paper. Had his face always looked that twisted?

To my surprise, everything was going very well. All the accent marks, crescendos, and staccatos were not a beat off. My chords were crisp, and the pedal wasn't muddying my notes. Although as time went by, the heaviness was becoming overwhelming.

Just keep pushing through, don't stop. Don't stop. Sleep later. Tire later.

My thoughts came in my father's voice. By the time I got to the middle of the piece, reality wasn't as close as it should've been. Each piano key blended with the one beside it, transforming into a mesh of melting paint. The space around me was morphing into a euphoric spiral. I felt my body moving with it, tilting and stretching with it. My hands... My hands were starting to tingle.

Keep going... Keep going. I have no... keep...

The feeling of a static television switched on, starting with the gnawing at the bottom of my feet. Its movement was slow, inching its way to my knees, locking them in place. My foot was now frozen onto the pedal, stretching the sound of notes into infinity. Then it attacked my arms, turning them into a pair of concrete blocks. My fingers tried to escape, swarming to the surface, as if it could outrun whatever had taken hold of me.

Stop... No stopping... I can't...

I wanted to scream. My mouth couldn't move. Nothing of me could. By then, the music stopped, and the world had turned on its side. The stage was no longer a horizon but a surface for me to lay on.

What's this now?

My face pressed against a new texture. It was cold and mixed in with the tingles pulsing throughout my body like a swarm of bees. An aching slap stretched from my brows to the heels of my shoes as I fell down.

Get up. You need to keep playing. Get up! Please get up!

Someone or something up there must have heard my plea. Because the only thing I remembered before all turned black was the shuffling of shoes, the murmuring of voices, and hands wrapping behind my back.

CHAPTER THREE

MALORY

NOT SURE IF IT WAS A BLESSING OR A CURSE to awaken from my blanket of sleep. I crawled into consciousness, climbing the ladder towards an aching pain on my temple doors. Though my eyes were closed, I felt a constant sting of kisses across my eyelids. It was the sensation of closed eyes up towards a bright summer's day. I lifted a limp hand towards my head, hoping to suppress the splitting pain. There was a slight tug at the bend of my arm. I traced a hand up my arm and something soft bumped into my fingers. It was long and slender. A continuous road my fingers paced onto as it reached my arm. Only then did I realize how uncomfortable the area felt. A rubber tube disappeared into my arm from where it was taped down. My mind grew nauseous as I took in the clean and synthetic-smelling air.

My memories were faint. All my mind could piece together was the feeling of something soft and white, then a swirling hard color of brown. I was clad in black, my body laced in a darkness that reached to the floor.

White snow

I saw it, I felt it. Snow was scuffed on the sides of my shoes while I held the music score in my gloved hands. I wore black that day, as I usually did at any other performance. But when had this happened? Was it yesterday? The day before? A ghostly instrument made its appearance the more I concentrated on this cloudy vision. The being struck a few keys into my head, the song slowly growing in volume. It was a beautiful song, something that seemed too perfect to be real. It was Chopin, soft and lovely. The sound continued to play as fingers twisted and convulsed into branches. The notes grew louder and louder, creating a sound so menacing. The notes contorted like rotten bark swelling in the marsh. Then the twigs snapped, the tree fell, and I saw myself crash to the floor. My eyes snapped open, panic placing a heavy palm against my ribs. The quick movement of rising up brought my brain into a whirl.

The room's brightness brought my pupils into a pin-pricking size. But the light didn't come from the windows that were pitch black with night. Instead, the light came from bright panels above my head. Through my frantic state, I focused on a figure shuffling towards me.

"Where am I?" My dry lips stung. Cream-colored curtains welcomed the night with spread legs. It was a simple room. Not much was inside except for a few wooden drawers and a soft beeping sound in the distance. It was a heart rate monitor beside me with a clamp over the tip of my finger.

"Please, lie back down sweetie! Try not to move too much!" The looming figure turned out to be a woman in nursing attire. Her voice and appearance were both foreign to me. Royal blue scrubs with small clusters of flowers printed on the fabric. Her hair was tightly spun into a brown bun. She wore thick mascara, clumping her eyelashes into the resemblance of fly legs. I could have sworn the smell of cherry medicine was lingering around her.

"Where am I?" I rubbed my throat. "I'm supposed to be on stage."

The nurse grabbed a pitcher of water off a small desk near the bed. Hearing the water trickle into the Styrofoam cup made the crevices on my lips feel that much drier. As soon as it was filled, I snatched it from her, drowning my lungs in water, feeling my parched throat soothed by the cold moisture.

"You're in the hospital sweetie. Do you remember anything at all?" Her voice sounded worried, strained to an unnaturally high pitch.

I ran a hand against my lips, smearing the water up my arm as I gave her back the cup.

"I was performing… It was my final round." I curled my fingers into my palms, feeling the dreaminess in my body begin to escape. Yes, I had performed, but that was all. Playing and playing and playing… and…

"I-I stopped…" My body tightened, still haunted by a looming weight in my chest. Two warm throbs came from the IV tube nuzzling clear chemicals into my arm.

"Stopped what sweetie?" Her big brown eyes blinked at me. The dozens of fly legs clashed with one another.

"My body started tensing… I… I couldn't control my hands, I couldn't move!"

The bubbling of darkness around me, how I couldn't hear anything. The way my hands lost control, having a mind of their own. Then the rest was blank. No, flashes. Flashes of something in the colors of red and blue. These feelings that I had no idea of expressing stayed in the pit of my stomach, stomping onto my bladder. I grabbed for my hair, hoping it would stop. Instead, my hand felt something soft pressed on my forehead.

"What's on my head?"

"I've applied a cleaning solution and band aid there." The nurse rolled a chair next to the hospital's bed and sat. "You weren't bleeding badly. Don't worry, it was just a scratch."

I leaned back into the bed, rearing my head deep into the pillow. The stage kept moaning for me, its tongue lapping at my fingers and chest. I wanted to go back but my chances were gone, ruined. All those hours and pain building up into my wrists reached into my eyes, turning them dewy. Father wanted me to play well. He made me try harder than my limits, staying with me for all those hours in the night. What was I going to tell him?

Getting back up, the nurse spoke again in that kind yet artificial tone. “I’m going to let the doctor know that you’re awake. I’ll let your father know as well. For now, try to rest more.”

My intestines knotted together as I heard his name.

I practically gave that competition away to Oliver like it was some easy gift!

The beeping of the heart monitor went into a short sprint and then slowed back down again. So many artists were successful at a much younger age. This was my chance to make a mark and break the everlasting ties with Oliver. Honens’ next competition would be two years from now. The age limit was twenty one, Oliver was only nineteen. He could join again, possibly breaking another record and gain more recognition. For me, it would be over.

A light knocking was heard on the closed door accompanied by a lone shadow.

“Come in,” I said.

What I expected to be father ended up being professor. His shoulders raised as if invading a private area.

“Malory? Are you feeling alright?”

“Professor! Yeah… yeah. I woke up a few minutes ago.”

Professor’s hands weren’t hidden behind his back like the last time I saw him. Instead, they folded in the front, cupping each other. He also hadn’t changed from his uniform except for folding up his dress sleeves above the elbows. That must have meant that I hadn’t been here for as long as I thought. He took the padded seat that the nurse was on and slumped into it.

"What happened to you? Did the doctor tell you anything yet?" His voice was softer than usual and appeared timid. As if afraid that anything louder would have shattered me apart.

"No… Not yet… I messed up… Didn't you hear me? I stopped playing! I just froze there!"

"You were playing wonderfully, but that's not of concern right now." He tried to reassure me with a smile slowly showing wrinkles of age. Then the smile disappeared. "I've always told you to take care of yourself. I didn't realize you were breaking yourself though. Had I been too hard on you?"

"No! Never! I know you always tell me to be healthy but this week… I just practiced too hard…"

"What did you do?" He leaned in closer with his hands gripping onto his knees. "Now's not the time for lying."

I bit my tongue. "I-I stayed up later than usual. I had to get that one passage right!"

I'm not sure why I hid the truth from the professor. Nothing was wrong with what my father did those past nights. His tactics were bound to make me play better. Even if it happened until the sun rose. And yet, it caught myself off guard how I stored that information away.

"Forget the competition. That should be the least of your worries right now." His frown told me that he wasn't completely convinced with my story. I wanted to protest. But from how tired his eyes looked and how raw my throat felt, I quieted myself.

"I was so shocked when I saw you collapse." He began again. "Oliver was still in the waiting room when I arrived. Grabbing his books and getting ready to leave. When we saw you collapse, that boy ran so fast. Damn it. I couldn't move."

"What happened to me?"

"I really wish I knew. I spoke to the nurse that just left and she said to wait for the doctor to return." Andre's face still looked yellow, colored by bloodless skin.

"Hope I'm not intruding." The door slid open after two knocks, revealing a middle-aged doctor. He wore a white suit, black shoes and a small tag with the name Dr. Smith.

"You're Malory Hawkins, correct?" He eyed me up and down, like a blank list of diagnostics he had yet to check off. Not giving me a chance to speak, the doctor turned towards my teacher and reached out a hand to shake. "And you must be her father, I presume?"

"Oh no, haha! I'm her music teacher! Andre Petrov." Professor got up from the chair, shaking the doctor's hand.

"Pleasure to meet you both." The doctor rolled a computer on a stand towards him, typing on the keyboard before bringing his attention towards us again. "Sounds like you've had it really rough today, huh? Scratched yourself up too. I'm sure that didn't mess with your memory too much though, right? Want to give me some of your insights on what happened?"

"I was performing, and my body was getting really tired. Then my hands and the rest of me started to tingle."

"Tingle?"

"Yes, like sleeping on your arm for a long time."

"And has this happened before?" He typed more, pushing his sliding glasses further up his nose.

Before? The closest thing I could come up with were my episodes at night. There were other times that I'd experience this. Usually, it was during intense practice sessions. But I ruled it out to be pure exhaustion and strain I placed on my body.

"I'm not really sure..." I answered. "But sometimes at night, I'd get headaches and can't move my body. Or when I'm practicing for a long time, I'd get the same feelings but would be able to make them stop

tually."

"Interesting. For those times during the night, around how long did it take you before being able to move again?"

"I usually can't move until morning."

"That long, huh?" He adjusted his glasses again. Must be a habit of his. "This sounds like sleep paralysis. It most commonly occurs from the lack of rest or having too much stress on your plate. As you've pointed out with your practicing. But in most cases, it goes away within an hour or two. Most people with a similar problem told me they were able to snap out of it themselves."

"How long does it take for it to go away?"

"Sometimes that can depend on how good you're taking care of yourself. Although there is a load of factors to think about."

I dared not look at my professor and forced my concentration towards the doctor.

"But from what I've been told, it looked to others like you were having a small seizure? That does worry me, but we can't be certain for sure though." He walked to the other side of the bed and took my hand, unclamping the heart monitor clip from it. "And how are your stress levels doing? Getting enough sleep?"

A seizure?

"I do practice a lot of piano. I try not to, but sometimes I find myself staying awake really late in the night." My eyes darted towards professor for a moment.

"How late would you say that is?"

"Not that late... Three, maybe four?"

"Four hours of practicing?"

"No. Four in the morning." I peaked at Andre again. His eyes seemed to reveal more worry. I looked away, guilt in my chest.

"And what time do you wake up?"

"Usually around seven."

The doctor's head cocked to the side, as if to crack his neck. "And you're only twenty?" His eyebrows came close to his eyes, arching low enough to tickle his eyelids. "You still live with your parents?"

"Yes, with my father."

"Ah yes." He turned back to the computer, hunching his back to look at the screen. His glasses didn't seem to help his sight that much, judging by how close his nose was from poking the screen. "I do see Wilton Hawkins in your records here. Now I know you're past your teenage years and are an adult now. But does he know about your sleeping habits?"

"Yes, he does."

"And what does he have to say about it?"

"Nothing really. Sometimes he stays there with me as I practice late in the night."

"Sounds like he is just as dedicated as you with your music… But apparently not your health. You have a job? College maybe?"

"Only music. Father says I don't need a job yet since my music is our main priority right now."

"Then why wake up so early if all you're going to do is practice?" The doctor brought a chair from the side of the room and sat a few feet from professor.

"Because I need the hours if I want to get to where I want to be."

I proceeded to answer the doctor's questions. All the while, my professor's head kept resting on one of his hands.

"I want to talk with your father. I'm getting signals of you simply suffering from the consequences of sleep deprivation. But I don't want to settle for that just yet. I'll try to have a nurse contact your father. He was here a while ago but might have left the building."

"How long will I have to be here?" The distance between me and the piano made my fingers itch.

"I'm going to take a few tests since we aren't sure what this is. Urine samples, a few blood tests. It may take an hour or two. Sometimes it takes longer to get results back depending how busy we are. I've already given you some liquids as you can tell by your arm. You were severely dehydrated." The doctor raised his wrist, checking the time on his leather watch. "Barely past one… I'll have one of the nurses come back in a few minutes to remove the IV." He brought the two of us a reassuring smile before reaching for the door again. "But I'm sure it's not too serious. All it sounds like right now is that you haven't been getting enough sleep."

Not a second after he left, I slumped into the bed.

"Malory, this is for your own good." Andre rubbed the back of his neck and cracked it to the side. "I know you worry about practice, but…"

"health comes first. I know…"

Things felt just as they did back in the waiting room with Oliver. The ticking of Professor's watch, the stillness in the air, wanting to speak, yet not knowing what to say. Deep in my chest was the feeling of disappointment of not taking care of myself for me, but for my professor.

Not long after, a rattle of the room's door swept away the silence. Father walked in, looking at professor before eyeing me.

"Where have you been, Wilton?" Professor said as he stood up. He wisped through his teeth. "It's been hours! And you look like shit."

"You're one to talk." Father stared at professor before speaking again.

"And you reek of beer! Have you been drinking this whole time?"

Father dodged his question, pushing forward his own. Then his gaze turned to me. "And you, do you realize the trouble you've caused me?"

I was scared the two were going to lash out in a fight, judging by my father's possible alcoholic state and professor's white knuckled fists. The tension continued to hold, even after professor's phone lit up in his pocket. He finally grabbed for it. "Hello? Yes. Yes, that's right… I'm with her right now." His eyes made a final glance at my father. "Fine, give me a few minutes. I was just checking up on her." While turning off his phone, he let a curse out from under his breath. "It's Clarice, one of the judges from the competition. She wants to meet up with me." Though the words were meant for me, he continued to stare at father.

"You're not needed here." My father moved closer to professor, his height a head below his.

"Malory." Professor turned to look at me. "If you ever need me, call."

Father continued to stare at me, the corners of his lips glazed in a rustic yellow. His coat had darkened spots from some unknown liquid and his bed of aging hair looked like it had never been combed.

"What did you tell him about me?"

"Professor?" I hid my fingers under the folds of my dress.

"No, not your damn teacher! The fucking doctor."

"N-n-nothing. Just that I had practiced a lot and that you were with me."

I so desperately wanted to embrace him. If it weren't for this situation, I really might have. Though, it wasn't something I'd ever done before. Him being here, finally coming to see me, that was enough.

"You not only raised the expenses I have to pay now because of these medical bills, but you lost the one thing you were barely good at. Isn't that why you play? Now you can't even do that?"

His words pinched two tight fingers in my heart. He was right. The only thing I seemed to be able to mutter was, "I'm sorry."

But it didn't get through to him. Maybe my words never would.

"I'm going to see what they're selling in this depressing hole since I have to waste time waiting for you."

He turned around, leaving me there alone. Not bothering to look at me, not bothering to heat the icy furnace in my chest, not bothering to acknowledge my presence… As something more than another human being.

The doctor, my father. Neither of them came back into the room. Only the nurse to remove the tubbing in my arm. I was so close to asking her to stay. Did father decide to drive home? If so, I hoped they had cabs driving nearby at this hour.

Father wouldn't leave me like this, would he?

The room grew a little smaller. Covered in the thin sheets of the hospital bed was the only thing shielding me from the chilled room. A colder feeling came from my chest. It spread to my fingertips and knees, making them bounce nervously.

No, I know he wouldn't leave me just like that.

The night was spilling through the windows and creeping up my limbs. They grabbed a tight hold of me and halted my jittering legs. The night's weight shifted onto the bed and rested heavily on my neck and chest. I thank whoever decided not to put traditional moving clocks in these rooms. It would have made my mind go haywire as I waited for someone, anyone to be here with me. I peered off into the square electrical clock propped onto the wooden desk. My eyes were the only things that could move at this point. It was almost two in the morning. I could have stayed up for another hour or two with the presence of this unknown being taking hold of my body—filling my thoughts with distorted violin strings. But the weight was too heavy on me. It wrapped its appendages around my toes, poking at my knees like pins in a cushion. The headaches transpired, bringing my body to a dizzying state of weakness. Did the lights in the hospital get dimmer? Or was my vision dying out?

Was the night staring me in the face?

The sensations of light static continued to roam slowly like a cancer in my body. It buzzed in my ears like bees. I was then greeted with the unbreakable stillness of my body and the waning of consciousness. I never liked the feeling. Never. This time, I embraced it. For it was the only thing that seemed to erase my worries of going home alone.

CHAPTER FOUR

BEN

ALL THOSE DAYS OF STARING AT THE CEILING, it was all I could ever do. My body never wanted to move when I tried to, always stuck to that bed. It wasn't something I minded though. I always watched the shadows stretching and hovering over that familiar ceiling, all the while straining my ears to hear voices or creaking movements down below. I was like a useless immovable guard. Definitely not the traits of a protector…

A few nights ago, the numbness I always had was beginning to die off in one of my fingers. I remembered it tingling, bending and stretching the finger while feeling the soft mattress under me. That lone finger told me something.

You're going to move someday. Someday real soon.

Today wasn't going to be different from the rest, coming into consciousness with that knuckled pain in my head. As I blinked my eyes, the hairs on my back stood on end. Skin like plucked chicken crawled down to my pale feet. The air was uncomfortable, chilling my skin with uncomfortable kisses.

Morning? No, that can't be right.

I darted my pupils back and forth. The room was decorated with a synthetic hue from a stapled row of lights.

Knew it. Of course, it isn't… It's always night when I'm here…

There was a single window beside me, cloaked in frost and darkness. The more I continued to look around, the more uneasy I became. The ceiling was nowhere in sight and my feet were under something smooth. My toes curled, their ligaments popping as I gripped onto the texture. The mattress I've grown so fond of disappeared.

The hell? I'm... No that can't be... I'm actually... Could I actually be?

Standing. I felt every part of me. Not only a finger this time, but my whole body fell into a swirl of consciousness. The heaving in my lungs with each breath, the warmth of my skin, the bumps on my neck from the cold. Was this what it was like to feel?

I nudged a foot forward, preparing for my legs to buckle and fold under me. That never happened though, this body wasn't weak at all. The corner of my eye twitched as I looked down at my hands. Too small to my liking, too fragile, like the limbs of a porcelain doll.

Where am I?

The cream-colored ceiling I watched night after night was bleached a vivid white. I traced over the room, then over myself. My clothes looked like an oversized shirt draped over my body. They copied the same color as the bed next to me, a baby blue. Slammed to the wall were a row of wooden cabinets and drawers. The room displayed a typical electric clock with green glowing numbers on it. **1:30 a.m.** Coming closer and getting a better look at the bed, it was strange. Instead of metal, it was made of a thick white plastic. The end of the bed was arched up, as if it had feet of its own.

I must have been in some type of doctor's office or clinic. I knew about them, but never had to be in one. They were for sick people, for ones that were seconds from drinking death through their teeth. They were also very busy places from what I'd heard. But no one seemed to be around. No sounds of busy voices, or a collision of shuffling feet.

Nearing the door, I cringed as I felt long hairs sway against my back. It never bugged me before, since I always laid on top of it. Now every bit of movement made the hair tease my back. On a wrist that was too thin to call my own, I pulled off a thin hair tie and lopped the hair through it.

Much better.

There wasn't much left to see in that room. I left and stepped out into the hallway. The lights above were the same yellowish hue as in that room. Two nurses passed by me as they spoke in foreign terms. A doctor strutted in the other direction with his head lifted high. He gave me a glancing smile before turning the corner and disappearing. The door must have been somewhat soundproof. These hallways were alive compared to the dead in the room. A sign was propped on the wall near a set of elevator doors. **3rd Floor. Rooms 30-50**. Right next to the elevator was also a set of stairs, one leading up and the other one to lower grounds. This might've been my only chance to experience walking and feeling and living. So, I took the stairs.

Each step leading to the fourth floor was surreal. It was strangely… enjoyable. Midway up, there was a large outstretched window. I came close, my breath inking onto the canvas. I jolted back like a spooked animal. The reflection revealed a distorted figure on the other side. Black hair… black eyes… were staring back at me. The skin was so pale. Its height the size of a dwarf. And the body… My stomach belched, tipping a sour taste on my tongue. I quickly swallowed it back down, my hand ready to shovel the liquid back into my throat. My head began to whirl, my head draining of blood. My knees had an episode of their own, tilting from side to side. Two fists gripped onto the handrail as my body slumped to the side. Thick crystal water dribbled from the corner of my lip as a single droplet fell to the floor. The simple fact of not being able to accept that thing as my own, wriggled my stomach full of maggots. It took me a while, but I was finally able to regain my composure and I headed further up the stairs.

Maybe I should go back. I have no business here.

Being back in that room seemed like the best option. I had no idea where I was or why I continued to climb up. And yet, my eyes didn't want to stare back at shadows on a ceiling for hours. I didn't want to be strapped down by an invisible force any longer.

Unlike you, I won't be a puppet.

My feet ushered me further as I arrived on the fourth floor lined with doors. Every few steps or so would be another room, probably identical to my own. Judging by how dark it was and how no one was around must have meant that this floor was some type of resting area. I rose to peek through one of the door's open window, my weight distributed on the fatty parts of my toes. I didn't want to be this height. It was a feature that never fitted the way I viewed myself. Then again, who has ever had the choice of looking a certain way?

There was a patient wrapped in a coffin of blankets, sleeping soundly as the dim clicks of a machine rattled beside him. Many others looked the same. Row after row. My eyes scanned each room, witnessing many that looked days from being kissed by the reaper. It was more of a mortuary than a hospital, which made me wonder... *Was I dying too?* I had to go somewhere else, somewhere that had more life than death.

As I turned my feet around, the sound of a thud struck through the silence. My head snapped towards the noise, nearly cracking a joint in my neck. My pupils squeezed smaller as I tried to grab a vision of where the noise came from. Nothingness enveloped me again. Back and forth my eyes went. First to the stairs, then to the room beside me, then straight down the hallway. I wondered why I didn't go back. And I continued to wonder as the rapping of knocks playing on my chest pushed feelings of fluttering bees in my stomach. The only noise that replied to that ominous sound was the steps of my sticky skin creeping off the floor.

I passed the first door, the second, the third, then the fourth. Each one was tightly sealed until I came to one that was ajar. Getting on all fours, I spied through the half-inch gap. A crumpled figure was on the floor, skinny appendages bent under its body like a squashed bug. The creature's hair was grudge-like. Sweaty strands spiraled on the floor with a few pieces still clinging onto the bed beside it. The thing wore the same hospital gown as me and whimpered soft sounds into the floor like a mut. I didn't know what drew me to the creature. Maybe it was the energy of finally being able to see, to experience terror.

It took me a few breaths before being able to open the door. I winced by the soft noise it made. Not a second later, the thing's head cranked towards me. Its eyes were black pearls in the moonlight. Pieces of hair that didn't cover its complexion revealed two slim cheeks. The lights in the room were out. Although, there was just enough moon glowing to see a sickly girl with chestnut skin.

"Get away from me! I don't need your help!" She swept a hand into the air before turning away. Her face plastered on the floor. "Go! Go away!"

Her scratchy voice nearly made me jump out of my skin. The thudding in my chest that curled up to my throat might've taken my feet away from that place. But her eyes... They were lined with a dark purple and laced with sunken skin.

Those eyes... Those tired eyes. I recognize them. They almost look like...

"Y-you're not a nurse…" The girl took a glance at my clothes, seeming to be fixed on the similar colors we wore.

"Um, I can call one. If you want." Hearing my voice's high pitch for once rather than in my head, brought my stomach onto another sourly episode. The girl didn't seem to notice my body slumping against the door's frame.

"No!" She hissed through her teeth, eyeing the floor along with her voice diminishing. "I-I don't want them near me."

The girl's elbows propped underneath her, shaky hands grabbing onto nothingness scattered on the floor. Her feet remained limp and she soon fell back down.

"Well… Can I help you at least?"

"Why are you here? I don't know you. Go back to your own god damn room!" Her peppermint cheeks shone brightly in the room as her voice began to rise.

"I heard a loud noise and went to see what it was. Then I saw you on the floor and wondered if you were hurt."

"Well, I'm not, so you can g…"

Her voice trailed off. She must've heard it too. The sound of footsteps was coming closer.

"H-help me up. Now!" It shocked me how much someone's voice could change in an instant. First like a deadly serpent, now a swan on the run.

I paced towards her and reached an arm out. Death's cold grip was clinging onto her fingers. A shiver shot up my spine as I kneeled down and wrapped my hands under her armpits. Her body was slightly taller than my own, but it wasn't as hard as expected. This body I had wasn't the strongest. Yet compared to hers, she was a brittle bag of dried twigs knotted together with paper skin.

"Hurry! Set me there!" She turned her head towards a wheelchair a few feet behind her. The sleeve of her nightgown revealed a bony shoulder as I dragged her closer. Like a person with a fever, her hair was slicked with sweat and smeared against my chest. Getting a better glimpse of her revealed green veins mapping themselves on her arms.

I was surprised how fast I moved. Within a few seconds, I managed to situate her in the iron clutches and began setting her limp legs on the rectangular plate extended below it.

"What's going on here?"

A nurse opened the door right as I jolted away and stood beside her.

"It's late and both of you should be in your own rooms."

"Sharron, it's fine." The girl smiled at the nurse, but I could tell that her chest was heaving up and down at a fast rate. "Um, t-this is my friend!"

The nurse stared at me far too long to my liking. "Really huh?"

"Please Sharron, I'm only going to be here for a day or two longer. Let me catch up with them for a bit."

"And where do you belong, huh?" The nurse with tightly fitted clothes looked at me.

Where do I belong?

"Downstairs on the third floor."

"Does your doctor know you're away?"

"Yes, I told him I wanted to see an old friend for a few." I continued the lie. "He said it was fine since my blood tests were pending."

The woman didn't bother to hide her eyes rolling to the side. She looked at us, her watch, then scratched at the many rolls tucked under her chin. "It's my break time… If I still see ya when I get back then I'm…"

"Oh, thank you so much! You don't know what this means to me!" The girl squealed softly.

The nurse was already waddling her way back to the door, her eyes continuing to stare at me. "Just don't make a ruckus. Ya ain't the only ones in here."

The tightening of the door released a sigh in both of our chests.

"I hate that bitch so much." The girl rubbed a hand on her chest before speaking again. "Thanks… For helping me up. Guess I owe you a favor for how rude I was."

"It's alright, you just startled me. And that nurse too."

"You? Startled by me?" She let out a wheezing laugh. "Shouldn't I be the one saying that? A stranger prancing into a cripple's room?"

"I told you. The thud made me curious. Did you slip out?"

"Hardly. It was me trying to get out of this damn chair. Sounds stupid… I know. I had a dream that I could do it. It was so real… I really thought I could." Her hands tapped on her legs. "But in the end, I couldn't feel a single thing down here. And these nurses don't care about what or how I feel. And you saw that one just now and how she acted."

I rubbed my arm, still sticky from when I carried her body. "She did sound a little rude. Maybe the night shift was getting to her."

The girl laughed again. "These people! The doctors and nurses… They are all assholes. No doubt talking shit about you too."

Her eyes didn't look weak anymore. Rather, they burned, charring my mouth shut.

"One day, after setting me into this chair, I heard that same bitch talking to another nurse about me. The door was closed but my hearing isn't as bad as my legs. "'What a hassle! Did you see how scrawny her legs looked all turned inward? Disgusting!'" She wasn't looking at me anymore. Her eyes were pried on her legs, her hands tugging down her nightgown. "I know it was dumb of me to think I could walk again. But those kinds of words made me feel so nasty inside…"

I wasn't sure what to say. I scratched the side of my cheek, hoping to pull up any answer. Conversations were nothing but fairytales to me not too long ago. Almost anything was. Now that I was being exposed to everything, it was overwhelming. Addicting.

"Not one for talking, are you?" The girl's face so rigid and boney, collapsed into something a little softer. "Now you know what's wrong with me. So why are you here? It was obvious that those blood tests were a lie."

A canvas of white painted over my mind as I sat down on the bed beside her.

Why had I awakened here? She knows as much as I do… Honestly, maybe more. How crazy would I sound if I said I didn't know? Would it make me crazier if I told her the truth? Now, that I could never do.

"I really have no clue. I woke up here, today. I'm not even sure I'm supposed to be here." My hands didn't make me as sick when I looked back down at them. The idea of not knowing did though. If this was the feeling of vulnerability, then I wanted no part in it. "My memory… Hasn't exactly been the most reliable."

"Maybe you're in the wrong hospital then." Her voice grew into a sarcastic remark. I actually believed that she was serious for a moment.

"Really? Where should I go then?"

"Geez, I'm only joking. I felt the same way when they wheeled me in though. Being lost in the nightmare. Replaying the incident over and over, thinking I'll wake up soon. Don't worry, I'm sure you'll remember soon. Shock can be one hell of a repressor though." Her hand suddenly stretched out. "I'm Elizabeth. What's your name?"

Me? My name? Is that something I have? I was born, sure... But no one had been there when I was. And no one had told me what I was here for. I already knew what it was the moment I took my first breath.

It was then that I realized I did in fact have a name. It had always been with me; from the moment I heard the screams of a voice below. I looked at Elizabeth's mangled black hair and warm skin. She was a swan in a river tiddling ripples of questions into my brain. I rolled the name in my mind. It sounded right, almost perfect.

"It might sound funny since it doesn't match how I look... But I go by Ben." Hearing the name created, being spoken by my own tongue and voice I hated to call my own. Nothing could have sounded better. It matched how I felt, even though feeling was a word I was barely starting to understand.

"Really?" Her eyebrows were arched low, scanning me up and down. The sourness wanted to come back up again from my belly. Then she said something, something I never thought she would say. Elizabeth's words startled me more than the flash of seeing her for the first time.

"Ben... I like the name. It really suits you." She took my hand, and squeezed it firmly.

That Sharron must have forgotten to check up on us again. But I knew I had to leave soon before someone saw I left my room. Being able to do these things... Seeing, hearing, feeling things, feeling alive. This girl, this stranger girl with matted hair and sunken cheeks. I swear it seemed like she knew more of me than I did. She gave me the chance to say my true name out loud. It might've been the only chance I'd ever get to. It wasn't like I was going to meet her again, so I didn't have to worry about anything.

Not long after our farewells, Elizabeth called for me to wait. From the desk beside her, she took a scrap of tissue and a pen, scribbling something down. She then handed it to me with the number sixty-eight written in scratchy handwriting. Right below it was a series of numbers, a telephone number.

"That's the room number I'll be transferred to. Just in case you ever want to visit again before I leave."

Her voice continued to haunt me as I went back into the hallway, turning away from the window as I made it down the stairs. The loudness of the second floor came pounding back into my ears as I entered my empty room. I checked the time to see that only thirty minutes had passed by. The bed was stripped of heat as I laid back down. Something had taken form on my face and I traced a finger across the unfamiliar pattern. It was the touch of stretched skin and teeth against my fingertips. Was this what it felt like to smile?

CHAPTER FIVE

BEN

WITH EACH LONG STRIDE, the doctor gracefully entered the room. Along came another man with oiled back hair and looked far too thin for his age. He wore a brown coat that must have been washed ages ago and a shirt that looked more stained than white. The smell of his terrible habit seeped through the fabric. Did hospitals really let people come in looking like that?

The doctor spoke in foreign medical terms while giving me back the results of some tests I didn't remember taking. He seemed to be speaking with the man more than me. That, or keeping an eye on him. I hadn't paid attention to their conversation, only hearing a few words of 'extremely dehydrated', 'possible stress' and 'lacking sleep'. I was busy revisiting the memories of meeting Elizabeth and how I was finally able to speak to someone.

"So hopefully that fall was from the lack of sleep and not anything more since it seems to me like you haven't experienced anything this extravagant in the past. Keep an eye on those late night freezes too. Just bring these papers over to the next room for your prescription."

The loud smack of a chomping stapler on paper brought me back. I gave a simple nod and took the thin stack, feeling the paper moisten under my fingertips.

"Alrighty, then it looks like we are done for the day. Try to get better sleep and come back in two weeks for a follow up." The doctor gave a small smile at us both and left.

We never went to grab those pills. Instead, Wilton buzzed nonsense as we walked to the underground parking lot. Each step grew easier as I focused on balancing myself with these heels. I tried not to look down at my clothes, feeling the silk wrap tightly around my chest and underarms. Each tease of the dress brushing up my knees was violating what masculinity I had in this… this thing!

The car was disgusting, smelling like booze and guilty pleasure. Stains paw-printed every inch of the poor damned thing. The worst was the floor. Pieces of broken bottles were crushed like salt near the passenger seat. All the while, others swayed drunkenly as he drove in his drunkard ways.

"What do you have to say for yourself?"

So, this was her father. I couldn't remember if I'd ever met him before. Really hoped I didn't. If I had, it must have been years ago. Back when the past was much more real to me. I didn't bother to reply, and he didn't seem to care. The way this man kept himself shone through his car. Black paint chipped like eczema and beer bottles continued to rattle along the floor like a lost cause. Guess he wasn't much for conversation, mumbling as he drove while I listened to the grinding of his molars.

The damn fool nearly swerved into the driveway as he parked, grazing against a dry shrub that must have once been a hedge. The house wasn't as bad as his car. Though I would've been lying if I said things looked great. Beer bottles stood like soldiers on the kitchen counter and a thick smell came from the small trash can choking with garbage. I almost forgot about the alcoholic as I scanned the mess of what was called a home. He was pacing back and forth while eyeing the receipt the front desk gave him after paying the hospital fee. What type of low was he? Malory was his daughter and watching him fuss over a small fee was irritating.

"It couldn't have been that expensive." I watched him through the blinding lights of the kitchen.

"That isn't the point! I'm on a tight budget already and you swinging by the hospital isn't going to help that!"

"Well that just makes me wonder where all that money is going." I traced my eyes over each bottle, each tiny soldier. Looking at a ceiling was much more pleasant than this.

Wilton planted the receipt on the greasy countertop and grabbed a vase sitting near the sink. The small pink flowers cascaded down as algae-colored water swished out from the lips. It took a loud clash onto the floor, splitting the porcelain body into fragments. The water now in puddles, traced the hem of Malory's dress. Wilton's head fizzled the color of pork as he stood over his mess. His first few breaths were loud, exaggeratedly loud. Then they grew into puffs, then nothing.

"See? See what you make me do?"

It felt nice to think about it. To take his head between my fists and pound him into the sink. I saw myself doing it, feeling the rush of relief as his head crunched into the faucet's neck. That was all it would take for her to be free. Free for a moment… then trapped in a cell. Even if I really did want to do it, this body was no match. Not to mention the cage that hung around this body and cupped at the cancerous fat around my chest. I would have planted a foot into his chest, if only they weren't compressed into these small black heels. I could have silenced him forever, but her hands were too small. Would his anger have broken me? Maybe. But I couldn't afford to let that happen because I wouldn't have been the only one broken.

"Do you realize how much this medical bill was?" His eyes didn't look at me but through me, escaping somewhere else. He rammed the receipt into my face. I eyed each knuckle, wondering how many pounds it took to crack the marrow out. The numbers on the paper weren't a lot. In fact, she would've been able to paid that on her own. But Wilton was in control of her money and all her earnings.

"You screwed up with beating that faggot!" Wilton stepped through the shattered vase, kicking the chips into the air. "What will this do for your reputation? This is an embarrassment! And what about the money? Huh! How are we going to pay for this shitty home? Two-thousand! Two-thousand dollars down the drain!" He took a full spin, arms outstretched like a ringmaster preparing for his circus act.

"Money? Shouldn't she… I be the one asking that? I'm sure I made enough to pay for many medical bills. Unless you used my earnings for your little addiction. And don't you have a job of your own? Because it sure doesn't look like it."

Wilton turned to an aluminum fridge, popping it open and rummaging through its contents. He pulled out a beer and hit the cap against the counter.

"How dare you speak to me like that! You did this to me… You made me drink!" He swerved his head close to mine and I took in the smell of his rotting teeth. He wasn't speaking to me anymore, but to the yellow-colored walls around us. "And we have that stupid Walker boy's gathering tomorrow. Oh, he is really gonna give it to you good! His damn bitch of a mother too! Especially on me!"

"I don't have to go. It's your pride that wants to."

His breath came to the top of my forehead. I focused my eyes on his, watching their yellowed rims grow plump.

Did this lost cause actually believe that he could intimidate me?

The smell of plaque pinched my nose. My body remained still.

I couldn't show him any fear. He needed to know that we weren't scared of him.

"That will make them think you are weaker. Weak people will always be stepped on by others! And I will not let them think that! You're going there because it's better to go as a loser than as a weak shit!" The bastard turned away from me and sat down at the dining room table. His foot tapped slowly, and my heartbeat followed.

"Clean the mess." He toggled the bottle in his sloppy fingers towards the scattered vase.

I hated that I couldn't do anything about him. Being the protector didn't mean beating those that harmed you. Although I wished that was the case. My job was to protect the body, even if it meant doing things that I didn't want to. I faced those facts as Malory's father locked eyes on mine. I wouldn't be able to overpower him. Maybe one day, but not now.

I gritted my teeth as I knelt down, feeling the chalky taste of the hard bite. Bending by the sink, I began searching for a sweeper. My back turned away from him made the feeling of vulnerability skyrocket.

"No. Use your hands."

This asshole.

With my right hand, I grabbed the pieces with my tips, dropping one by one into my palm. This was going to take more than a single trip, so I got up steadily and made sure not to step on any other pieces.

"Oh no, I'm not letting you get off that easily. Not from how you've been talking with me so suddenly. You're usually much more obedient. What happened?"

"Look I don't know what you want. You tell me to throw it away and that's what I'm doing."

"No. You pick them up all at once, then you can throw them away." Wilton took a loud sip of addiction.

"Can't you see that they don't all fit in my hand?!"

"You'll figure something out."

Reasoning wasn't something this man had. I trailed onto the remaining pieces. There were still handfuls of portions riding on the puddles.

I couldn't use the sweeper, I couldn't make multiple trips to the trash can, and I couldn't murder this man. I gave a hard swallow when I looked down at my clothes. It was long enough to work as a basket, and hopefully enough to cover most of my insecurities. I lifted the edges up, immediately regretting it as his eyes relaxed on me.

"Finally using that brain of yours. Guess that fall knocked your bolts back into place."

I picked up the pieces fast enough to finish, and slow enough to show that I wasn't scared. With both sides of the dress lifted, I pressed a heel down on the trashcan's pedal. A cold chill ran down my spine as I turned my back from him. I felt something right behind me, its body so close to mine. Hot air smothered against my neck and made the hairs on my neck rise. My eyes froze at the rubble in the trash, taking in the smell as my vision warped with sickly stomach aches. I was trapped, stuck, vulnerable, weak.

Is he touching me?

I snapped my head in his direction, fear buzzing in my ears. There he was. Far away. Sipping his beer and not giving me any notice.

It was a relief to stare at the ceiling again. Despite the things I'd seen and the things I had been able to feel, nothing felt better than this moment of escaping Wilton and losing myself to this room. The moment I closed the door, I tore off that dress and threw the heels away from my vision. I became a host to the blankets, hoping the layers were enough to cover the curves of my body. The headaches were already kicking in even though it was still night. Night was supposed to be my time. It throbbed across my forehead and bent around the bandage near my temple. I guess it was from not being used to coming out in this world. This body needed rest and I knew I was partly responsible for that. Should I have just closed my eyes each time I awakened? Probably. But being able to control my own breathing and feeling myself alive in this world rather than the one that existed in this mind, felt that much more real. I guess there was also the fact that I feared sleep. That if I let sleep take hold of me, then something could've happened to the body. That probably wouldn't ever happen. Wilton was busy with his moaned cries somewhere downstairs while on a date with his beloved booze.

A vision of Elizabeth came as I closed my eyes. My first interaction. My first conversation. The aches became a buzzing hum that infected my body. It didn't take over my vision though, and I was able to see the two of us in the hospital one last time before drifting.

I wonder if I'll ever see her again.

CHAPTER SIX

MALORY

Since when had I gone home?

My clothes were lying in sloppy lumps on the floor and my heels were toppled near the wall. The room I was so fond of became foreign during those few moments of waking. The hospital bed I expected to wake up in had softened into my own. The yellowed lights I waited to squint at turned into natural sunlight. I immediately slipped on clothes the moment I saw my bare body. And though I wasn't sure of the events leading up until now, I did feel better. Refreshed. I was happy to wake up to the peaceful quiet. My mind felt more alert rather than in a swampy haze. But I was parched. I took down the tap water from my bathroom sink and rinsed the cup after.

"Is father home? It doesn't sound like it… He would have woken me up by now."

I came downstairs and found him sleeping soundly. His spots were usually on dirty clothes in his room or the storage room during nights. Today had been the couch. One hand loosely hugged a beer bottle on his stomach and the other hung down to the floor. I crouched and leaned close to his stubbled face. Father's eye bags added a decade to his fifty-year-old skin. The sides of his lips hung tiredly, revealing creases resting on both sides of his crusted mouth.

Would he ever look at me like this while awake?

I turned to the hallway, noticing his room door was wide open. Of course, weeks of dirty clothing toppled over each other on his bed. The most bizarre thing was that there were no bottles there. Hopefully, one day it would be like that for the rest of this house. I went into his room, eyeing the cow-printed stains on his blankets, which I hoped were coffee.

I came back to him after tearing off the bed's thin lining. I rolled it in my arms and closed the door behind me. As I came close to him, my body nearly jumped as the blanket came on top of him. His single finger twitched, making my body crawl back.

One... Two... Three... Four...

Nothing. Father remained asleep and I didn't think twice to give him back his space. I went back to the upstairs hallway. The first door led to a packed and musty storage room that always liked staying locked. It was the place where father kept his beverages to soothe his never-ending addiction. On really bad days, I'd hear him unlock the door while I practiced. Long hours of practicing would be nothing compared to the time he spent there. Each time he went in, fear came over me, wondering if he would ever come back out again. My piano room came next, then lastly mine.

I came to the second door, checking behind me to make sure father was asleep before closing myself inside. No windows, making the only source of light come from my lamp on the upright piano. Its jade body stood shyly as its long golden neck hung. Clicking on the light, welcomed the shadows. Some of the dark figures laid dormant by a stack of books just a few feet from the ceiling. Others laid stretched on the floor by bitten yellow pencils and scattered music pages. That day before the final round really made father angry. I was practicing with the sheet music to make sure I wasn't missing anything. Father told me how I shouldn't have needed to use the music score—that seeing me using it—showed how unprepared my memorization was. So, he tore it up, telling me to keep playing, and scattered it on the floor. A lot of mistakes happened after that, resulting in his fist banging on the side of the piano and a whack to the back of my head. It wasn't intolerable; he never really meant to hurt me. I needed the discipline. I knew the piece, I really did. But the moment the sheet music fell to the ground, I heard it again. Simply thinking about that day brought them back into my ears. The sound of strings, screaming louder and louder into my head. Father's hand became a metronomic conductor to this mental symphony, and it was only when I looked back with a drenched face that he left. That, and those strange strings I'd hear sometimes.

What was I supposed to do now? Professor hadn't given me a new piece yet and the one I did for that competition was useless now. It turned into a reminder, a terrible one.

I traced a finger on the piano, clearing the dust away. Right about now, Oliver must've been getting ready for his gathering. It had always been a tradition for winners to have performances after competitions made by staff members. With his black suit, his black shoes, the black piano, and my black shadow stretching behind him.

I gathered up the torn sheet music, and threw it into the trash, watching their purpose be nothing more than crumpled garbage. A bottle clicked behind me. Father was clad in a blanket and resting against the door frame.

"What time is it?" His back made a dry crunch.

"It's close to nine."

"Damn. Almost forgotten about that Walker child's little party."

He left the room and clamped downstairs. I followed behind as we entered the kitchen.

"Garbage is too full to put in. Deal with it, yeah?" Father nudged a finger to the empty bottles and other broken pieces.

Did he drop the flower vase? How did I not hear that?

"Of course, father." I picked at a loose skin on my lip. "Are you going later tonight?"

"Why? You think I'll embarrass you in front of your friend?"

"What? No, I was just wondering since I wanted you to g…

"Well don't worry. I'm not. I've got a meeting with the boss around that time for a possible client. But I'm sure that your beloved teacher will come scurrying on by."

Father headed towards his room, already unbuckling his pants. "What time is that brat's party?"

"Oh, I have time! It's not until seven."

"Well fucking good for you. My meeting is in thirty minutes for who knows how long." The pants slipped off. "Make yourself useful and find some competitions to sign up for while I'm gone, yeah?"

I took father's laptop that had collapsed at the side of his bed like an open book and sat on the living room couch. The bed sheet I gave him laid on the floor like shed skin. I brought it around my body. Some competitions were free, others required a fee to join, others were too far and the payoff was small.

"Done… Done… Already done…"

I already won several of the competitions I was looking up. With the exception of organizations that required a hefty fee to join. New York had a long list of competitions. Living here all my life and always playing the piano, the list grew increasingly shorter. There were strange times of trying to apply for a competition, only to get turned down because I'd already won. Of course, I never remembered applying, so the only thing I could do was resort to the inevitable. I must have joined during those earlier and foggier years.

Finally, a fresh one came across my eyes. It was a hundred dollar fee to join and the due date for the audition was coming quite close. It was also something different, being international rather than by state or country. I knew father wouldn't like this idea; the steaks would've been too high. The expense would've been more. But it also could've been the thing that redeemed me.

CHAPTER SEVEN

MALORY

I could redeem myself… He would forget all about losing to Oliver. Ten thousand dollars… Ten thousand… dollars…

"Father?"

I looked to the driver's seat, watching his sun-spotted hands grip the wheel.

"What."

"I did some research on competitions while you were away at work. Just like you said. And I was able to find one that has a…"

"Do you have any respect for me at all?" Father let out a groan, running a hand through his hair. "The last thing I'd ever want to hear right now is that shit. I'm already taking you to someone else's winning performance. The performance that should have been yours."

"But I thought you…"

The car came to a thudded halt in front of Carnegie Hall. He continued to look through the side mirror. "Thought nothing. Don't make a fool of yourself in there. That's the least you could do for me right now."

The continuous screeching of rubber turned through my mind long after father left. I tugged at my brown jacket tightly, not used to seeing this building vacant. I waited for shuffling, muffled speaking, anything to show signs of life. Most of it was shut off for a different event later that day and the room given to Oliver was a separate area where weddings sometimes took place. It took some time to find. But after searching the vacant halls, I heard the sound of clinking glass. The Hall Foyer shone through crystal chandeliers. The walls were caramelized wood, and marble pillars stood proudly around the room's perimeter. To the far back of the room was a small bar and round tables aligned with assorted foods. Though it was an hour before the actual starting time, everyone seemed to be here. I spotted professor around a cluster of teachers much older than his age. He took a sip of bottled water while his group held fragile glasses of red and white wine. Mrs. Walker stood nearby, her laugh vibrant through the room. Oliver was both her son and student, making her proud as both a mother and teacher. As I passed through the entrance, the chatter had gone quiet. A small group of musicians took a quick glance of me before continuing their conversation. One pranced around them in her billowing dress and came up to me. Her frills spun around her legs like fallen petals, her head being the center piece for all the cosmetics one could ever find. Finally, a memory that was much more real to me.

"Isn't it a shock?" Her eyes fluttered. "To finally find yourself other than first place."

"Well, he did perform really well." My smile only seemed to make hers go wider. Each tooth was a clean and aligned stick of gum.

"Oh, of course you'd say that! But you have to admit that your loss wasn't entirely your fault. Well, kinda. As much as I'd be happy to see you second, the judges should have given you another chance." Kira was a well-performing artist herself. In the past, she'd compete beside us, nearly beating Oliver a few years ago if it weren't for her bad habit. I do admit, her skills could've been better than Oliver's and mine combined. Yet the fact that she always hurried to finish was what ultimately destroyed her. That or the fact that she was trying to outrun the verge of her mid-twenties.

"Well, it's nice to see you again. Can't wait to hear what you've got for this thing next y..." Kira's hand went up to her lips. "Right. You're like me now. Sort of. Well, welcome to the older raking bunch. Maybe it's time to step up your game internationally. My daddy thought I should show everyone my skills. So, that's what I'll be doing now! I've began to feel like I've outgrown New York anyway." After taking a sip of alcohol, Kira scurried off to the bar.

Was that what would be happening to me now? Being here in New York was best for my father. We didn't have the money to use on plane tickets or registration fees. But if I somehow convinced him of this one... Maybe, just maybe the prize would've been enough to waver him.

The small taps of a microphone adjusting turned the room silent. Clarice twirled a lock of corkscrewed hair back in place, only for it to bounce back. Hanon stood close in his suit and held the glimmering embodiment of my failure. "I want to thank all of you for joining our branch! To all the students of this year's competition and to our sponsors who have been so generous with their donations. I also want to thank our judges who had the difficult decision of choosing our winner! We couldn't have done it without you. Now, without further ado, please give a hand to this year's young winner, Oliver Walker! "

Young...

Oliver came up to the stage, his face like plaster. He took the trophy from Honens and gave a small nod.

"The stage is all yours!" Honens patted his shoulder before heading to a group of people who must have been the sponsors. Oliver's eyes didn't leave the trophy for quite a while. As everyone remained hushed, he took a deep breath and finally faced his audience. No, not his audience…

Is he looking at me?

"Thank you for coming and supporting me with this… This win."

With that, he walked back down and headed for the back of the room where the food was. My eyebrows weren't the only ones that raised up. Clarice looked at Honens but he simply cleared his throat.

"Short and sweet I must say. As you all saw, the refreshments are in the back if you follow Oliver. Anyway, thank you all again. We hope to see you next near."

"That's it? That's all we get?" I turned to see Professor standing beside me.

"I guess so. Maybe he got nervous?"

"Oh, please Malory. That boy has the ability to hide all emotions. I've seen it and heard it in his playing."

It was right to feel off by Oliver's speech. Professor obviously displayed that attitude. The boy had always been blank, simple and straight to the facts. Knowing those facts, maybe it shouldn't have been a surprise to anyone that he didn't prepare a heartfelt speech.

"If you ask me, he doesn't seem satisfied with the win."

"But he has been wanting this since forever. Maybe he isn't one for crowds.

"No joke there." Professor uncapped his bottle and took a long sip.

"Oh! I've done some research on more competitions this morning."

"You never seem to give yourself a break, huh?"

"I think I've rested enough. It's time to pick myself up again. And this time… I-I well, I want to start going international."

"You do know that it would mean flying out to places. And flying out means cash. Those places usually won't provide that."

"Yes, yes, I'm aware. But the prize money isn't small either. It's ten thousand. And look at me, I'm already in my twenties. I'm getting older."

"Really? You're still in your prime. And I'm much, much older than you. But look? I'm still kicking."

"You've seen those little kids." I looked off to a small group of children by their parents. Probably siblings of my competitors. Or maybe the moms and dads were already starting them off young. "Kids like those are learning piano since they were four or five. I needed to catch up."

"But you also can't compare yourself to them. And as much as I'd love to see you get out there, you haven't exactly been able to take care of yourself with competitions just minutes from your home. Let's try to enjoy this party and talk about it later. Sounds good with you?

Oliver's parents didn't seem to be bothered by his speech. Both the Walkers' eyes shined as they watched their son up there, not caring how simple and plain his speech was. It was a bizarre concept to me. How such little effort brought such bright emotions? After Oliver came down, everyone dispersed into their own sections again. Many of the pianists were busy congratulating Oliver in a circle while my professor continued having a chat with older musicians and teachers. Despite not winning, I found myself also surrounded by a circle of performers. I knew of them, but usually never spoke to them. A few mothers of children also came closer. Asking of my future plans or mentioning that their child looked up to me. Really? Looking up to a girl collapsing on stage?

I pinched at a few sandwich sliders stacked on top of themselves like a pyramid. A little doughy, but it satisfied the emptiness. The smell of alcohol usually tore away my appetite. Somehow, a room filled with wine was a different feeling than the usual brown.

From the far corner of the room, a glimmer of silver caught my eye. My throat tightened around the swallowed food and a large weight came down on my shoulders. Two spinning wheels tracked across the room, tying a rope to my legs and pulling myself forward. It was too far to see who it was, but I was able to distinguish long locks of thick hair. My heart rolled up my throat and the sound of swarming bees infiltrated my head. Had the room always looked so warped? Since when had the room gone darker? Unless…

It's happening again. I'm going to collapse right here in front of everyone again. I need to get out, I need to get away. I can't, I can't, I can't. I can't disappear again.

It really suits you. I like the name. B…

"Ah! There you are!" The silky echo of a female voice came behind me. Mrs. Walker in her stunning red dress, one bold cut in the fabric that rode up to her hip. Her dark Indonesian hair swirled up like a honeycomb sprinkled with tiny diamonds.

"Oliver told me what happened. How are you feeling dear?"

"The um… The doctor hasn't told me the results yet, but I'm feeling much better. He said it might not be anything more than exhaustion and dehydration." I peeked behind her back, but the wheelchair was gone.

"That boy I swear! He confuses me. One day he talks all about you and the next he acts like you two are strangers!"

"Well, we don't really talk that much."

"You mean you don't talk very much?" Her large eyes and ruby lips puckered at me. "But I really do hope you two speak to each other again. I don't know what happened, but I'm sure it isn't something you can't fix. Isn't that right?"

Somehow, a man had teleported beside her. His head was down and busy on his phone like a young teen. Mr. Walker's skin was much lighter than his wife's sunny tan.

"Honey, be nice. She just got back from the hospital." He tucked the phone into his pocket and pushed his thin glasses up. "Maybe we should all have dinner sometime."

"Ah yes, I agree!" Let's do it at my house." Mrs. Walker clapped her hands together before linking an arm around her chubby husband.

"Our house."

She seemed to ignore her husband's voice; her pitch hitched with excitement. "Tomorrow! Tomorrow evening around seven or eight. How does that sound with you?"

"I'll have to check with my father but I'm sure I can go."

She gave a hard swallow, loud enough for me to hear. "Oh, oh! But maybe alone? I don't mean to be rude but your father can be a bit…"

"Your father is as welcome as you are. Right?" Despite having a tall frame, Mrs. Walker looked shrunken by his tone.

"No, it's alright. He might be busy anyway."

"How is he doing by the way?"

Clean the mess. Use your hands. Do it in one go. See? See what you make me do? Weak shit! You did this to me!

"He's doing better."

"Well, I've always found it strange that he doesn't join many of your piano recitals or gatherings such as these. Then again, he could see my son as a competitor to you. That's one thing I could agree with him." Her laugh tickled her golden hooped earrings. "Now if you'll excuse me, I'm going to get more wine."

Her hips swayed as she walked away, and Mr. Walker craned his neck after her. "Sorry about my wife's behavior. She really likes to ruffle her feathers. We will be seeing you for dinner, yes?"

"Of course, sir. Thank you for inviting me."

"Same to you. It's been a while since we've talked. You take care, alright?"

I wasn't able to congratulate Oliver that night before receiving a buzzing text from my small bag. Father texted that he was outside, parked and waiting for me. I looked around for Oliver, but he was nowhere in sight. At least I was able to thank the judges and see Hanon again. He gave a ruffle to my head and wished me the best. He might have had too much to drink, judging by how pink his cheeks were. I also wanted to thank Clarice and reached to shake her hand. She brought me into a tight hug, her perfume overwhelming but welcoming. She whispered something in my ear. But age was taking a toll on her voice, making the words hard to distinguish. Clarice wiped a tear from her eye and gave me a final smile as she walked away.

While on the drive home, I barely heard the rattle of bottles or picking of the steering wheel by father's hands. I was still in that ballroom with everyone. With the sweet smell of wine and tiny sliders. With conversations that weren't a necessity but rather spoken for the sake of simply speaking to others. Would I ever see any of them again? Would I ever see Oliver again if I went international?

I placed the purse on top of my bed as I tasseled my fingers through my hair. Each strand felt oily and thin.

"I really do need to start caring for myself more. Maybe I should shower."

Showering could've waited another day. Things weren't going so well with my father downstairs. Since he picked me up, his smell had been more sour than usual, his eyes so red I thought they were going to burst. Guess his job was really taking a toll on him. I could've only imagined the stress. Comforting him was tempting, but avoiding his anger might be the best thing tonight.

I glanced over at my mirror while unzipping. My figure had slimmed down a size or two, the muscle in my arms growing tighter around my bones. Since when had my wrists been so small and ball-jointed? Taking my dress, I tucked it into the laundry basket and grabbed my purse to put away. Its mouth opened wide, as if begging my fingers to be stuck inside of it. *Open me up,* it said.

I peered inside, only to dump everything out. Receipts, pens, an empty wallet, and somehow a piece of broken glass that might have jumped in during the car ride. I grabbed the receipts and found a small paper crumpled in with them. The thing was neatly folded up into a square. As I peeled the corners back, my fingers slowed. The thumping in my chest grew loud and jumped at each number on the paper. Scratched in pencil was a phone number.

It meant nothing to me. All I had was my professor's and father's number. A strange heat traveled to my cheeks, tempting them to burn. I stood up, feet pointed towards the trashcan near my door. But they wouldn't move. I pulled and squirmed my toes into the carpet, but my heels refused to be lifted.

Don't. Don't throw it away. Please.

The voice of a young man spoke close to me. I turned but found no ghostly apparition in the mirror. Only my stretching irises and lips tucked into my mouth. The voice should have scared me, but it brought warmth to my body. So warm that it tingled at my fingertips and picked at the raised hairs on my skin. Then came the sound of three nails tapping on glass. Father slouched against the wall, taking a long sip while continuing to look at me.

"Father? Sorry, I thought I closed the door."

"You did."

Father groaned while rocking on the balls of his feet. A loose grey tie licked his chest.

"Why are you dressed like that?"

"I w-was getting ready for bed. And I thought I heard someone here…"

"Well, don't worry. I'm the only one here." He came over, his body tilting with each step and sank into the bed. "Ya know how bad ma job is? Keep goin to that place even though ah can't pay for my own? Only damn time I can get him on my side is if I do what he wants. One day though jus one day I'll find ah way. Then I can rest my fucking brain before it blows."

Father took another drink, a stream of beer driveled down each side of his lip. Most of it splattered onto the bed rather than in his mouth.

"And now you're the cause of dis mess. You ain't supposed to be in the picture ataall…"

His words, loud and brittle like twine, were starting to blend with one another. Father swung close to me, his arm raised above my head. Once his hand tilted, there came a coolness over me. The smell overpowered me, making my face burrow down close to my chest. The beer continued to pound over my eyes, the world turning yellow. It crawled on my skin, worms and maggots writhing their bodies in me. Multiplying, thriving, dying.

His warping figure was fading away, but the coolness continued to pour. I almost convinced myself that the stinging drink became tolerable. My arms wrapped around my chest, compressing the beating of a lazy heart. One blink, then two, the liquid turned clear and soothing. It came in like a storm, pounding at my back and streaming down my face. It seemed impossible for this to be from one bottle alone. I looked down at my feet, pink and wrinkled. The brownish stream was gone, replaced by a pearly white floor.

When had I gotten into the shower?

It wasn't scary. In fact, it was better for me this way. Not to remember. The presence that I felt in my room with father was still with me. Whatever it was, the *voice* that spoke to me. I almost saw it from where I rested in the back of my mind, taking my body and slipping it on. The first sleeve it took was my arms, then my legs. My vision turned to carbonation as it zipped itself inside. Only as things turned dark, was my body able to relax a little.

CHAPTER EIGHT

BEN

"HOW CAN SHE KEEP DOING THAT?" White mountains peaked from my knuckles. Just the thought of that bastard's mouth speaking words fouler than the smell of his spit…

"Why can't she understand that this was all wrong? What will it take for her to snap out of this shit hole?"

I splashed water into my eyes, not sure if I was trying to erase the alcohol or his gaze. It felt like his eyes were all around the ceiling, looking down at this nude and skinny body. I tried to rub the tension out. It didn't feel natural, but I had to be there for her. Of course, I didn't want to stand here, waking up to the splashes of water on these breasts. Taking front wasn't entirely out of needing to protect her from a situation. Guilt crawled in my belly. After she found Elizabeth's paper, I couldn't contain myself. Sure, I knew that I wouldn't have been able to call her. Probably never see her again. But it would have been nice to pretend to.

I scrubbed at the many layers of skin on the body and hair sticky with beer. I wished that each layer would've fallen off to reveal the person I was inside. Then came the masochistic mindset of wanting to look, to see if I really had the parts I hoped for. Looking down… Shit why did I keep doing this to myself? My eyes met two small mountains I never wanted to climb. I should have stopped there and turned off the bathroom lights. I traveled lower, biting into the side of my cheek, becoming more overwhelmed by the audacity of my heartbeat.

Just before I was met by a pair of milk-colored ankles, I saw a dark round bundle of hair slicked down by water. It was a parasite that clung to the middle of my thighs, being a thin slit instead of a hanging pair of flesh. The soap coming into my eyes snapped my head back up. It should have lessened the torture. A suction-cupped mirror stood a foot from me. Her eyes were red from trauma, her body sucking the minerals it needed from her soul. No matter how many times I saw myself in my head… A tall man brimming with maturity. I'd always be greeted with her face. The face of Malory.

Why don't you change how this body looks if that's how you really feel?

Since I've officially awoken, that thought kept prancing into my mind.

"You know I can't do that." I replied to Malory's reflection.

It's not only hers anymore! To heat up a knife, those little lumpy lumps would slip right off like butter…

"I said stop!"

I wanted to believe I was real, but staring down there… That wasn't my purpose anyway. Not to look like a man or to think and to feel. This body had to be protected so nothing could ever happen again. I couldn't afford to simply be a watcher.

I turned off the shower, stepping out onto the floor. Puddles spread below me, and I quickly wrapped a towel around myself. Staring at the bathroom sink, then the towel hook and under the cabinet. Nothing.

"Shit…"

That damn puppet of a daughter didn't get herself clothes. She spaced out long before that. Leaving this way was far from comfortability. How did I know for sure that Wilton was sleeping? Or what? Wait for myself to dissociate before letting her take control again? Who the hell knew when that would be?

The lights were off which was a good start. All except for a smoke detector on the ceiling, a red bulb glowing in the center. After taking the damp towel and wrapping it around me, I didn't miss the chance to speed out of the bathroom. Finally, being back in her room gave such relief. This was the place I felt most comfortable, the place we all felt the most comfortable. She really should get a lock though.

"Why did he have to stench it up?"

I looked at the ceiling through the darkness. At the end of the day, it was a nice remembrance of simple things compared to the complex world.

The room didn't have much light, leaving the curves of this body to blend in with the night. The moon tried to peek, so I went over to the window to close the blinds. Reaching up with both arms to grab the curtains, the water seeping in my hair grew suddenly colder. The blood pumping through me grew warmer, almost burning. I turned towards my door. I'd forgotten to close it. From the corner, two white marbles with tiny black specks hovered in the air. Coming along with them was the smell of vinegar and sugar. Its gaze was crawling and crawling and crawling. The pair of whites bobbled back and forth. Something told me that they would eventually grow closer. Before they did, I came towards them. To think she had to deal with this… this…thing.

"Why the hell are you looking at me like that for?" The green eyes narrowed as they spoke.

I stopped, now a small distance from the pair. They were connected to an oval shape. The figure stretched high off the floor.

I didn't need to reply to him. She never needed to reply to him.

"Answer me!"

That fucker tried to swing the bottle at my face. But the man barely had an aim. If she was out, she would have let her face break the glass. Never wanting to fight back, trying to be the perfect girl that never existed. I grabbed it, my hand gripping over his. Wilton's face contorted and two rows of yellowed teeth snarled back at me. Then, on the side of my cheek came a swarm of heated tingles. It was quick, the tension from his hand disappearing into a throb.

"Don't you ever do something like that to me again."

He tugged his hand away from me and gave my body a solid push. The bed was nearby and its iron frame was enough to leave a nice gash mark. Then I could have dragged him to the door while he was stunned and used his head as a door opener, continuing to slam it in until his brain pulped out from his ears like cheese whiz. I could have.

Wilton left after drinking the rest of his bottle, mumbling to himself as he closed the door behind him. I wiped a hand across my cheek, still feeling the gross stain of his palm. If this wasn't covered up somehow, then tomorrow was going to be quite interesting. Deep down, I wished she would let it show, every purple streak and green print. Those marks would've been enough to shout to the world every damn word he ever called her.

CHAPTER NINE

MALORY

I TOOK A MOMENT TO GLANCE into professor's glass door. Hair swooped over my shoulders and I hoped it was enough to cover the greening imprint on my right cheek. Too much foundation had made the skin cakey, but it was better than what would've been shown underneath. It might have looked better, but rushing while hearing the screams of father saying to hurry didn't give me much time.

I turned back to look at his yard after pressing the brass doorbell. Crispy baby's breath grew in large groups, flourishing around stone pebbles that led to his side gate. A simple pink savanna that looked more like cotton candy in the spring. For now, their little bodies were covered in sprinkles of sugared snow.

"Well good morning!" Professor swung the door wide open while ruffling a small towel draped over his head. "Sorry I took a while. It's hard to hear that bell while in the shower."

"It's fine. I was busy looking at your garden. Are these the only ones you ever grow? I never see any others."

"They have always been my favorite. So, I find no need to plant other flowers. And their maintenance isn't so bad either. They seem to keep growing everywhere on their own."

After getting inside, I took my boots off and rested them on a wooden bench. No matter how many times I'd been here, his house never ceased to amaze me. Wooden flooring and walls, jade-colored fans that spun slowly with their mellow hue.

We came to the living room. Sitting proudly on top of an outstretched antique carpet was his Grotrian Concert Piano. Professor pulled back the curtains as he spoke.

"Now that I think about it, you do look paler than usual. Sleep enough?"

"I'm just trying to get used to how things are again." I let the music bag slip off my shoulder and sat on the leather piano bench.

"With how your father is, I doubt that would ever be something to get used to."

"Don't be like that. He isn't as bad as you think." I touched my cheek, nearly forgetting what hid underneath.

He let out a soft laugh as he pulled a chair next to me and sat down. "As I think?" Professor stared up at the flowing fan before letting out a sigh. Summer or winter, those fans never stopped spinning. "Well, I guess that doesn't matter. But Malory, it's so obvious that he isn't treating you right."

"He hasn't done anything wrong. All father wants is for me to be the best I can in my craft."

"And don't you think I want the same? Look, I'll stop bringing him up, alright? I know you care for him a lot. But mark my words Malory, if I do find something against him, I won't hesitate to call someone."

There came a strange silence between us as professor got up and unlocked the piano. I couldn't miss this opportunity. The deadline was too close to waste any more time.

Now is my chance.

"You said we could talk about it later, right? Well, I still want to do it." I held onto my hands.

"Do what?" A soft click came as the piano opened up.

"I still want to go international. Look here. I have the requirements."

I quickly took out the printed sheet I got from the website and brought it to him.

Two fingers pressed against the side of professor's temple. Each passing moment of looking at the paper made his eyebrows grow narrower. "You do know that it says the next video send is due in a month, right? There's no rush. You could always join it next year when you're more…"

"But I am prepared to do this! I can do it! I can practice hard!"

"And that's your problem. You always work too hard and look where your health got you these last few days. Not to mention in the past. Do you really want to scare the living life out of me again? How would you think it would be if you decided to tackle this? Another *bathroom scare?* And do you really think that father of yours will pay for flight tickets?"

Bathroom scare?

I was confused in thought for a moment, being lost in his words. I gripped the paper and forced it into his hands. "But it's here! Look!" I dipped into my pocket, pulling up my phone and went into my internet tabs. "See? The prize money is ten thousand. We would get more than what we put in!"

"That's how things usually go… I guess that changes a lot of things. Especially with that mindset your father has with…"

"Professor."

"I know, I know sorry."

"Please."

He must have noticed my desperation. He rolled his eyes to the side, looking at his shelves to the back of the room, then at the form again. His eyes suddenly grew wide. "Wait, this is in Russia?"

"Yeah! Haven't you been telling me that you wanted to go back and visit your hometown? This would hit two birds with one stone, and you'd be able to help me there!"

"You know that I'm still unsure of what's going on with my performances. Although that one conductor is on and off with me, if I end up having a concert during that time then I won't be able to go there with you."

Of course. How could I have forgotten that professor had a career too? I looked down with disappointment, but I still wanted this. Even if he wouldn't be there to cheer for me. "It's alright. As long as I get in the practice, I know I can take it."

"Ugh… I really can't if you look like that at me." Professor shook his head and handed me back the application. "I…I guess then it's fine."

"Oh professor! Thank you!"

"But if you're joining this competition, you're going to have to play something like this." He got up from his chair and walked behind the piano to his three wooden shelves. They reached to the ceiling and were crammed with books. He hummed as he tapped a finger on each one.

"One…Two…Ah! Here it is!" He pulled out a minty book and came back to me. "You need to learn this."

The pages barely looked used. A familiar crackle of fresh dry paper came as I opened it.

"This is Liszt's La Capella. You know this song, right?"

Of course, I did. I too was a fan of Liszt, and every other composer that ever lived. But I seldom touched his pieces. I'd always done more lyrical and slow pieces for my performances. Professor said that feeling empathy was better than feeling the speed of a song.

"Yeah. But doesn't this piece seem a bit short? The time limit on each piece is eleven minutes. This is barely half of that time."

"Don't let the number of pages fool you. Can I see that for a second?" He reached back for it and ushered me to move from my seat. He pushed the bench farther away from the piano and sat. Professor looked at the notes for a moment. His eyes moved like the arm of a typewriter and I stuffed the form back in my bag.

"Wow! I really haven't touched this in ages. Wonder if these hands still got it." He examined it for another minute before pressing the first key. I wasn't sure how long it had been since he played this. Though it barely seemed to matter. The moment his fingers pressed down on those ivory keys, they played and played. He went through each measure as if it were nothing, as if he never needed practice. Each arch of an octave to the crescendo of the rising tides of notes. Perfect. Absolutely perfect. Then his fingers became faster. His pace, my pace. My chest didn't dare breath, watching whatever creature had taken over his hand. I heard it starting to become more powerful as the leaps grew quicker and wider. His hands didn't want to stop. Neither did the trills. His fingers so precise as if playing faster than sound itself. And his fingers would keep going and going until…

"Well, that was close enough. I always hated that part!" He straightened out his arm which made a small click in his joints. "But my hands are getting a bit stiffer. Guess age is creeping in on me… " I barely heard his words, making out a muffle of a voice until he snapped the book closed.

"Think it's too much for you?"

"What? Oh, no! Not at all. I'm sure I can do it. I want to do this!"

But do you want to?

I turned to look behind me.

"This isn't something that can be pulled off in a night or two. This thing usually takes months. If I see you going back to the hospital because of something like this, then the competition is off. Deal?"

"You have my word." I smiled back at him.

"Alright. Then I guess that's settled. Let me write in the fingering for this, then I'll have you start it on your own for today. Got to meet up with the stingy conductor today."

As professor kept himself busy with writing in the music, my eyes looked with curiosity around his room. The aesthetic seemed similar to that of an elderly woman. A desk with small drawers attached underneath rested near his window. Small and curious antiques made a home on his shelves. The middle shelf had a small shine of collected sunlight which strung its beads down on a small glass bowl. It shimmered like opal with a warm glow in the center. I was immediately locked on it, entranced by its beauty and by the thin linked chain draped teasingly down the bowl's side.

"Is this yours?" I let it slip into my hand, feeling the cool shape of the heart-pendant nuzzle in my palm.

"Oh. Oh that?" Professor placed the music score down, his eyes seeming to keep contact on the fragile item. "Yes. No… It was uhm… A gift I was supposed to give to an old friend years ago." He carefully took it from my hand and brought it close to him.

"From here? Or when you were living in Russia?"

"Well… She and I both used to live there. I actually met her there. We came here through separate ways, but I never had the chance to give it to her. Her love life… Was a bit complicated."

Professor rubbed a thumb around the heart piece. He must have forgotten I was there for a moment, nearly jumping when he caught me glimpsing at him. A cough caught up in his trails of soft laughs. The necklace slipped out of sight and into his back pocket. Once again, professor went back to the music score lying on the bench.

"Okay um… So, practice getting the fingering down and a rough idea of the first page or two with both hands. We'll start the real work next class. And don't overdo it today. Got that?"

"Well, you won't have to worry about that! I have a dinner later tonight."

"Really? With your father?"

Have we ever had dinner together?

"Actually no. I'm going to the Walker's home!" I took the music back from him and carefully slipped it into my bag.

"Walkers? As in Oliver Walker's house?"

"Yes! His mother invited me to come for dinner."

"Now that's something I thought I'd never hear again. Just how long has it been since you've been over there?"

"This is my first time going. But both his mother and father were kind enough to invite me and father."

"First time? They're really alright with him going too? Not sure about that… Well, then you have fun." I got up from the bench and slipped my shoes back on. Professor opened the door for me. "Just remember, you two are competitors. And sometimes Brighid really has a way of showing off her son."

Professor followed me outside to father's car. His windows were up, and he slumped in the seat like he was asleep. I got into the back seat and watched as professor stood next to the driver's side. His smile was gone and he knocked a knuckle softly on the glass. My father let the window roll down, but only enough to his eye level.

"Wilton. Taking care of yourself as usual, I see."

Father grunted and let the window roll up. Before it did, professor slipped his fingers through and gripped onto the glass. My hands went over my lips and I gasped in terror. Father stopped the window from going up further, fear in his eyes. Professor's hand was hairs away from being trapped and his free hand tapped on his cheek.

"I hope you're taking better care of your daughter. Makeup can do a lot, but I know when it's being used to hide something."

Father looked at the steering wheel as professor pulled out his hand and examined it. "Malory, I told you. If you ever need my help, I'm a single call away. Don't you ever forget that." He stepped away from the car, heading back to his porch. "I'll see you later Wilton."

CHAPTER TEN

MALORY

IT HAD BEEN HOURS SINCE FATHER dropped me back home. He didn't deny me from going, but he also didn't say he'd take me. It was my mistake for assuming. It wasn't just his appearance, but his attitude seemed on high alert. Telling him of going international seemed to slip past his brain. Giving me replies like *Uhuh* or *yeah, uh huh, great.* He kept repeating strange mannerisms like scratching roughly at his scalp or kneading a palm across his inner thigh. By the time I'd gotten into the bathroom to get ready, the house grew quieter. Then as I slipped into my clothes, a loud rumble came from outside. By the time I'd gotten to the window, my father along with his car was gone.

I figured that he might had gotten a call from his boss or coworkers. It was the norm, especially at night. Most of the time, it was an offer for a house he'd been trying to sell. Father must have been pretty successful. Although he never told me if he made a sale or not, he'd sometimes come back quieter, much more relaxed than his usual. Most of the time he would be too tired to speak to me, going into his storage room upstairs and spending the night there.

I took my phone from the moist bathroom counter. It was almost seven and still no call back. Contacting him was something I never did nor something he ever allowed. Father could have been in the middle of work, maybe even close to making a deal. But something made me want to know if he was alright.

Dialing the numbers felt foreign, and waiting to hear the telephone ring was unnerving. What surprised me more was that he picked up. He actually picked up. And I should have felt happy, overwhelmed in fact. He was actually taking the time to answer me! Yet the booming in my ears wouldn't let me. Laughter crammed through the speaker and the crackling signal didn't help with hearing his voice either.

"Why ah you calling me?" His voice slurred.

"Remember the dinner with the Walkers? We're still going… Right? The dinner is at seven and it's almost time to lea…"

"I told you never ta call me during businessss meetin. Can't hear I'ma busy? An I aint eatin with those snakes."

"Well, I wish you might have told me because I don't want to keep them wai…"

"Bcause I hama own friends over here! Right? Donneed them shiheads!"

The speaker vibrated through the metronomic bass and a loud shrill of voices overclouded him.

"Is everything alright over there?"

He continued to yell and gargle, the voices around him only growing louder. The call soon flatlined.

The phone rested on my cheek long after the call ended. If I kept it there long enough, maybe he would have called back and explained everything. So, I waited, hearing nothing but the patronizing sound of that ticking clock.

Click. Tick. Tock.

"Of course, he isn't calling… He's… he's at a business meeting after all."

The loud strumming bass kept host of my ears as I slumped onto the couch. The smell of alcohol made me want to retch. And the longer I stared, the closer those bottles seemed to be getting. As if trying to intimidate me. I checked my phone again, letting father's number burn into my brain. That was when I called for a cab.

I never asked for her address, so thank god she called. I never recalled giving Mrs. Walker my number. I quickly told her that I was on the way and if she could text me the address. Soon after, a bright, almost orange-looking taxi pulled up. My head rested on the glass as I watched the trees passing by the hand-smudged window. Why did it feel better to be in here? The car of a stranger filled with the scent of cigarettes and laundry detergent? Why did anything feel better than the words that came out of father's throat not so long ago? I tried not to linger on that thought for too long because the noise might have come back if I did.

The driver sped off after I paid the fee. His car gummed up with dark purple smoke that hovered like a spirit. I turned to my destination, checking to make sure this was the right home. They had hedges like mine and frozen grass that stretched across the lawn. Two wide windows were filled with lights and looked down at me. A large camphor tree slept in the winter breeze to the right. The only difference was that their plants were sleeping, not dead.

"Oh Malory! Welcome!" Mrs. Walker opened the door, surrounding my body with the light from their home. "I didn't think you'd actually come!"

She closed the door behind me as I smiled back at her. Her clothes and hair, even her skin, was completely different from when I last saw her. Her blouse was red, plain. The sleeves tightly clung to her skin. No heels either. Below her white shorts coming close to her knees were a pair of fuzzy brown house slippers.

"Thank you for having me. And sorry I'm late. I actually forgot your address, so I'm really glad you called me."

What a surprising yet refreshing feeling it was, to be speaking to someone in normal clothing rather than dresses or tuxedos.

"Your father won't be joining us?" Mrs. Hawkin's voice cooed, looking behind me for another body. I followed her gaze to the sounds of that loud bass and female screams.

"No, he... He has work."

Through her clear dark skin and makeup-free cheeks, I still heard the sternness of a teacher leak out. That and the tone of an overprotective mother.

"Now that's a shame. But work is always important!" Mrs. Walker turned away from me, her lips pursed up towards their lovely staircase. "Oliver! Come down! Our guest is here!"

"Jesus Brighid, can you speak any louder?" Mr. Walker entered from what I guessed was their kitchen door, a phone in his hand and a coffee mug in the other. "You're gonna scare the poor girl."

"Hi Mr. Walker! It's nice seeing you again."

"Please!" He chuckled. " Save that formality for the stage. I always tell you Samuel works just fine. Make yourself at home."

A soft beeping came from the other side of that door and Mr. Walker turned back to the kitchen. "Be right back. The chicken is calling me."

"Follow me. Oliver should be down in a minute. Dinner is almost ready."

I took a few steps behind her, only for her to stop me again.

"I'm sorry, but could you please take off your shoes and leave them at the front door? We don't like to track dirt in here."

"You mean you don't like to track dirt." Mr. Walker mumbled from the kitchen.

She led me towards the kitchen door and my pace slowed with each step. My feet were cautious of stepping onto any beer bottles that might have been around.

Had they cleaned them all up before I came?

I kept my eyes to the ground, ready to maneuver my feet around a possible bottle or crumpled piece of garbage. Nothing. Absolutely nothing. Just an outstretched sheen of white marble sprayed with black freckles. My ears searched for the noise of my father's grunts as he took a bottle to his lips. Nothing. Only a friendly bickering between husband and wife.

Their home seems so different... Unnatural...

They had an uncluttered dining table and four seats instead of one. Father had broken the other one when I made him upset a few years ago. We haven't gotten a new one since.

The couch that laid on the border of tile and carpet was so fresh that the plastic cover might've just been pulled off. There was a smell of freshly lit frankincense and a smokey trail left behind. Yet, no candles were in sight.

"Sorry about the mess. It's been a while since we've had guests over." Her fingers picked at an invisible mess on the table.

"N-Not at all! I actually think your home looks very nice! It's really different."

"Different?" She smiled before I finished, as if she knew those were the words I was going to speak. "Well, I'm not so sure about different. Just a little home that we try to keep together."

I could have sworn I heard Mr. Walker let out a sarcastic laugh. From above our heads came the sound of banging keys.

"Oliver! I said come down here!" Mrs. Walker shouted.

The music refused to stop.

"Oliver! How many times do I have to say it? I know you can hear me!"

Mr. Walker scratched at his chin, quiet eyes following the direction of the melodic music. "Actually, do you mind fetching my son for us? He can be pretty stubborn when he's in the zone! Especially with his mother."

"Well, excuse you." Mrs. Walker gave a playful slap to her husband's shoulder.

"Me? Sure alright. You said upstairs?

"Yup. It's the first door to your right."

The music grew bolder as I climbed their wooden steps. By the time I reached the top, the entire floor was rumbling with his dancing fingers. Oliver's door was untouched by any dents or holes.

"Oliver? It's me, Malory." I knocked. "Your parents want you to come down."

A moment passed. The only reply I received was more musical passages.

I knocked harder and this time the music came to a halt. A soft squeak came from the other side. Probably his bench. The door flung open. The room's odor was of warm sweat and old leather. It might've been from the thick pieces of foam against the walls. Their job was to muffle out any noise coming from the room. Though from what I've just heard, they hardly did their job. Or maybe the smell could have been coming from Oliver. His hair wasn't up in waves of brown, rather a moist flat confusion hovering over his eyes. His skin glistened under the dark hue of the room, looking almost blue.

"I didn't believe it when she said she'd actually invite you over." I knew his eyes were fixed on mine, but it didn't feel that way. His gaze pierced through my pupils.

"Well, here I am?"

"And after all this time? Outta be the sickest joke you've pulled in a while. Congratulations. You won first prize."

Oliver... What do you have against me?

Oliver's shoulder roughly bumped into mine as he went down the stairs. After closing his practice room, I followed behind.

"Not even going to try, huh?" Mrs. Walker stared at her son as she put down a blue-rimmed porcelain plate.

"What's the point? We always try and you know it's never gonna happen."

"But this is different. We have a guest over."

"I'd hardly call her that."

"Oliver Walker!"

"Fine! But don't blame me if an argument happens all over again. There's enough bad energy going on in this room." He gave a hard glare before leaving the kitchen.

"So sorry you had to hear that." Mrs. Walker slipped on a pair of red oven mitts that were hovering by a silver hook.

"Is Oliver alright? He seemed pretty upset."

"Oh, that boy is always upset. And it's not him... Our daughter never wants to join us for dinner. The last time she was down, fingers were being pointed at everyone and things just got out of hand." Mrs. Walker shook her head as she went back towards the table, placing a tray of chicken and herbs on a large coaster.

"Oliver has a sister?" I raised an eyebrow. " I thought he was an only child."

"Oh yes, he does. You've never known about her because... Well, you know how quiet Oliver is. And she never enjoys watching his performances. She is always busy with her own stuff. I'm honestly surprised that she came to that winner's performance."

From the other room, an electrical hum murmured. Mrs. Walker's eyes grew large, making both her and her husband turn heads.

"Well, that's unexpected. She's actually coming down." The sound continued for a moment or two before coming to a cranking stop. From the kitchen door, her chair barely able to fit through, came a girl. Her long black hair hung like two hurricanes battling against one another. The room reflected a sickly glow off of sunken prunes lined under her eyes. She sat in a steel chair, cloaked in a thin white dress that hung loosely.

"Oh Oliver, I do wish you would have made her change out of those clothes at least!"

Mr. Walker looked back at his wife and shook his head.

"Let's be glad she actually came down instead of you nit-picking at her, alright?"

His wife's face went a soft red before clearing her throat. "This is our daughter Elizabeth. Elizabeth this is..."

"Ben?"

How long had she been looking at me? Lively energy gleaned from behind her eyes. I wasn't sure what it was, but I felt it too. Somewhere deep down in the back of my head and down my throat—there was a pounding—a rapture of soft locks at the sides of my temple. It was almost speaking back to me, flickering my view hazy. My mouth opened. It wanted to say *Yes.*

"No? This is Malory. You've heard about her before, no? She and Oliver are usually in the same competitions."

She passed by her mother, both arms rolling the wheels until we were a foot apart.

"I never thought I'd see you again! How are you?"

This girl never existed to me. And yet, her existence made the pounding grow louder until it reached all the way down to my chest, locking my knees in place to stop them from shivering.

Again! Again! I never thought I'd see you again!

Her voice continued to play rhythmically, each reply making my view dimmer and dimmer. I felt the nothing creeping in on me, ready to trap me in its box. Ready to slip me on and zip me up. I didn't want to go. Not here, not ever! I refused to listen to those strings again!

What's your name? What's your name? Your name. What is my name?

It was that *voice* again. No, no, that voice was not real! It was the silence, it had to be! Just like how the booming was not real! Father was at work, there were no voices. No. No. He wouldn't be like that! You can't continue to replay a moment that never existed!!!

I dug my nails into my palm, trying to consume the pain, anything to bring me back.

My name. Is that even something I have?

The boy's voice kept at it.

Now, where was I? Where had I gone? Was I sleeping back at home? That couldn't be right… Had the dinner already finished? Why couldn't I see?

I blinked and blinked for the Walker's home to return. Slowly I began to lose feeling in my body. Everything had gone dark as the voice of that boy spoke to me. No longer was it a voice. Attached to that voice was a body. His back turned towards me while looking out the window of a room. My room.

My name. Name. Name. Name. My name is

"Malory?"

Steam pressed against my cheeks. I looked down to see a white plate, my shaking hand holding a silver ladle. I looked up to find eight brown eyes staring at me. It was the Walkers,

I was back. Mrs. Walker smiled at me with a bowl of mashed potatoes in hand.

"Would you like any?"

"Where? Um. Yes please. Thank you." My voice grazed while I grabbed the bowl. I still felt that darkness clinging onto my shoulders, wanting to take me back.

"Anyways, it's a shame. Isn't it?" Oliver's mother turned back at me. She smiled, but it didn't feel like she was. Oliver was sitting across the table from me, his head staring off in another direction as he ate.

"Shame? I-I guess? Sorry, but I'm not sure what you're saying…"

"What I mean is that I know competitors are always rough around the edges. Trust me I know from performing in the past. But we can only keep our music so close before we get consumed in all that madness. Right?" She turned to look at Oliver, his plate nearly empty with a smudge of gravy and mashed potatoes left.

Oliver kept quiet and his sister mumbled something under her breath. "It still doesn't matter, does it?"

"Elizabeth. What are you talking a…" Her father was cut off by Elizabeth's voice, now more raised.

"Exactly. Even now, don't you see how I look? What I am now? What I'll always be!" The family members straightened their backs as she slammed a fork down.

"Hey, watch your manner…"

"And yet the conversation is always the same. Brother this. Brother fucking that!" She brought her palms to the edge of the table, pushing herself away. The plates rumbled angrily.

"I thought coming down… I thought I might be able to hear something different for once. Now I'm back, and it's still the same!"

In an instant. She reeled her way out of the kitchen and towards the front door. The sound of her chair clanked as she slammed the door behind her.

Mrs. Walker quickly got up and was brought to a stop.

"Mom." Oliver caught her arm. "Leave her alone for now. If you go out there it'll only make things worse."

"What does she think she is going to do out there! In the cold with what she is wearing?"

"That isn't the point! You always talk like this with her. She likes it better when she's alone."

While they spoke, I seemed to surprise myself. I was standing, although I wasn't sure how long I had been or when I stood up. My jacket was halfway on and my senses continued to tell me to go for it. The pounding was back. It wasn't in my head or in my chest. It was a rush of adrenaline that coursed through me.

"I'm really sorry but I think I came at a bad time. I appreciate the food and all, but I think It's time for me to go."

"Jesus, I really am sorry Malory. You getting all caught up in this family's nonsense..." Mrs. Walker sat back down, her husband's arm already around her.

"It's fine really. I know things can be difficult. Maybe I can come over another time?"

"Of course. You're always welcome."

I was out of the kitchen after both husband and wife gave a small bow of their heads. Oliver hadn't looked up from his plate, sliding a finger across the grease. I slipped on my shoes and zipped my coat up. My body was on a high, fuzzing with static and breathing that I couldn't catch up with. The drive of anticipation followed me out the door as I began my search. I walked further from the house, looking right and left. Beside the camphor tree, a small glistening of silver hid behind.

"Elizabeth? Are you alright?"

She was there, alright. Thank god.

"Oliver and your parents were worried about you."

"Worried? Now that's something I haven't heard in a while."

"Aren't you cold?" Her dress was already speckled in snow drops. But she wasn't shaking. Her stare punched what warmth I'd built up in my body. That burning fire in her eyes…

"I can only feel half of it anyway. Coming out here, I actually believed for a second that I would feel more."

Beside her was a dead bush thick with snow. She shoved her hand into it, grabbing a chunk and spread it on her legs. Elizabeth's laugh croaked as she flicked the snow off her fingertips.

"See? Nothing! I can't feel anything at all! Hahaha!"

Through the night, I saw her shoulders shaking against the chair, her laugh going to the beat of it. I took off my jacket and placed it over her chest.

"Even if you can't feel the cold, some parts of you still can."

She gave a bewildered look, as if what I had said was something so bizarre. Elizabeth traced a finger across her snowy leg while I began feeling the weather lash back at me. It was a good thing I decided to wear a wool shirt and thick jeans before coming here.

"So, they call you Malory huh?"

"Well, that is my name."

"Back in the hospital, I know it was you. You called yourself Ben."

Ben huh? I like it. It suits you.

"I'm sorry…" I massaged my forehead. "I don't think we ever met in a hospital. I don't ever remember going to one."

I gnawed at my gums. The muscles in my tongue were beginning to stiffen. In fact, I didn't seem to bother going into those untapped memories. I figured that I worked too hard, passed out, and was driven home. That should have been the end of it. Yet here she was, this girl that claimed to know me. To know a name I didn't have.

"I mean... Maybe we have met." Saying this should have felt like a lie. "But sometimes it's hard for me to remember. I don't remember where my nights go sometimes."

"You said something similar at the hospital too. Still... I'm sure we talked long enough for you to at least remember me. I gave you my number!"

"I'm really sorry..." My head ached as my body continued to chatter. "What about we start over? Start fresh?"

"Seriously?" Elizabeth let out a loud groan and looked up to the sky. "You're a damn weird one... But I did like talking to you there. So fine. A restart I guess? Just how can someone forget an entire night's conversation like that?" Her finger snapped once.

"Well, it does make sense that I'd be in a hospital after collapsing. But I really can't recall anything."

"Well, there you go. Maybe another screw got loose in your brain and jumbled some memories." Her hand grip had a familiar firmness. "Maybe someday along the line, you'll remember me too."

But I do remember you.

"As you heard Oliver and your parents say, my name is Malory."

"Elizabeth. Although I think Ben suited you better."

She must've had pity on me. If it wasn't for my intense shaking and bluing lips, I'm not sure how much longer she would have stayed out there. We came back to the front door. My hands ready to swing it open and gain that lost heat. Mrs. Walker got to it first. She flung back, staring at both of us in misbelief.

“Goodness, you two are covered in snow!”

“So?” Elizabeth blew the snow off her shoulders. “It’s not so bad out there.”

“Do you see the weather outside? And Malory! Look at her Elizabeth, she is pale!”

“You’re treating us like we’re still children.” Elizabeth chuckled as she rolled past her mother. “I’ll see you later, Malory. Don’t forget about me next time. And don’t change your name again either!”

“I’m so sorry about my daughter. She can be very… blunt at times!”

“She was actually very nice to me. Also, thank you for the dinner. I really enjoyed coming here despite the things that happened.”

“Of course, dear! You’re always welcome to come back anytime.”

My stomach held the weight of a brick as I caught view of a car screeching into the street. The paint chippings and blackened windows made me gulp down my guilt, only to feel fear bring the bolder back up again. I gave a quick wave to Mrs. Walker as she closed the door and came close to the car.

I should have told him. How did he know I’d be here? Why did I forget to tell him!

The window rolled down a crack as I came close, my hands gripping for my shirt.

“F-Father? What are you doing here? I thought you had a meeting with your boss and coworkers.”

“Get in the car.”

"I swear I was going to text you and let you know! You know I never do things like this. It just slipped my mind over dinner was all. And I-I didn't know when you'd get back!"

"I said get in the car. I don't plan on making a scene here."

He took a quick swerve around the corner, beating the light before it turned red. I in return clutched onto the backseat. Almost immediately I let go again. Not because of the laced underwear I saw bundled up under my feet. But from the stringy yellowing liquid that came between my fingers. There were smaller speckles of it nearby. Dried and hardened. I swiped the mucus away from my hand and rubbed the rest on my jeans.

"I trusted you ya know that?" He slurred.

There it was again. The new smell he came back with every time he went to work. In fact, it wasn't only coming from him this time. The smell of cheap perfume left its vinegary scent everywhere. For once, I actually missed the smell of beer.

"I know and I'm sorry. But I didn't have any of their numbers. It was Mrs. Walker that called me… Somehow."

"So, what did she say to yah?"

"Elizabeth?"

"Who? What? No! That bitch mother!"

"Mrs. Walker? We w-were all just eating dinner."

"What dishe say about your playing?"

"We actually weren't talking about music at all. I did get to meet Oliver's sister…"

"What the bitch say about me?"

"She didn't mention you either. Just that it was a shame you didn't come."

"That oughta be the fakest shit I ever heard." Father grumbled as he took another turn. To the right, he nearly grazed a van that was parked at the far end of the street. "Where did you go before this?"

"I only came here…"

"Don't lie to me! I need to know!"

"I'm not! I swear to you I didn't go anywhere else!"

Since when has this car been so small?

I looked around. The smell of dampness coming up from father's seats grew stronger, making me nauseous with its sweet rubber smell. The car continued to swerve in its boat-like motion. Had he turned on the radio? The loud repetition of a stringed melody kept playing in the background. When I looked in the driver's seat, my father had disappeared. His place was taken by a dark figure that loomed right up to my face. It took my head in its arms. What I mistook for a soft embrace grew tighter. Its claws mowed through my hair, its other hand slipping with the precision of a tongue to my ear and down my chin. The hands rested around my throat as the world grew two times darker. I must have been underwater since I could no longer breathe. Only bubbles floated up, as if this car was at the bottom of a lake. The pressure in my eyes increased as it kept a firm hold. I should have tried to get free. But I couldn't move. More so, I didn't want to move. Small shadows had taken the form of fish, swimming around my eyes to the point of not being able to see anymore. The radio—the strings grew louder and then came a buzzing. It was similar to the one I felt at Oliver's house and during my performance. But this buzzing wasn't delicate. Not even nauseating. It came… in sudden forceful tugs. As if I was going to be dragged down past the car and into the earth.

You know you can't keep us living like this.

The strings were violins and the voice that spoke was new. The instruments screeched bloody wails and I smelled the deceiving color of blue.

Are you going to forget this moment too? Are you going to smile away everything in the morning?

I grew full of fear as I coughed on mind bubbles. They popped in white flashes. What was I doing in this car? Was I in a car? Maybe that was all it was. A dream, a dream, a horrifying dream that would just disappear in the morning.

Close my eyes, Close my eyes. All I need to do is close my eyes.

CHAPTER ELEVEN

MALORY

WHEN THE WORLD FINALLY SHUTS ITS ONE EYE and the light begins to die, all should be at peace. At rest. The music of silence would bring everyone it touches to sleep until dawn took its place. Only then, would things be alive again.

In this place, this cramped room, time didn't exist. Nothing felt alive... Just a ticking metronomic moment that never played onward. The only purpose this place had, was to play a single moment over and over again in the form of a repetitive melody. This was a place where light was banished.

I felt for the walls, trying to find a door or opening to leave. The walls didn't end and seemed to stretch on for an eternity.

I'm so sorry... I'm so sorry honey I won't do that again... You believe me, right?

"Hello?" I gripped at my throat, feeling my lungs wrap up in dust. "Is anyone there?"

My voice was drowned out by a frigid silence and melody that wrapped itself firmly around my wrists. It didn't matter how far I tried to go. The farther I walked, the hotter the pain grew. It went all the way up and pressed against my neck like a steaming iron. But I needed to hear that voice. To know it was him. He needed to know I was here!

I would never betray you like that. I swear I'll never do it again! What can I do? What can I do to make it up to you?

"You don't have to do anything! Just come back! Please! Don't leave me here!" My right knee gave in, sending my body face down to the ground. I tried to plow through, but my legs became useless, shrinking to half its size and no longer able to carry my weight. It was inside of me, filling me up. Every orifice of my body filled with grainy sand. My limbs gave way, turning into heavy sacks ready to burst. My body had turned small, shrinking to the size of a child.

"Where are you? You have to help me! Someone! Anybody!" My voice sounded too young.

The shouts were louder now, speaking in a continuous slur of mumbles.

Oh, what have I done, what have I done!? What kind of father am I?!

The music grew louder as I tried to overpower it.

"Is that you father? Can you hear me?!" The pain swelled, but it kept me going. The voice was coiling into the shape of a screw, the words sending a jab to my spine. Something from behind grabbed at my ankles and tried to pull me from the walls.

Oh,, oh, but I have to do it! Don't you see I have no choice?! As a matter of fact... You made me do this! If only you didn't look so much... So much... Oh god oh god what have I done?!

I squirmed as a sick warmness came over me, moistening my skin with the smell of sea salt. The stuff was coming from somewhere above, leaving small droplets to come into my eyes. I squinted to see and pressed my knuckles into my eyes. The darkness had turned to colorful speckles of firecrackers and by the second time I blinked, I was staring at a ceiling. It didn't matter if my body was only covered halfway. My head was soaked with warm water, its salt stiffening my hair. Being awake, I thought all those terrible feelings would've been gone. The memory simply lingered in my wrists, but the same couldn't be said about my neck. Somehow, a dry fever was hosted around my throat.

Cold wheezes of air licked their way from outside and into my room, bringing an ache to my bare skin. I turned to the clock.

"He didn't wake me up?"

Usually on days when my alarm was faulty, father would come in, making sure I was wide awake. It was past eight, hours longer than I should have slept.

I hurried to my dresser and found an oversized yellow shirt. A swarming pain came as the fabric nuzzled close to my neck. I winced as I pulled it down fully and looked into the dresser's mirror. My fingers traced four snake-like patterns around my throat.

The bang from downstairs made me jump. It came a second time before a doorbell followed. I pulled on my white shorts and headed downstairs. Each step was another bell ring. It wasn't common, but sometimes father would forget his keys, resulting in a series of loud knocks and kicks to the door.

"Hold on!"

I would've opened the door right away if it wasn't for the voices on the other side.

Did he bring someone back with him?

Being too short to look through the peephole, I drew back a corner of the curtains.

"What are they doing here?"

Standing with his hands in his pockets and head nuzzled into his phone was Oliver. Beside him was the busy hand of his sister, never stopping at the button.

I opened the door, taken back a moment by her appearance. Though she still had a yellowed tint to her skin, she didn't seem as sick as before. Her hair was straight, all strands slicked behind her ears. Her cheeks shone prettily in the sunlight. Of course, Oliver looked the same as ever. Same swooped up prickles of hair, same expression, same slouching posture.

"Finally! I told you she'd be home!" Elizabeth punched her brother's elbow. "Good Morning! Sorry if I woke you up."

"She's not the only one you've bothered…"

Elizabeth gave one more punch to her brother. This time to his gut, making him yelp.

"Oh, good morning." My voice couldn't reply the same amount of life. It was still tight from the clutches of sleep.

"I won't be long, but I got something here for you." On Elizabeth's lap was a brown paper bag. Her hands reached inside, and she pulled out a jacket.

"Thank you for yesterday. For talking with me again. Oh, and letting me borrow your jacket." She dusted off a few small pieces of snow on its fur. "It looked worn and kind of gross. No offence. So… I washed it for you. Don't worry, it didn't get hard from the dryer. I air dried it."

I took it from her. The cotton that had been worn down by the weather and smell of unnamable drinks was gone.

"Wow… It looks brand new! Thank you! You really didn't have to."

"And you didn't have to lend it to me." Her smile broadened.

"It's nice to see you again too." I looked at Oliver, his eyes staring at something in the snow.

"I'm only here because someone needed to drive my sister." His eyes rolled to look back at their car.

"And also!" She began again. " I swear I won't make a scene next time, so you have to come back again soon. It's not like Oliver has any buddies of his around anyway."

Oliver scratched his head aggressively and began walking back to his car. He left the passenger side wide open and hopped into the driver's seat.

"Wow. Rude much? Guess he wants me to go now. Sorry about his behavior. He's always been like this. Well… Not always, but mostly nowadays."

"It's alright. He's probably stressed about music or the winner's performance."

"No more talk of him. I've honestly had enough. As you could see from yesterday…" Elizabeth looked back at him one more time before her eyes grew large and bright. "I know! What about us then?"

"Us?"

"Yeah! Let's go out and eat somewhere else instead. Only if it's not a bother of course. I want to leave the house anyway."

"That does sound nice. I'm sure if I ask my father then he'll agree." I caught my hand pulling the shirt higher onto my neck.

"Text me if you want to or not. Oh yeah!"

She pulled out her phone from her side pocket and handed it to me. "You might have forgotten about this too. But here is my number again." She shone her screen at me as I pulled my phone out to create a contact for her. I licked my lips as they grew dry.

I've seen this number before somewhere.

"I swear you better not lose it this time."

"Don't worry I won't. I'll have it right here." I showed her my screen after pressing save.

"Good, good. I'll get a text from you soon kay?"

Elizabeth's smile faded as she cocked her head to the side. Her eyes looked steadily at something below my chin. She must have realized that I was following her vision because she immediately snapped her eyes back up.

"You uhh… Call me later if you decide to go or if you also need someone to talk to. I'll see you for the finals."

"O-oh right. Of course! Thanks, I'll make sure not to forget."

I'll see you for the finals

Finals? What finals?

The moment I closed the door was when I heard a quiet wailing. I searched in my father's room downstairs and the kitchen but soon realized that it was coming from upstairs. Specifically, the storage room. My feet paced up the stairs. I knew better than to go in, but the temptation of seeing it slightly unhinged was enough. I needed to make sure he was alright.

Two fingers to the door made them nearly chop off. The door swung open again before closing behind father's body. His face had grown puffy with sags in his eyes that seemed to stretch down to his cheeks.

"I tol younot to comein here."

"But I was worried."

"Who was that out there? Andre?"

He's only getting worse day by day… Does he realize what he's doing to himself?

"Father… You need to stop drinking. It's ruining your health."

"I said who was that? You can't just open the door whenever you please."

"I-It was Oliver and his sister. She wanted to return my jacket to me."

"You gave it to her?!"

"She returned it."

"What do you think we are? Rich? You're going around and letting people borrow stuff?" He pressed his thumb to my forehead. "How much of your brain is left? You really think people like that who are smothered in money need your clothes?"

"But she was outside in the cold."

"Well, that's her damn fault! And I still can't believe you had the nerve to go there on your own! How did you get the money, huh?! Did he take you there?"

"I-I found a little extra in my bag and used it for a cab."

"Wow, the effort you'll go to steal from me! Wow! This is why that happened to you last night! Now you see it really isn't my fault! For you to think you're innocent!" Father pushed by me while stumbling to the stairs. "You don't actually believe that you'll be seeing them again like that do you? He is your competitor. Your enemy. You've seen how he acts towards you. Yuh really want to be around that?"

Father's words were always absolute, a law that I never wanted to break. A law that I always wanted to respect.

"Well? Do you?!"

"Of course, I won't. I told them I was busy anyway."

To my horror, those words spoken just now weren't the one's I'd expect. Ever expect.

He didn't seem to believe me at first, eyeing me for a hidden lie stuffed somewhere in my pocket or ear or flinch from the corner of my lip. But I wasn't lying. I never lied to my father. And yet, someone else did.

That voice...

It took every effort to hide the fear I felt. Then I was struck with something worse than the lie. The fact that I... Was alright with it.

After father walked down to the kitchen, I went back into my room and came to the pile of scraps dumped from my purse. Lying at the very top of the mound was the creased piece of thin paper. I didn't realize how shaken my hands had been as I pulled it out from the rubble. I took out my phone and went into Elizabeth's contact info. My eyes must have looked over them ten or twenty times, hoping one number didn't match. And yet each and every time, I was never given that satisfaction. Only denial.

"I really did meet her at this hospital..."

It took a while before I was able to speak my mind. Father was going through my scattered music books in the hopes of finding a new piece. I bounced my leg up and down as the burn around my neck grew stronger.

"Father? I..." I barely heard my own voice. "I talked with professor about it."

He turned around, nearly hitting a stack of books by his elbow.

"I need to go international. I already told him, and he finally agreed."

"You were telling him before you told me?"

"I have tried though! Each and every time you were dr..."

"I was what?"

"I know that the tickets will be expensive, but the winner gets ten thousand dollars."

"What if you don't win like last time? What if you have another atttack? Where will all that lost money go then?"

My neck writhed in agony.

"Well I..."

"Exactly." A loud thud came as father dropped the books to the floor.

"There are only so many times that I can join these competitions and I'm getting older! Please, I'll try to help with the money too..."

Of course, it had to ring. Of course, father's phone had to go off right when I finally had the courage to speak. His eyes narrowed at me while picking for the phone in his jeans.

"Who is this? Oh! It's nice hearing from you. What seems to be the problem?" Father's dismembered voice disappeared.

Someone talked at the other end. I strained for my ears to hear. The voice was much too soft.

"Yes. Yes of course! Thank you so much for giving my daughter and I this opportunity again. Yes, yes, of course we will. Alright. Thank you!"

The phone skid on top of the piano as he let it go. Father paced to the trash bin and began pulling out pieces of torn sheet music.

"Good thing your lazy ass didn't do the trash." He began straightening out the sheets and piecing them together. After doing a messy job of taping, he shoved them in my arms. "This is all you'll be doing today."

"But father." I looked with confusion at the music. "I already used this piece for Hanons' competition. Don't you think I should be learning another one?"

"No, because you're not done with that place yet. You're back in."

"I don't understand."

"Hanons called and said the judges were willing to give you one more chance tomorrow. I refuse to let you make another embarrassment of yourself again. No more stupid talk of going international. The only thing I want you to be doing is showing how much of a fuck up that son of Brighid's is. Now get to it. You're gonna stay here all night."

CHAPTER TWELVE

MALORY

YES, MY ARMS ACHED. Yes, I did get hit to the back of my head again. Did I take a break to drink water? I couldn't recall. I needed to make him exhausted somehow. The screaming and banging on the piano didn't seem to do the trick. Despite the rage I brought him after making that one mistake over and over again. It was only after doing it the fourth time that I realized I was doing it on purpose. Father had left a scattered mess of fresh empty bottles while I slaved on the Black Beast. He seemed more exhausted than I, slumping onto the piano bench while he told me to grab him another drink from the fridge. If things went the way he wanted, I'd be practicing till dawn. I watched my feet travel downstairs with eagerness. Alcohol never tired him unless it was in ravenous quantities to the point of being poisoned. That tiny plastic bottle in the cabinet told me it could help him. I hesitated at first, nearly slicing my nail off as I crushed the pills with the back end of a knife. Sliding the powder into the bottle felt like a betrayal. Watching it all dissolved however felt like an open door.

I need to see Elizabeth again. It's not like this shit will kill the bastard anyway.

I looked into the reflection of the kitchen window. Of course, I only saw myself staring back. I was the only one here.

"About fucking time." Father snatched the tonic and took it down in almost one go.

Drink it, drink it, drink it old man.

The ache in my neck was gone, replaced with a daring desire for his eyes to finally close. After an hour of practicing, his yelling grew to grunts and his hits turned to smacks. He was down, slouched on the living room couch while on the way for another drink. It felt wrong as I put a blanket on top of him and as I dialed for Elizabeth's number.

"Am I really going to do this?"

Maybe not. But I sure am.

The *voice* spoke to me and that was when I heard the ringing of my phone. Elizabeth shot me a text on where to meet, making me surprised that she was alright with meeting this late. It was almost eleven and the wind wasn't being the kindest. What was more surprising was that I started losing control of my hands again. It could have been anxiety; maybe fear from the shameful thing I did to my father. The surge of energy pulsed in my brain and warped at my eyes while I ran to the bathroom to grab my foundation. It didn't take much to hide the marks.

Hopefully, this stuff doesn't stain.

I came to my closet, feeling my hands rummaging and throwing clothes on the floor. I could've worn that pastel shirt with the white trim, or the broken in heels from two autumns ago. My hands went deeper into the cavity, pulling out a button up shirt that hadn't seen light in so long. I swore the thing was turning grey with dust. Bundled tightly in and far back hung black slacks. I snapped the clothes in the air, dust releasing its grip

Going into the bathroom, my bra fell to the floor as I felt the tight metal clasps of an undersized sports bra hug my chest. On went the shirt and over went my pants. It took a little bit of effort, judging by how sticky my body was from sweat. Two hands that were supposed to be mine grabbed for a dampened hair tie on the counter and pulled my scalp back into a tight ponytail.

"Father would be mad... No... He would be furious!"

My feet carried me downstairs and into some broken in flats. Next, my hands vibrated against the foggy rubber buttons of our alarm system.

Beep. Beep. Beep. Tick.

Each mechanical noise stung my ears. A weary eye looked to the living room couch; father's shadow cupped in the cushions. My breath grew heavy while grabbing for the keys by the door.

What am I doing?! Do you realize what's going to happen if you go out? Father... Father will never ever trust me again!

When had he ever trusted you? You're just his puppet.

Dark patches warped my view. One blink and I was by the door, the next I was in the driver's seat turning on the ignition.

I'm going to see her. Let me have this! Save your performing duties for another day!

I looked to the passenger seat. I should have been sitting there, not here!

"I can't do this! I don't know how to drive!"

I know you can't.

I took a final glance at the empty seat before turning back to see my hand on the stick and backing out of the driveway.

But I can.

The yellow from the glowing streetlights ran away from me. Somewhere that wasn't my room, somewhere that wasn't the stage. I felt it, being in those fearful students' shoes. They feared the stage, and I felt that fear coming right behind me as

I pressed on the gas. Patting rhythms on the steering wheel, my foot thumping onto the pedal.

There came a brightly lit building as I made a right. The place stuck out like a sore thumb from everything else around it. Just a simple cafe smacked in the middle of a nearly empty lot. I checked the navigation a last time before parking. This didn't seem like the place judging by Oliver's truck being nowhere in sight.

"Maybe it's not too late to turn back."

Taking out the keys, I got out of the car and felt the wind twisting around me. I was blacking out on my own drunken state of adrenaline rush followed by howling scolds in the wind. I walked closer to the cafe. If it were in the spring, the place would've looked more lovely. The frozen plants hanging around the roof's rim would have been a perfect contrast from the cafe's sunny color. The dying succulents would have been plump and dewy. The flapping wooden plank that read Camie's Home Cafe would've been resting calmly above the door.

All it took was a single glimmer for me to open the door. The same I'd seen during the party, the same I saw at their home. Elizabeth's wheelchair was folded up on the other side of the window as she sat alone at a booth. The inside was small and filled with flowers that were too bright and stiff to be real. Besides an elderly man that sipped loudly on his coffee while reading a pocketbook, the place was empty. I followed the glimmer of Elizabeth's chair to the far end of the room. There she was with her tanned skin and dainty hands resting on an aging menu. Her wheelchair was the opposite of her, propped up and folded tightly. Had she sat down by herself?

"Hey! Over here!" Elizabeth waved at me. I returned the gesture with two more blackouts.

"Took long enough to get here! I was about to ditch this place and walk out!"

"Is Oliver here? I didn't see his car in the front."

"Really? Common! I don't need him to drive me around. I got here myself. Ever heard of a taxi?"

My eyes grew so heavy, they were about to fall out of my sockets.

"So, are you ready to kick my brother's ass this time? If not me, then it's gotta be you."

"I'm sorry? For what?" I sat down across from her.

"Oh, you know! For the competition."

"I'm not too sure about that but it was nice for the judges and Hanon to do that for me. I know how hard it is to reorganize things like this so I'm pretty thankful for that."

"Judges? Hanon?" Elizabeth let out a comical snort, murmuring laughs through her arching lips. "The judges didn't plan on ever doing that round again. Like you said, too much hassle for them. It was my brother. You didn't know?"

"Oliver?" I sat deeper into the chair. "But… But he won? After all these years of being tied? That doesn't make any sense."

"Funny guy, isn't he?" She took a loud sip of her water before clearing her throat. "All I heard was him saying how it wasn't fair. That he couldn't accept something like this. I wonder if this place sells alcohol."

"What about the orchestra? They already set up for his piece, didn't they?"

"Yeah, a real hassle he gave them. There's no use for them to be playing with a ghost though. He outright refused. So, they had no choice but to give a redo. Anyways, according to him, the orchestra was ready to play either one of your pieces since the winning performance was only a week after, right?"

"Right... I still can't believe it... I'll really have to thank him later."

"Oh, I doubt he'll talk to you." She shooed a hand at me. "I tried to bring you up at home, but he ignored me. Like what is that all about?"

You're always defending him!

Two feet came beside me, and I looked up to find the figure of a woman. She stood tall, one arm behind her as if grabbing someone else's hand. Two large hoops danced under her ear lobes. They shone golden from an unknown source of light. She looked down at me with disapproval in her eyes.

Don't you ever think of doing that to my little boy again.

"Then again, that's probably none of my business."

"What?" I blinked hard as the woman faded. "Oh no, it's fine. I really don't remember ever fighting with him. I assumed he never liked talking with people since he's so...

"Robotic. Yes, I do agree with that." She pulled out the straw from her glass and tapped it on her temple.

When had I gotten so thirsty? I looked down at the glass of water in front of me. Melting cubes floated near the surface while the cup bubbled with sweat. It wasn't the only one. I tried to reach out and take it, anything to quench my thirst. But my hands remained still on my lap. I struggled to lick my peeling lips only to find my tongue resting inside my mouth like a piece of meat. By this time, Elizabeth's voice had grown so distant that I couldn't comprehend her anymore.

In. Out. In. Out. There. There it was. The feeling of hands gripping at me again. My weak state fell into their grasp, pulling my vision away from my sockets and taking me somewhere else. Almost like watching a driver. You're in the passenger seat, watching everything happen that you have no control over. And yet, you were still there. I tried to scream, talk, anything. Only empty air came out. Now a victim of my own body, I heard myself speak.

"So, uh… You come here often?" The *voice* rang.

"What kind of question is that?" Elizabeth let out a snort. "Is this your attempt at trying to make a conversation?"

I needed to break free, use my hands to tear away this invisible wall. But I had no hands, I had no legs, no feet. I was nothing more than a thought, a perspective.

"Well, it doesn't hurt to try. You always seem to be the one interested in me with all your questions. So, I thought I'd have a swing at it."

My body knew exactly what it was doing and knew exactly what it wanted. The banging in my chest to the fumbling of clammy thumbs from under the table all pointed towards a single cause. Every single strand of nervous twitches tied to Elizabeth's warm smile. None of those feelings belonged to me.

CHAPTER THIRTEEN

BEN

Really? You've got to do better than that! Did I actually tell her that she was interested in me? Stop slipping!

"Sure weirdo. And yes, to answer that question, I do come here often. It's a place my family used to enjoy before their nose got stuck up their asses."

I took another deep breath. The smell of burnt coffee and over-perfumed waitresses was so much better than the mold between Wilton's teeth.

To think being around Elizabeth made things easier to get control. I honestly feel pretty proud with the pills. It made the escape so much easier, but I really didn't think I'd be able to talk with her like this again. And damn I sure didn't think I'd drive that well.

"Unless that's too hot for you?"

How long was I staring at her dress? Should she be wearing that in this weather?

"Who?"

"The coffee? I'm thinking of getting one. What do you think I was talking about?"

"Oh no. Nothing. Yeah, coffee is good."

"Mhm sure." Elizabeth raised a thick eyebrow before looking back at the menu.

I uncrossed my legs, feeling the aching relief of comfort and space for a body part that wasn't there. It was the third time now I'd seen her. And yet, this was only the second time that

I'd been able to talk with her. Maybe one day I would let her know, I did want her to know. My name again, and that I did remember her. It'd already made complications, so I could only imagine if I started it up again. It was fun to wonder if I'd ever hear her lips murmur my name. I itched my cheek and hoped they weren't too red.

"Hi, I'm Martha! I'll be your waitress for this evening." The woman nearly jumped me out of these damn shoes. She was middle-aged and came up to us in a buttoned-up mint blouse and skirt too tight for her body. On her left breast was the name **Martha** etched in red. The waitress pulled out a small notebook from her pocket, ready for our orders with the click of a pen. She seemed normal, almost looked it. It was only when she turned to look at me that one eye followed and the other stayed behind.

Want to start off with any drinks?" She smiled kindly.

"You guys don't sell alcohol, do you?"

"Sorry mam, we don't."

"That's fine. I'll get black coffee please. Sorry. Make that a strawberry milkshake." Elizabeth handed her back the menu, seeming to be unaware of the waitress's lazy eye. "And a blueberry bagel with cream cheese. Thanks."

"A bit cold out for that no?" the woman jokes.

"Well, only half of me can feel it so it ain't so bad."

"U-um, oh right. Sorry." The waitress took a sneaking glance down at Elizabeth's legs before looking up again. "And for you, mam?"

I continued to wait for Elizabeth to answer Martha until I saw that her eye was on me.

"Right… Of course…" My heart fell six feet under. "Just an iced tea and bagel then."

"Alright! I'll be back with you ladies in a few."

I'm not a damn lady, lady.

After sweeping our laminated menus, Martha and her busty hips were out of sight. Elizabeth leaned closer again, her arms cupping the cool glass in front of her. She swirled the straw in the water before taking a long quiet sip. My cheeks grew hot as I looked back at my glass.

"Do you also play an instrument like your brother?"

"Oh, hell no! My family tried to push that on me when I was barely five. I told them I had other ideas in mind… They never supported them."

"What idea was that?"

"It sounds silly since I'm like this." Elizabeth cleared her throat. "But I always wanted to be a dancer. Obviously, that never happened… As you can see." Elizabeth outstretched her arms to the wheelchair as if displaying an expensive object.

"Well, I don't think that's silly at all. Do the doctors know if you'll ever recover?"

"Oh yeah, no. I'm through."

Well shit. What was I supposed to say now? That everything would be alright? That there was still hope? Nonsense. And yet, my idiotic brain seemed to come up with worse.

"Well, I'll find a way."

"What."

"I'll find a way for you to dance someday."

Are you actually a full blown idiot?

Now was the time to wait for her face to blow up and tell me she'd never want to see me again. She'd slap my face and that would be the end of it. But to think she would laugh? A laugh so wonderfully obnoxious that even the waitresses from the kitchen were popping their heads up to see the commotion.

"Oh god. Now that's funny! Wow, you never stop surprising me honestly!" Elizabeth went into one more episode of wheezes and tearful eyes before forcing herself to stop with a series of hiccups. By the time she quieted, Martha made an appearance with a towering shake and a teacup barely half its size. On separate plates, she placed down two large bagels squeezed shut by gushing cream cheese.

"You two enjoy your meal!" With that, Martha headed to the front where an old man had fallen asleep with his nose in a newspaper.

"But I'm up for this challenge." Elizabeth raised her glass, almost toppling over the large mound of melting ice cream. "I can't wait to see what you have in store."

That damn phone buzzing in my pocket was hard to ignore. Elizabeth rubbed breadcrumbs off her cheeks before looking down at my seat.

"You want to get that?"

The phone replied with another buzz. Annoyed, I finally took it out, finger ready to silence the noise. That was until the bold print of fear printed on the screen. It wasn't my worry alone. Deep down where puppet girl hid, I felt her fear build up as she read along with me.

Missed call from: Father.

"That phone of yours seems pretty busy, huh?" Elizabeth took another bite, squeezing a dollop of cream on the plate.

I could have stayed, maybe I could've run away. I had a car; I got enough gas to last me miles. Money would come eventually. Yet all the arrows pointed back to the most logical yet most illogical route of all.

"It's fine." I stood up from my seat. "It's uh… my father. He wants me to come back."

"Already? But we barely started chatting! I'm sure he'll understand if you shoot him up a quick text."

"I really wished it worked that way." I put the phone into my back pocket as I came to Elizabeth's side of the table. My hand squeezed onto her shoulder softly. "Let's do this again sometime alright? It was really nice to relax and talk again."

"Geeze, not even offering a ride home?"

This is the worst timing ever

"I'm really sorry Elizabeth."

"It's fine, I was only joking. I get it. Parents tripping up and stuff. Just don't let it consume your life like mine tried to do."

I sped towards the door, nearly tripping on the wire that welcomed guests as they opened the door. The parking lot had grown darker. No, it looked darker, dimmer, fading.

Shit. I need to hurry back before I switch out

Once I managed to shove the keys in, I reeled out of the parking lot. I dug my nails deep into the steering wheel, listening to nothing but the static of a bad radio channel and the huffs of steaming breath. One throb of my brain and I was back inside the mind. Another and I was back out again, nearly running over a white blob that had to be a dog.

Shit. Shit. Shit! At least let me get us all home safely!

Oh god, father is going to hate me! Why did I do this?

"You didn't, just calm down. This is my fault so let me drive!"

The front wheel grazed the curb that wrapped around this depressing neighborhood. The edges of my sight were disappearing which left a thin amount of road for me to see. If it wasn't for my gut, I wouldn't know where the hell I was.

The sudden stop woke my dazing head as I banged into the rim of the steering wheel. I slumped into the seat, unbuckling the viper's grip against my chest. The house was completely dark. Maybe he butt dialed me while at a whore house. I looked back down to the phone in my pocket now greased with sweat.

Nope, no imagination here. This crazy loon had called over ten times while I'd been driving back.

Things didn't look so bad when I was in the car. Maybe a small dent or two. Getting out however, the entire garage door crumpled inward like a smashed can. The face of the car scrunched its nose back, scowling at me with a twisted look of disgust.

Why did you have to hurt me like that?

I brushed the echo away. I didn't bother to look back, facing forward and clenching my teeth as the porch light caught my figure. The crackle of suicidal moths had a duet with the pulsing at my temples. Each clash of their burning wings sent a strike of pain to my head, as if they wanted me to feel their pain. I gripped at the knob to find it unlocked and slipped myself in. The room's entrance was etched with shadow and thin streamers of light traced from the circular window above my head. The thick shadow of an empty couch and tossed blanket screamed at me from behind. I turned to follow their screams, only to feel my head seconds later spun around by a fist curled into my hair. The force jerked my head back, stretching my neck to a max.

"Where have you been?"

I didn't reply. Rather, my eyes shivered at the three moons in the sky. The one peering through the window and the two glowing balls planted above each of Wilton's cheeks.

"I was out." I sucked on the raw of my tongue, burnt from the tea.

"And where is out?"

"A friend. You were sleeping so I thought why not. It's not like I had anything better to do anyway. She… I already practiced that song long enough."

"Oh really? Is that all?"

In Wilton's free hand, he pulled out a familiar plastic bottle.

Fuck

"What were these doing on the counter?"

"I was going to take them later. To help me sleep well for tomorrow's performance." Seeing that bottle made me forget the finger's tightening around my head.

"Oh well, what a wonderful idea! You really thought you could get away with something like this?" Wilton popped off the cap and jingled the pills inside. "You'll really have to stay true to your words now."

"I-I think I'm fine now actually!" I tried to pull against his hand. "Why don't I get back to practicing yeah?

"Oh no. You're so right! I think it's time for your nap time daughter."

With the bastard's palm at the back of my head, he began shoving me forward. The pills now inches from my mouth.

"Say AH!"

My teeth slipped past the bottle, sinking into the fat of his fingers. Wilton let out a loud gargle before setting me free. I ran the corner, nearly hitting my knee into the baluster. The bite didn't do much. Nearly five breaths away from me was the raging man and a bottle of poison. For a drunk, he was too damn quick. I cursed as he grabbed onto the ends of my hair. The back of my head hit the floor; the rest of my body being pulled like a heavy rug. Wilton's grip was a continuous clench, my eyes only able to stare back into the ceiling as I felt the rubble of fallen bottles under me. I didn't think I'd meet my old pal again like this.

The border from carpet to kitchen tile had not been made well. Screws hidden by the edge were sharp enough to scrape my skin and weak enough for this old shirt to outlive a terrible tear. What hurt more was the small button that came unclasped near the middle of my chest. The flat blinds brought darkness, but I felt the coldness of the counter as he pressed my cheek down on it. Blind to his actions, I raised a fist to his gut. His grip loosened for a moment before tightening again. The hand around my scalp dug into me. Wilton turned on the sink and warm steam bloomed from the sink's mouth. He closed that too, letting the water fill up.

"I want to hear you apologize!"

"Fuck you! I did nothing wrong!"

"One last chance!"

"Go to hell old man!"

"Fine!"

I forgot he had the bottle. Being pressed against his chest, Wilton shoved the pills into my mouth before placing a hand over my nose and lips.

One two three.

Four five six.

Seven e-eight nine t...

I can't take it!

The pills went down and so did my head into the sink. The world grew nauseating, swarming, raging hot. I had to close my eyes before they melted out of my skull. The light touches of what must've been my hair floated around me. Right when the dizziness was about to take over, Wilton lifted my head, barely giving me a chance to breath before launching me back into the water again. I kicked at his leg, scratched at his side, hoping to have him release me. The drunkard kept at it while I continued to wonder when this baptism would end. I felt my pupils touching the top rims of my eyes, struggling to keep awake. Poor puppet, poor Malory. My fears went away, and I couldn't feel her close to the surface. That was a good thing. It had to be. Being in the front meant that she wouldn't need to feel or experience these things. That was my purpose I needed to prevent. But what was the point of preventing it if I died? I tried to give one more kick, my leg barely lifted an inch.

Had it ever felt this heavy to lift an arm? The skin around my fingers felt so tight that they might have burst. I breathed in, only to receive more water gurgling up my nostrils and flooding into my brain. It didn't matter if my eyes were wide open. I was staring at nothingness, sparks of white light crinkling back at me. Wilton raised my head up a final time, letting it hover over the sink. At this moment, I nearly gagged from the amount of water sloshing in my lungs and stomach. My head went back down until my face was pressed against the bottom of the sink. As much as I wanted to be stronger than him, at least it was me that took the degrading beating, not Malory. She suffered enough already.

CHAPTER FOURTEEN

MALORY

"No, baby please I didn't mean it. Don't go, don't go, I swear I won't do it. I won't do it again. You saw her right? I had to do it."

It wasn't real. It was something I made up just like before. There's no way father would do something like this to me, right?

"Come back to me please! I didn't mean to turn out this way, you know that right? You still love me, right?!"

No no no... No! There's no way. There has to be a misunderstanding. If I put this away and stop thinking about it, I'll forget. I know I will! Then everything will be normal again and he'll forget about ever being mad at me. We could be happy if I just forget!

It stayed. Everything stayed. It should have gone away, it should have been a dream.

The first time I opened my eyes, it was night. The kitchen window had been wavering from the winter's howls. Stars peeked from the window's frame, blinding my eyes. They felt boiled and my body was drenched. As I continued to look around, I traced another light source. It was a bright light from the farthest door in the hallway upstairs. It leaked onto the floor and I swore it was sunlight. I looked once more, only to see the night again.

"Aria, please, she wouldn't listen..."

A murmuring voice came from deep in the hallway. Father. His cries were loud enough to be heard, but too far for him to be seen. As my vision adjusted, I found the glow to be coming up the stairs again. Not from my room or the practice room, but from the storage room. There he was again, drowning in the taste of vinegar and grapes. While I laid here with a frozen cheek to the tile.

The second time I opened my eyes, the moon was gone as well as the winding trail of father's voice. I traced the source of the aching light. The burning sun hadn't stopped the cold. The room was a freezer, striking every inch of my constricted muscles. A lake had formed under my drenched hair. Any cooler and it would have frozen over.

"Father?" I drew back my voice as I called his name. "Are you still there?" It didn't matter that I was soaked. My throat was cracked, sounding like I swallowed a bucket of nail clippings. Biting hard on my lip, I hoped to feel something. Nothing. I must have been turning blue. I curved my elbows in and tried to hoist myself up. Only to come crashing down moments later, scattering more droplets of water on the floor. The morning drummed its bright colors into my brain like a jackhammer.

From the living room not far from me came the faint noise of a door opening.

Footsteps? Is father home? But why would he leave me here like this? He would never do that!

The creaking of the floorboards was slow. Then the steps came faster with the loud clunk of some metal object falling down to the ground. Just as suddenly, my head was cradled by someone's hands. Father's hands.

I knew he wouldn't forget about me.

"Father? Where did you go? Who were you talking to?" I tried to blink the haze away.

Of course, there was nothing to fear. He would take care of me.

"Oh Jesus, Malory! Why are you down here like this?"

The mellow voice stung my ears. More so, it stung my chest the more I listened to it.

"You're freezing cold. A-And drenched! What happened?"

Another hand slipped onto my forehead, bringing a light warmth I hadn't felt in a long time.

"What are you doing here? I thought…"

"Wilton! Damn it! Where are you?" I wanted his voice to stop shouting. It hurt too much. My muscles, my brain. Guess he was able to tell. He went quiet, though his voice filled with a raging fire. Professor… I wasn't sure why he was here or how he got in, but that didn't seem to matter. He sat me up on the couch, his wool coat already taken off and wrapped around my shoulders.

"What are you doing here? I thought we didn't have class today."

"Why am I here? Thank god I came! I was here to bring good news but didn't think I'd see this! Where's your father? He left the front door wide open. His car hit into the garage."

Boom. Boom. Boom.

Bcause I hama own friends over here! Right?

"I-I don't know."

Professor walked over to the kitchen, kicking bottles in his way and unplugging the sink. Hanging at the oven, he grabbed our used hand towel. One turn of his hand and the water soaking up my hair grew hot. The droplets on my skin were ablaze. I was drowning in that sink again. And at the same time, I wasn't there. Just a viewer, a spectator, a disconnection. But I felt it… The faucet turned all the way to the left, scorching my face, boiling my eyes. Father was there when I fell, talking to someone, standing over me. While I stayed… Doing nothing… there…And he…

"Did he do this to you?"

Tick. Tick. Tock.

"I don't remember."

Professor sat down and handed me the warm washcloth. I pressed it against my forehead as water rolled down my face.

He did do it to me. He did hurt me. Whether it was his intention to kill me that night... Or as he said, to teach me a lesson. I guess a part of me wanted to keep believing that everything was a lie, that he still was what I believed he was.

"No... No it wasn't. He didn't. I showered... I was showering, I think I was just too exhausted... from practicing."

Why do I keep protecting him?

Because you love him as much as I do.

I looked around but only professor was there. This voice... didn't sound the same as the one talking with Elizabeth.

"Can you get up on your own? You need to get out of those clothes."

"Yeah, I think so."

As soon as I put weight on my ankles, they buckled, and I was back down on the floor.

"Here. Hold onto my shoulders."

Professor wrapped my arms around his neck, reaching his arm down to my back and lifted me off the floor. He brought me to the bathroom along with his now soaked torso. "I'm going to turn on the heater and get you some clothes from your room. Wait right here, alright?"

"Thanks. Sorry about your shirt and jacket." I waved one of the long jacket sleeves at him.

"Don't worry about it, alright? I'll be back."

I looked at my thighs and covered them with the jacket. The only flowers father gave me were the purple and green ones forming on my skin.

Fifty seconds later and the rumbling from the heater was on, probably blasting past its limitations. Professor's pace was fast up the steps and was back in a matter of seconds with a long sleeve shirt, fuzzy pajama pants, and a starchy towel.

"These should keep you warm. I'll be just outside in the living room."

I nodded and he left with the door closing behind him. I wasn't sure how I managed to pull it off. My arms were sore, and my entire body felt blistered. With a few maneuvers and quiet strains, I was able to slip on the oversized maroon shirt and ginger-colored pants. Taking a few twists of the towel, I managed to squeeze out most of the water in my hair. As for the drenched clothes, I left them to dry over the shower. Back in the living room, professor was looking out a window near the front door with watchful eyes. The metal clang had to be his keys. I suppose being in a drowning, almost dying state made things seem louder than they seem. I picked them up from the floor and brought it back to him.

"It makes me sick..." Professor zipped his duffel bag. "You're like a daughter to me. How could he..."

"He didn't!" My voice squirmed. "Father does care about me... But you were right. I do need to take better care of myself... I mean look what it did to me."

All he did was stare at me and shake his head. Standing by the door was his mug decorated in music notes. He placed it into my hands. "Whether you're right about him being good or not, I've already told you. Once I have something on him, I'll have your dad where he belongs. I feel like I have enough already. But you're also an adult. You need to tell your story too."

"Why?"

"Why what?"

"Why did you two end up this way? You two were supposed to be close."

"Life changes. And people change. I just didn't expect Wilton to turn out this way. The way he treated you… The way he treated Ar… everyone else around him… I don't want to associate with people like that anymore. Even if he was once my closest friend. Can you believe it?" Professor put a hand to his heart. "I've caught a voice or two gossiping about me. That I was the reason you collapsed. I mean I don't care what others think. It just hurts a little to be thought of that way."

"But that makes no sense!! You've done nothing but help me."

"And I'll continue to keep helping you. All I ask if for you to be more truthful to me. I promise if you let me help, then he won't have to hurt you anymore."

I looked out the window, already feeling the wheels of that chipping car coming closer.

"You should leave before he gets back. I know he'll want me to get ready for the competition with Oliver."

"Your father doesn't scare me." Professor took his satchel from the floor and looped it around his shoulder. "As your tutor, I know you're in no shape…

"This competition is giving me another chance. I've got to prove that I can win this." I passed behind him, opening the front door. "And I'll try to make sure those rumors about you stop after this."

Professor smiled at me, but it wasn't filled with happiness. "You always care about the ones around you. When will you start doing that for yourself?"

The clock became my companion during those moments, my eyes continuously attracted to its pendulating tick. The moment the ticking turned into the sound of running water, I left the kitchen in hopes that it would stop following me.

"It's barely been an hour…"

The clock struck nine. I was plastered on the couch, sipping tea from professor's mug. If things hadn't gone the way they had, I might have actually enjoyed the sun pressing against my cheeks. Instead, it pressed hot blisters into my skin. One pound was enough to get me up. The sound nearly scared me off the couch. Then came a quiet creak.

"He's back."

My hands tugged myself up onto the stairs while my feet slid onto the wooden floor and nearly slipped when I made the curve to my room. The moment I shut the door, the front door swung open. My thoughts were severed short as I heard the moans of stairs creaking from the weight. Then it stopped.

Minutes past by me. Although it might as well have been seconds. Time was hidden from me under those sheets. Maybe if I dug deep enough into the mattress, then I would have disappeared too. It didn't matter how far I'd go, how far I'd try to suppress these feelings. His hands always seemed to find me.

"The hell you lying there for?" The usual stench of alcohol was barely present through his yellowed and chipped teeth. Although, judging by how tightly my father rubbed his palm against his head, a hangover must have taken a toll on him. I nearly threw up from that smell of apples and peaches. The number of bruises on his neck only seemed to increase.

I told you never ta call me during businessss meetin. Can't hear I'ma busy? An I aint eatin with those snakes.

"The competition is tomorrow, and you bother to sit there wasting your life away?" He came closer, nearly knocking me off of the bed. I scrambled up, sitting on my knees, pulling my large shirt down.

"I-I must have forgotten to set my alarm."

His eyes nearly folded close. Why had it gotten so hard to smile at him? I usually could. I always would. All I managed was to do was bite my lip and bring blood up from their blue tint.

"You're lying again. Do you really want to do this all again? How long have you been up?"

Why am I feeling this way?

"I told you, just now."

"You haven't been downstairs yet?"

"No, I was sleeping this entire t…"

"I saw it downstairs." In his hands was professor's mug.

"No, I…Y-Yesterday! I woke up in the middle of the night… I made myself tea because I got cold…"

"This isn't ours! Was Andre here… What are you looking at?" His eyes caught mine focused on the purple splotches. "Really? This? I told you I was at work."

"Yes, I know that, but I was wondering why you have a bruise agai…

"You think I'm betraying her or something?! You think I'm a

fucking low life, don't you!"

Am I really going to keep telling myself this? That those were from some accident in his office?

"Well guess what! It doesn't matter what I do now because she's gone and you're still fucking here!"

I can't keep doing this

Do this for papa's sake. He cares for us.

Does he really?

I looked off to the stack of books that never seemed to end, this life I lived that never seemed to end. How much did it take to make father happy? More than that, would I've ever been able to experience a smile on his face? Was that really too much to ask?

Father pulled me off the bed and dragged me to the next room down. The Black Beast awaited me, and he shoved me towards its leather seat.

"You will not leave that bench until it's time to leave! No more of your little schemes! And oh, if you think I'm not going to watch you perform this time then guess what missy? I'm not scared! I'll make sure I can hear every fucking note you pluck from those damn keys!"

Him watching me? Since when was the last time he'd done that? Never. At least from what I remembered. And lately, I was beginning to think that I couldn't rely too much on my memory. I didn't want to believe it before, but I pushed it off as him being too nervous to watch. I get that some parents might be like that, judging by how tightly Mrs. Walker clenched her hands as Oliver performed. When I used to ask him in the past, I became surprised at how quiet his voice grew, and how active his eyes bounced around, leaving before my performances began.

"You won't be making an embarrassment out of me again. I better not find you spasming on the stage! According to your little doctor's orders, I've given you plenty of water yesterday."

The memory came like a scorching tidal wave as I looked down at the keys. Black and white blended together as the room turned into a silver hue. My throat grew tight as more water swarmed into the room. Only when I was able to let in a deep breath before playing, did I realize that I was no longer underwater.

CHAPTER FIFTEEN

MALORY

Tick. Tock. Tick.

"Again! Again!"

Tick. Tick. Tock.

"AGAIN!"

Tick. Tick. Thud.

Numbness grew in my hands and ears each moment I restarted. Time and time again… Fifteen minutes, then thirty minutes, on only three measures… Whether it be paranoia or father hovering by me, it all came out wrong! Every note and slur that swept across those monochromatic planes!

"Don't understand…" my head collapsed onto the keys. I knew it was hard… God, I knew it took me twice… Three times as much effort than other musicians to get a piece down. I had to believe that it'd eventually stick. But this was impossible. I pressed a hand against my ears which were in a continuous battle with the phantom symphony. Why was my mind always tormenting me?! Its strings began grinding the moment I saw my father. I thought it would have quieted down eventually. I hoped for nothing but the last few whispers of a freshly plucked string. He was listening to my every movement, every breath, every heartbeat… That made it all even worse. He couldn't hear the violin strings, of course he couldn't. I looked around the room with panicked eyes. The shadows watched me from their places on the walls, judging me. The lines on the sheet music were bars that were coming for me. I heard the running water of a faucet plugging my ears.

"Father don't you hear that? Please tell me you do!" The shadows' eyeless faces stared at me.

He looked just as surprised as I did when I found myself clinging onto him. "You hear them, right?! The strings?"

"Get off of me! The fuck is the matter with you! Do you want me to punish you again?" Father pushed me to the ground, and I felt the strings rumbling on the floorboards. I pressed my palms against my ears.

"No. I just want it to stop! Why won't it stop?!"

To my horror, the strings weren't the only things that visited me. I swore I heard it, that *voice.* The *voice* that drove to see Elizabeth. It wasn't the same. The laughs sounded like they'd come from a child. It kept nagging! And laughing at every small mistake I created! The tension was so great that it was enough to shatter my skull with its force. I scrambled back to the piano and played over and over again to prove the voice's mockery wrong.

Perfect. Perfect. It needs to be perfect. He can't get mad, he can't get mad again… If I just play perfect.

You are far from perfect. And papa can see right through you!

It wasn't exhaustion alone. The keys grew hard under me. Like putty had sunk into their sides, making it impossible to play. I banged harder this time, nearly cracking the surface of my nail. The pain swirled up into my hand and arm. I held tight onto my wrist; my fingers locked into a claw. I looked back for my father, but everything was turning hazy. His body was like the rippling waves of a muddy pond. Then in a blink, the pain was gone. Not just the pain. The dark walls, the dim yellow light, the bench. The Black Beast. My father.

The focus came back to my eyes as I stared down at my notebook, hands curled and nailbed bleeding. The aching strings plucked. There were other eyes looking at me. Eyes which were hazel and wide in shock. His body leaned back into the chair, like the day he spoke to me. What did he say again? I won't let you win?

I didn't hear his song. Though it probably sounded the same as that day. My mind was so wrapped around needing to get every note right that I didn't realize he already came back to the waiting room. I paid no mind to him and looked down at my hands. Knuckles, like pomegranates. Warm to the touch, yet shaking from the cold fever inside of them. That day, was this how he felt… Was this what nervousness felt like? As if all those hours of nonstop practice didn't matter in this moment. Oliver… Not just him, all those pianists went through this too? Every competition? Did they also hear the strings? What fate was in store that made them so fearful? Was it something worse than mine?

"I think I get it now." My voice spoke solemnly. In the distance behind the waiting room's closed doors, I heard two men talking.

The only thing that spoke back were the lights in Oliver's eyes and the lowered arch of his eyebrows. Why was he looking at me this way?

"Your sister told me. You refused to play for the orchestra."

"I didn't do it for you." He looked at me with those empty eyes.

"Even so… Thank you. With this, you gave me another chance."

"With what? If you think I'll cave in with pity, then you've got another thing coming. I'm done trying to help you."

"No... I know that... I'm hoping this will give me another chance with my father."

The life that refused to live in the back of Oliver's eyes gave a moment of spark. I could have sworn that his hands clutching onto the chair looked tighter. Why did he look so frightened of me?

"What's that supposed to mean?"

"I can't agree to that!" From behind the door, whatever talk was going on grew into an argument. "I've done enough! I'm done, you hear me?! Done! She is not leaving here, ever!" The man shouted and cursed; the other voice was barely heard.

"The hell?" Oliver got up and went close to the door.

"Please why are you being this way? Your daughter said this was what she wanted." The quieter voice spoke.

"Why am I this way?! This is your fault! She doesn't know what she wants! Nothing about this is good for her! I'm ending this all you hear me?!"

"How would you be able to do that? And yet you're the only one that has allowed all of this, right? Wilton stop acting like the victim and go back to your home that you worked so hard to get."

Oliver opened the door and I looked out from where I sat. Professor's button-up shirt came loose around his neck. He was pressed up against the wall, father's fist twisted around his collar. From down the hall, Clarice came running. Oliver left the room and I followed behind with disbelief on my face.

"What is happening here? Stop this!" Clarice stopped near my father and he looked ready to punch her.

"Why are you hurting him!" I was surprised by my own voice. Before I managed to get closer, Oliver grabbed my wrist and pulled me back. He kept his eyes on my father and shook his head. "Stop it. You're always getting in harm's way."

"Me hurting him?! You're always on his side! But I'm your father!" Father staggered to look at me, his coil still around my professor. His lips were covered in yellow grease and fresh new patches of alcohol stains soaked his jacket.

"Malory, get back. Wilton! What is going on with you?!" Clarice stepped in front of Oliver and I right as professor pushed himself away from my father. His lip looked busted; his shirt halfway untucked.

"Nothing to worry about here. Just a little argument. Clarice you don't need to call anyone. Wilton was just about to leave. Weren't you?"

Clarice looked back and forth at the two. "But..."

Father shoved his way past Clarice. He looked down at me. Anger fumed in his eyes. There was something else hiding there. At that moment, it felt like it was only my father and I in that hallway. I stared at the aging jacket. The fabric was torn close to the bottom from all the trudging in dirt and snow. The collar stood rigid. Now that I was really able to get a long look at it, it was empty. Just a dark space where a body should have been. I squinted harder, hoping for his image to form. But he was gone. The static of strings grew louder.

How long had it taken me to realize that? Maybe it was when I was younger; that empty decade where nothing ever seemed to piece together. At the same time, I wanted to believe it. That the girl I sometimes saw in my head was me, holding the hands of this man that should have been in front of me. But now... Father had turned into this... This thing!

I took a step closer to it, seeing the body that took hold in the jacket. No, not a body, the stench and shape of a monster. This monster that once took the form of my father. It stared at me with red ringed eyes, skin folded around its face. It curled back when I took another step. All the hours it forced me to play. All the hits, punches, and screams.

And yet, I loved you. I still love you father.

I hated that I still felt pity for it. At the same time, I hoped it would've been able to feel everything it did to me.

"Leave." Professor scooted me to the side. "Come back when you don't smell like a liquor store."

Clarice stayed by my side after the monster left. She told me how I didn't need to go through with it if I was feeling uncomfortable and that the judges would've understood. Professor was with her, agreeing with everything she said. He buttoned up his shirt and wiped his bruising mouth. Oliver disappeared at one point after my professor apologized to him for having to see this mess.

"What happened? What made him so upset?" I looked at my professor desperately.

"There is never an explanation for what your father does. The entire world angers him."

I stared at my hands while sitting in the hallway. There was a yearning in me. I longed to play on that stage more than anything. I knew somehow, though it might've sounded dumb, that I still had a chance of bringing back father. All I had to do was win.

We sat there for a few long moments. I couldn't bear to look at his face. "I'm going through with it. I still want to do this."

Professor sat beside me, shook his head, and placed a soft hand on my head. He gave me an earnest smile and didn't argue. I guess he realized that arguing with me was futile. "That fire in you never does seem to go out."

There weren't any ropes on the floor. The backstage wasn't dark like before either. The velvet curtains had been pulled back, revealing the wooden boards that completed the skeleton of the room. The lights didn't focus solely on the stage. Rather, the entire auditorium was lit from the viewing booths of every empty seat. After Clarice took her seat, her and the other two judges stared back at me. Their faces, emotionless and straight. Maybe it was due to the fact that they had to be back here again and listen to both of us play.

Don't worry. It'll be over soon.

Clarice looked off; her expression seemed fearful.

I faced the judges and bowed. When I did, I spotted my father sitting up straight in a seat. I almost smelt the hint of alcohol from his face drenched in...What was that? Tears? By the time I sat and gave the stage a final glance, he was gone. Just the coat he left behind and the dark being that took form.

You have no right to look at me that way.

From the reflection of the piano was the silhouette of a girl. Her large sunken eyes stared back at me from the other side. Her skin was pale and thin like sheets of worn tissue. I raised my hands and she raised hers. I looked down at the keys, and she bent her head down in remorse. This blistered, bruised little girl.

I pressed the first key but didn't hear a sound. I played a chord, and empty puffs of air came through the slits of the keys. The Black Beast must've not wanted me to have the satisfaction of hearing it cry. It didn't give me the satisfaction of hearing it at all.

I pressed harder onto the chord, then slammed my thumb onto a B flat. As if resting at the bottom of an ocean, I heard a soft muffle of what might have been the music. No matter how hard I tried to hear my notes, only the strings in my head grew louder. That was when my body tensed in a sudden panic. With the phantom symphony as my only guide, I played against its melody, hoping that at least one of my notes could've overpowered it. My foot relied on muscle memory of pressing on that pedal for hours on end. I hoped through this chaos, that the pedal wasn't blurring the notes together. Never had I felt so much at war with my music.

No one seemed to hear this battle. I stole a quick glance at the judges. They all seemed pleased. Especially Clarice with her small smile appearing again. No red circle on my name, no nods of disapproval. Just the three of them with their eyes giggling at me. But it wasn't their faces I was after. I looked at the piano crouching in front of me. It rested perfectly still, perfectly composed. After everything I had done to it, the Black Beast remained looking at me with wanting eyes.

If it weren't for the heaviness that continued to grow in my body, I would have raced out that suffocating building. Every muscle in my body had gone sore as if I ran a marathon. A body passed by me, though I didn't bother to turn, afraid the tightness in my neck would snap my head right off. I felt his head turn towards me, the sound of his feet stopping as our distance grew.

"Hey, wait up!"

Oliver came to me, his dark coat draped over his arm. A music book dangled from the tips of his fingers.

"Are you doing alright?"

"Yeah." I leaned against the wall. "I'm... A little tired is all."

"Your dad..."

"He's also tired. I'm sure that's why he acted like that." I pressed a hand to my ear, trying to muffle the sound of violin strings.

"Look…" Oliver tucked his music book under one arm. "You always protect him. You always do. But something is off. For once, you're actually scaring m…"

"Oh, there you are! Oh, and Malory too!" Mrs. Walker swayed towards us, a hand on her hip and the other ready to snatch the phone out of her husband's hand.

"Do you really have to be on that all the time? I swear you're no better than a child."

"Please. As if that dress was fitted for a sixteen year old. Why not wear something your age for once?"

It wasn't only the Walkers, something else was with them. And that thing was actually laughing along with them! Of all the times before with just him and I? Why now?

Why couldn't I have that!

"Wow Malory. I didn't realize how much of a comedian your father is! It really is a shame you couldn't make it to the dinner."

"Oh well, I might come off that way. Probably the way I dress." The imposter pulled at the collar of his coat. "This thing was given to me by my wife and I've never seen myself wear anything besides it."

My eyes burned; Oliver froze in place.

"Now that's something. I on the other hand would never be able to wear anything Brighid gives because she never gets me clothes!"

"I got you those nice pants!"

Why couldn't they see what I see!

"Those were pajamas honey…"

"Are you serious?" Oliver shouted and went up to his mother. "Had you not heard how he acted?! Had you not seen anything?!"

"Oliver, quiet down. We got here a couple of minutes ago and ran into Wilton."

Oliver ignored his parents and stretched his neck up to look at my father. "You don't belong here. And for what I saw you do, it's only a matter of time before you get caught. Even if Malory never says anything."

"Oliver! Hush, will you?" Mrs. Walker raised her voice. Her husband lifted his eyebrow.

"Young man, it's so nice to see you again! It seems like only yesterday you and Malory were running around as kids. Sorry if I'd come across rude in any way but I do apologize. Her performances make me extremely nervous."

"Tell me about it. I know just what you mean." Mrs. Walker laughed.

Father kept that smile at Oliver. "He is right about that though. My daughter and I have to head back home now. Dinner does sound good though but not as good as in my own home. Maybe next time."

I looked away from the bickering couple and glanced at Oliver, his eyes stern on the imposter beside me instead.

Maybe he…

The monster put his claws around my shoulder. I listened to my supposed father, how the thing tried to persuade the Walkers with that soft-spoken voice. Listening now was almost comical. "I'll see you at the winner's performance. She's got a lot to do. Don't you?"

His car, his bottle wrapped in a brown paper bag, his stench of alcohol. My heels dug into the carpet the more I thought of it. I hated myself for thinking this way. That if he saw I'd won, then maybe I'd be able to see his smile. His happiness. The way he spoke to them…

Maybe things aren't as bad as they seem. I'm overthinking. That's all. Father would never hurt professor. Deep down I know they still care for each other.

After we got home, father waited in the kitchen. He had his phone resting on the table, ready for the buzz from the judges. I made haste to my room, changing as quickly as possible. I wanted to share the moment with him, and the moment of us smiling together. I had to believe that this life could still be real. That he loved me as much as I did. Raising my hair through the loops of the black elastic, I made a tight ponytail and tugged on my nightgown.

"This is it. This is what you worked for." I spoke to my reflection in the mirror.

By the time I finished changing, my father's voice echoed through the door. It was a calm voice, loud yet not as harshly pitched as before. It was enough to make my heart beat in excitement.

Father's feet stood planted at the bottom of the stairs. Phone up, screen towards me. The bright white light shone on his exposed teeth and curved lips. There was no way I was imagining it. He was smiling.

I won, I won!

My beloved father who was no longer a monster walked up towards me, taking two steps at a time. He was just as eager as I! The closer he came, the more my heart raced, my arms ready to lace around his neck for an embrace. God, I longed for this moment for so long. I would finally see the smile. He kept the phone turned towards me, his stomping movement making it hard to read. Father stopped, my eyes looking up at his. Then at his flaring nose, down to his mouth. It didn't look right. How Clarice encouraged me, how Mr. and Mrs. Walker greeted me. Their lips rose up towards their eyes, not stretched straight across their cheeks. The more I stared, the more I realized… Father's lips were flared up, exposing his meaty gums. It might have been my imagination, but I thought I heard the grinding of his teeth. It was faint, but I heard it again, the ghost of violin strings and a thick cello's moans. An orchestra began to play again as I stared upon the screen.

It was a long paragraph, but the words that shone out the most were: **Thank you for participating.** My eyes were stuck, hoping that if I stared long enough, then the words might've changed. **Please join us for the winner's performance. We thank you and hope for you to join us again next year. Best regards, Honens.**

"Father… Please…"

"YOU LOST!"

I was too slow to notice the hands that were sewn into my hair, tugging my nose down towards the floor, slamming my right cheek and shoulder onto the stairs. I should have kicked, I could have screamed. Was I worthy enough to do so? My orchestra continued to play; my body being dragged like dog meat. It was when I saw the kitchen that my limbs began to awake. I didn't want that feeling again, to lose control of my body, to fall back somewhere so dark that I had no ability to speak. To become a victim to the *voice* that walked and spoke for me. Making me feel emotions that weren't mine! And yet… Taking the pain I was supposed to feel and suffering the blow instead.

"F-Father you're hurting me! I tried!" The roughness of aged carpet ended, nearly slashing my cheek with the granite floor. Glass bottles danced in a waltz.

"After everything I've done for you! Look what you're making me do!"

The air was socked from my lungs, my chest clashing with the wood of the drawers just below the sink, their edges biting at my chest.

My fingers dug up into his torso, hoping to make him let go. My nails were too short. The water was already running, each wave a reminder for what was about to come.

What if I don't make it out this time?

My head was snapped back, each ligament straining to stay intact. With a forceful crank, he snapped my head towards him, my hair whipping at the faucet behind me. It was still running, teasing my eyes to run with them. The grip was so strong that it was hard for me to see the sink, my eyes... Going lower from each tug on my head. His teeth continued to grind while his tongue rested as a red lace in-between.

The water was boiling, beating my skin to a red pulp. At the same time, the loss of air puffed up my nerves, turning my skin a sickly purple. Seconds passed and the hot water was becoming welcoming, turning my brain to carbonation, millions of tiny hands, running sleepy fingers over my eyes.

I lifted my leg up, jamming a foot into his side. His scream came and he let go. I struggled to lift the black cloak of hair from the sink as he gnashed back at me.

"You fucking bitch!"

What is this feeling?

It tensed up my chest and ran adrenaline in my heart. I bit down on my dry tongue as I continued to run faster. Faster than my feeble body ever could. My face was burning, yet my fingers were icy cold. Wet tracks lead behind me and the raging voice of my father. No. It was only the imposter. His pandora's box must have finally set my voice free, for I screamed so loud that my ears began to ring. All around me the house grew larger. The furniture, the widening of the stairs, the outstretched floor.

No, I was growing smaller with each step. I felt my body rolling into the past, my age going to my empty years, to the years of being a teenager, the years of being five. I wasn't only running from the monster. Something else was but a few breaths behind me. Something much more terrible. And I knew, I just knew... That if I stopped running, then I'd see something I didn't want to remember.

The moonlight shone on the monster's milky eyes that rolled into the back of its skull. The floor came up to me as the thing grabbed my ankle. I shoved my heel into its jaw and continued up the stairs on fours. I slipped at the top, nearly chipping my tooth, and tasting the chewed in flesh from the impact.

It seemed to be the safest place, so I shut myself inside. How did I not realize that my door never had a lock? I tightened my knuckles around the knob, My body was almost thrown back as I felt his force pressed up against the door.

"OPEN THE FUCKING DOOR!"

The symphony grew louder and louder, making my ears fill with a static. I heard the boy's voice again.

Let me protect you!

A single cramp to my wrist and the door slammed into my face. I heard a crunch, then the taste of iron.

"From everything your mother and I did for you!" His fingers cracked as he uncurled his fist, getting a firm grab onto something from underneath his shirt. With the sound of metal against metal, the brown color slipped out from the nooses laced around his waist. His motion was so fast that the belt cracked at the air then lay limp by his legs. "You think your precious teacher is protecting you?!"

I can help you! Just let me take over!

I backed up into the darkness till I hit the wall. The fear in my eyes taunted the belt closer.

"He's the bad one here! Not me!"

Let me do my job! Please!

"N-No you can't help me."

"That's right. No one is going to help you. It's just you and me!" Three steps and father had my wrist in his grip. Two steps later and my body was plowed into my bed. One fast movement, and he was over me.

My screams muffled into the sheets, fingers scrambling to hold someone's helping hand that wasn't there. The rims of my nightgown were coming up, the sound of ripped stitching coming undone. The first whip nearly made me bite my tongue off. My chin tucked into the sheets as I lifted my head up. Back down went my face into the sheets. The pressure of his palm against the back of my head was enough to send a coursing migraine down to my neck. I tried to scream for him to stop, but the blankets took my voice away. The internal symphony thrashed their strings, choking me with their violent sounds.

The second lash left a longer sting to me. A warm thread of liquid ran down from my back. Blood? That or the froth coming from the monster's gaping mouth.

"I'M DOING THIS FOR YOUR OWN GOOD YOU HEAR ME? I AM NOT THE BAD ONE HERE! I'M GOING TO HIT YOU UNTIL YOU SEE IN THE RIGHT!"

With little strength, I managed to lift my head up, coming face to face with the only things that gave my life purpose. The tiny figure stared back at me, mocking me. The warping features of my face wrapped around its golden tubular body. In the middle was etched, **1st Place Winner.**

Another whip came. Then another. Then another. My lower half had disappeared at that point, drowned by raised skin and screaming limbs.

You don't have to do this on your own!

I stretched my arm to its limitations and reached forward to my wall shelf. My nail was close enough to graze the trophy closer to me. The whips continued and this monster didn't seem to notice. As it finally fell into my hands, the fear melted away. His anger, my hatred.

"This time stay down! It's the least you can do for what you did to your mother!"

Father's weight lifted from me and the bed gave a bending sigh of relief. He was buckling the belt back into his jeans. Was it over?

Maybe this is the last time…

Tick. Tick. Tick.

No! He'll hurt me.

Tick. Tick. Tock.

Maybe things will be better from now on.

Tock. Tock. Tock.

Papa will never love you! You imposter!

If I put this down and forget about this, everything… Then everything will be normal again. I'll forget about it just like before.

Stop being such a damn puppet and let me help you!

Tick. Tock. Tick. Tock. Tick. Tock. Tick….

The trophy thrusted backwards, the top point of the star nuzzling deep into something. There came a scream nearby. Then another scream, accompanied by a gash to the chest. The trophy came down again and something wet lashed across my face and soaked my hands. He stumbled off of me, his body flaccid and slumping into the corner. One of father's eyes looked larger than the other, as if ready to pop out of his skull. There came a deep breathing… who's breathing? My breathing. Ghostly weights latched onto my feet as I kept balance and watched. My father's body lay slumped in the corner of the room, mangled and indistinguishable. Starting from my father's head, I followed the path of dark red splashes on my walls. Frozen, I watched the twin behind the mirror, a stranger my reflection became. Red soaked her dress and splashed her cheeks with color. She looked at me with fear, the crimson trophy in her hand. Not fearful for what she saw me do. It was the voice that continued to mouth in my brain. My voice and my voice alone.

How could doing something like this...

"What have I done?" I dropped the trophy.

Feel so... so good...?

CHAPTER SIXTEEN

MALORY

MY HANDS CLUTCHED ONTO SOMETHING WARM AND ALIVE, a fleshy ankle in my fists.

"Somewhere but where? I need to go and put you somewhere... Oh no, oh no, what have I done?"

A warm thickness oozed between my toes. The tendons in my arms had gone tender from the weight. Even so, I continued to tread the endless span of my bedroom floor.

"It's not my fault. I-I was protecting myself. Don't you see that? How could you? You'd never u-understand."

A bubbling reply came from father's lips.

Somehow, I knew it would've stopped the noise, the strings screaming in my brain... The damn tickling! The voices! Eating away at my ears!

The world throbbed to the beat of my heart.

"Where should I go? I need to go... No... Hospital. hospital! He needs to go to the hospital!" But no, no, no, he can't he just can't! Why should he?!"

A peeping ray of moonlight stripped across the floor, revealing a thick pump of red spewing from father's head. Bumpy pink flesh... I could've sworn it was breathing. The liquid trickled like black soot down his face. Each rise of his chest came a throb of the exposed brain.

"I didn't mean it... I didn't m-mean it... You believe me? Don't you? Hey... Hey!"

Father's brain pumped once.

Believing in what I did, that this murder was of my own will…

Twice.

"Oh, father I'm so sorry… P-Please you have to forgive me okay?"

Despite the mourning voices of the violins coming quiet, a pain grew so strong, each stroke like metal wire tightening around my head. A feverish rush was infested in me. So firm, so powerful, it puffed my forehead with veins and burned at my eyes like cold bleach. My breaths unlatched from each other, a frenzied line of gasps and mucus leaking from my nose.

A scream came. It echoed through the rooms and scrambled up the stairs, shaking the foundation of the house, leaving the floor to warp underneath me. I dropped his leg and crammed my hands towards my lips. I tried to silence myself from the horrific shrills. But they kept going, bounding and arching and breaking my ears. Had I been screaming? Then why was my mouth shut? The internal wail continued to bang in every part of my body and pressed its thumbs to my forehead. The longer I listened, the sooner I came to realize that it sounded like the voice of a girl.

I stumbled back, slipping onto the mess of the body. It was everywhere, the voice contorting to the cries of slaughtered animals. Frantically, I scattered on all fours hoping to leave the sound, drawing streaked trails of my father behind.

WHAT HAVE YOU DONE?! WHAT HAVE YOU DONE? LOOK AT HIM! LOOK AT WHAT YOU DID TO PAPA!!! YOU HAD NO RIGHT!

I fled down the stairs and the voice continued beside me.

YOU CAN'T DO THAT! YOU'RE NOTHING! NOTHING!

An open door called me, and I ran in, shutting it behind me. The slam must have been enough to scare the voice away.

My knees found a way close to my chest as I crouched down, focused on the tiny army of beer bottles and dirty blankets. Only then, was my heart able to catch up with itself in this claustrophobic room. I looked to the door, waiting for something to bang and scream for it to be opened, for that voice to come back for me. For the sound of a flicking belt. It could have been five minutes, twenty minutes. The rapid fire of paranoid thoughts simmered down as I waited for my breathing to calm.

"I've got to hide him somewhere."

I stood up, grabbing onto the edge of his desk. A cold brass shape made a home into my palm. It was the key father always used to get into his storage room. Maybe there would've been enough room to put him there. Until I figured out what to do with him… And myself.

I stole a blanket off his mattress and walked up the stairs. There wasn't as much blood as I thought. Only a thin streak on the wood and smeared footprints around the house. The horrific thing was how the brain looked ready to leap out of his head. Throw-up ran down my mouth and onto my dress. I covered my mouth, but another lunge of bile spilled out.

"Calm down, calm down. Breath." After wiping my mouth with the sheets, I tugged it underneath the body and tied a thick knot on both ends. In this cheap boat, I dragged him across the hall with shaking legs to the storage room. Once unlocked, I pulled him in, closing the door behind us both. Sweat dripped from my forehead and my shoulders ached. The room was much larger than I imagined. Also wasn't crowded with acres of boxes. I came deeper into the room as my eyes began to adjust. I felt for the small dangling beads of the fan light and tugged it on.

"What is this?"

Not a single bottle was in sight. No cardboard boxes or scattered bottle caps. Instead I was presented with a pastel green room. A bedroom. With windows and a bed with delicate lace… A desk filled with jewelry and windows and carpet and… And lies. All lies!

Malory, Oh my sweet Malory.

I turned back to my father, his body still limp and unmoving on the floor.

"Everything here is a lie… He lied to me!"

I replayed my encounters with father over and over again. Him going in, me staying out. Hearing his wailing at night in what I assumed was a drunken rage. Him leaving the room in the morning and grabbing an empty bottle of beer rather than leaving the room with an empty one. Had he ever told me what this room was? Or was that simply… Something I just…

A small frame laid face down on the desk. Its hinges looked worn, as if whatever were in there had been taken out several times. I set it up, eyeing the three figures centered around a summer lit sky and lively rose bushes. To the left was my father. Younger-looking, happier-looking. Not a speck of grey and had a warm smile towards the other two. A girl in a sundress, no older than five. And a young woman. A dress of pearl white and hair that slept calmly behind her ears. Given a quick glance, she could have pulled off looking just like me. She had fifteen more years to her name and a smile towards my father that gave me jealousy.

A groan came from behind me and I quickly turned to find my father's arm twitching underneath him. His chest gave a sudden heave, as if he had awoken from a terrible nightmare. Only one of his eyes seemed to look at me while the other pointed towards his exposed brain.

Father's mouth gargled out nonsense as he tried to get up. I looked back to the hallway where my room kept that fallen trophy, then at the taunting picture. This prolonged treatment of a slow death might've been the worst thing I'd ever do to him. But if he was alive enough to speak, then he would've been willing enough to answer.

Since the adrenaline had calmed, his body had grown two times heavier. With enough force, I managed to ease his body up to that perfectly made bed. Taking the white lace around it, I fastened Father's limbs to the bedpost, tying four knots on each for secure measure. Two bloody stains to the sheets later and there he was, no longer able to touch me. What was I supposed to do with him? He continued to flick his eyes upward in a dazed state while I counted my options. There was no way I'd stay here, and there was also no way I'd call for help. He didn't deserve it. He also… didn't deserve what I did to him. This little key hid this room from me for so long. For now, it would be able to hide father too.

Before leaving, I noticed the desk's drawer ajar. Placed right in the middle was a manilla envelope tied loosely with string. The end of it bulged out and multiple numbers were written in and scratched out.

"Everything he stole from me."

If only it was everything. A mere three hundred dollars was all but left from the thousands. This much was enough to leave for now. But where would I go?

Professor.

I searched for my phone and quickly called him. Fifteen seconds later came the beep of a voicemail box. Three times didn't seem to be the charm and I was left staring down at my phone, then towards the door that hid my father.

I don't remember what I packed, only knowing that the smell of drying blood and leather belts was getting intolerable. Let an officer stop me from reckless driving, let him put me in cuffs. Let him be led back here and see what I'd done. This monster I felt I'd become. A part of me wanted to erase the guilt from my consciousness and end it all. Yet there I was wide-eyed, fear being an aid to my swerved driving. When professor's neighborhood came into view, I slammed the break, nearly hitting into someone's driveway.

"He knows I can't drive, let alone this car."

Taking a different route, I parked two blocks from his and took in the cold as I ventured back towards his home. Hopefully, no cop would be suspicious from how crooked the parking was.

Darkness loomed from inside his windows, soft music played in the air. It took me a moment to realize it hadn't come from my head. Several frantic knocks later and his porch light came on. The music stopped. I clutched my backpack as the door came open, revealing my tired and messy-haired teacher.

"Professor… You've got to h-help me. I think there's something terribly wrong with me."

"Do you know what time it is right now?" Tightening the robe, professor looked behind me. "How did you get here? And where is Wilso…" His eyes lowered to my body and I followed. My heart rolled up to my throat as I expected to find my dress torn up, a sleeve slipping off my shoulder and bits of blood flaking up my arms. Through all the chaos, it seemed that I still had enough mind left to change into fresh clothes. Though the same couldn't be said about underneath as I felt the blood crusting on me.

"I took a cab and left my home. I-I didn't know where else to go!"

"What happened? Did he hurt you?"

"I…" My eyes twitched as I felt father's belt travel down my back. "No. We had a fight and I didn't know where else to go. I tried to call you, but you didn't answer. I needed to get out of there!"

Professor looked past me one last time before opening the door wider. "Hurry inside."

We sat in the dim of the kitchen, professor rubbing into his hair and I shrinking away on the stool.

"Well, you need to give me more details Malory. Did he hurt you?"

I traced my hand up my sweater before pushing that eager hand away. "No. He could have. I haven't seen him that angry before… We got the results. I don't think he could take that I lost."

"I knew this was going to happen. Look we can call someone and file a report…"

"I don't think that's the best idea."

"Listen…"

"I just want to be away from there… At least so I can be back on my own two feet… I know it's a lot to ask but all I need is a night or two. Please."

"I know that face when you're trying to hide something." Professor turned on the kitchen light and scuffed into the living room with his slippers. "I don't know what happened and I'm glad you're finally leaving that hell, but eventually I'm going to need the whole story. For now, you can stay here as long as you like. I hope you won't mind the couch?"

Laying, I rubbed at my elbows and cheeks. Since when had sweat felt like blood? Professor was kind enough to give me most of his blankets to shield me from the cold draft that slithered through the closed windows. This place, how I loved this home and all the memories it held. I'd learn so much here and I hadn't realized it until now, but this was a safe haven away from father. I covered my head as the wind grew harsher and branches scratched to come in. I heard the wind gargling from outside. Deep down, I feared that they were trying to help guide father back to me.

CHAPTER SEVENTEEN

BEN

I STARED OFF INTO THE DARKNESS. Everything ached and everything felt wrong. This body was sweating, I kept smelling blood. God, the blood. I tried. Holy shit, how I tried. From the moment her father was at those steps, to the moment he dragged her down them. I pushed myself so hard… I knew that if I tried a little harder, then I might've been able to stop her. But then what? What was I really stopping? And fuck how I felt everything. The pain from every strand ripped from her head, to the rash of carpet on her legs and back. I knew I wasn't fooling myself. Of course I was scared, more by the fact that something was blocking me from coming out. Her doing.

I can't exactly call her Wilton's puppet anymore now, can I?

The pain and fear she had should've been enough to make her let go just like all the times before. I mean, I begged her! I knew she heard me! I replayed those moments of being able to see slices of her view… The trophy in her hand, how hot blood felt. Why would she want to experience something like that?

I watched the unfamiliar glow of Andre's ceiling. The words she spoke made the green fans spin.

Feel so good…

"Unless…"

I dug deeper into the blankets, shivering from the hoarseness of her voice, the touch of her skin that was burning with an unknown desire.

"Unless she wanted to watch…" I pressed myself into the pillow. "No, I can't think like that." My temples hung heavily on my neck, from a past that wanted to invade everything I'd done to protect Malory. All those faded memories… She wasn't the only one suffering those empty consequences! Didn't she know that I also wanted to remember what happened?

The draft came in stronger; it didn't matter if the window was closed. Chicken skin needled at my flesh. Each time I closed my eyes, all I saw was that woman in the picture frame.

"How long are we gonna have to stay here?"

The wind wailed.

And now this… This incident no better than murder… It wasn't the role any of us were supposed to play.

CHAPTER EIGHTEEN

MALORY

DEEP IN THE OUTSTRETCHED HALLWAY AND BLUE OF THE MOON, I saw father again. Had he drunk too much? Both of his feet rocked back and forth. Our distance shortened as he slid across the floor, all the while hearing the loud cracking of his bones.

Tick. Tack. Crench.

Father's skull fell apart like broken porcelain, his hair in swirls of thickening blood and flapping skin that took the image of fallen petals. His tongue had become that hideous belt. Its end rolled out; the tip lined with silver. In his hand was the glowing screen of a phone. The font outstretched and scrawny, almost scratched into the screen.

YOU CAN'T HIDE

My body was frozen, but I knew it wasn't another episode. I didn't feel as if I was going to disappear at any moment into the fog. No, this was all too clear. My eyes trapped themselves on the creature that shaped itself as my father. It knew I couldn't hide those guilty feelings, and this thing must have known. Its smile curled from one cheek to the other, revealing teeth so loose they were ready to fall out of his puffy yellow gums.

"Yooou can't hide!"

His words weren't about my escape but to the feeling I had as soon as the trophy banged his brains. It continued when I tied his body down and traveled with me to professor's home. A disgusting queasiness leached onto my chest, my neck, to the crooks of my mouth. Seeing my father on the floor, holding the cold trophy with splattered blood soaking in my nightgown.

It felt so...

The figure was on top of me. The weight bent my ribs inward and scorched the air out of me. It opened its mouth wide. Inside were my father's eyes pleading at me. The mouth closed around my head. The eyes turned vivid blue; the creature replaced by another figure coming close. It rushed at me like a tidal wave and ripples of black velvet followed behind. Professor swung his room door open and came running towards the living room where I sat up in a cold sweat.

"Malory! What's wrong?" Professor heaved with labored breaths.

I wiped my face for any blood. Sweat stuck hairs to my forehead, my clothes sticking to my chest. My fears rose as I looked down at myself. There were only clean clothes.

"It w-was just a nightmare..."

"Some nightmare that must have been. You screamed so loud I thought I was being robbed..." Professor pressed the back of his palm to my forehead. "You don't seem to be running a fever."

"I think I just feel a little sick from... everything."

"Understandable. I'll make you something light and get you some water. It might be able to help settle your stomach."

Food was the last thing I wanted. I sat up with dizzy eyes as professor clicked on a lamp light. "I think I want to rest for now. At least until the sun is out. What time is it?"

"Close to four." He shuffled back to me in his house slippers and sat on the couch's arm.

"I'm sorry for waking you up. I was having a bad dream..."

My professor wove his fingers together and sighed. "You weren't the only one with a nightmare. I got scared that Wilton broke in and was hurting you. Your scream in my dream turned out to be real and I hurried out as soon as I could. There's nothing to be sorry for. Wilton has done me a lot of wrong when we were younger, but never the amount he has done to you."

I clutched onto the blanket. "Why were you two fighting the other day? I've never seen him so upset in public before."

"Your father has loved power since I can remember. Even if he was with you while going international, knowing that it was out of his comfort zone… I guess he thought it was only a matter of time before you left him behind. I'm glad he was right about that part."

"Professor… I- I'm not as good as you take me to be." I heard it. The gurgling of father choking on his blood and the metal clang of the trophy picking out of his brain. The stranger I looked at in the mirror.

"That's the silliest thing I've ever heard. What makes you think that?"

His smile, his eyes, his trust. Of course, I couldn't. I could never tell him what I'd done. What would he have thought of me? He would've hated me. "You're right, it's nothing. I think I need more rest. My head hurts."

He gave me a solid pat on my back and rose up. "If you ever need me, I'm one call away. Just don't scream or I might have a heart attack." He laughed softly before going back into his room.

It should have smelled delicious. Instead, all I smelled was the bacon's burning flesh. Watching the scrambled eggs bounce onto the plate… Seeing father's yolk-like brain leak from the side… Pink ham sliced so thin like the flaps of a torn forehead. I didn't want food. What I wanted was to go back to that house and see him again. Even if it meant facing the agony that had been torturing me since last night. All I wanted to know was why… And who, just who was that woman?

"I need to go back." My fork took a stab to the tiny yellow membrane."

"Back where?" Professor rolled an egg into his cheek.

"Home. I need my things… My clothes. He will only throw them away with time."

"You can get clothes anywhere. You do realize how dangerous it is for you to go back, right? Judging by how you came here all…"

"He usually isn't home in the morning. It'll only take a moment. I'll be out of there before he comes back."

Professor stared at my full plate, his napkin dabbing the side of his cheek. Then he pulled out of his chair, as if already having the final answer.

"Look… If it really means that much to you… You could stay here, and I'll head back to your home and get your belongings. What will you do if the odds aren't in your favor and he's back at home?"

Pulse. Pulse. Pulse. Crunch.

The risks were high, and suspicion might come if I left on my own. There could've been chances of him calling the police if he suspected my father got me. "What about if you take me there? If father's car is there then yes, we can leave right away, or you can go in with me. If it's not, I want to go alone. At least see my home one last time…"

"I really don't like this idea…" He rubbed nervously at his neck. "Alright fine. But we aren't leaving till you try to at least eat something first."

I pinched at a hard clump of blood at the end of my hair. Looked no different than old hair dye. "Deal. Also, is it alright if I take a shower before leaving?"

“Sure, of course. You can use the bathroom that’s beside my room door.”

I didn’t want to be in the shower long. My thoughts turned cloudy the longer I stared down at the light pink running down my body. I scratched at my skin for any trace of blood to go away. Every time I blinked, I saw my father’s twisting face getting closer to me. The shower mist imitated his breathing.

Professor was kind enough to lend me his clothes. I rolled up the sleeves of his button-down shirt and put my jeans back on. It hurt sliding them on. I had forgotten about the lashes on my back and the puffiness didn’t seem to be going down. He still tried to convince me that it was a bad idea as we got into the car. His worries though subsided as the car I stole wasn’t there in my driveway.

“Guess he really isn’t home.”

“You see? And you’re right here,
so you’ll hear anything that’s going on or if I scream.”

Or father’s scream.

“Fine. But after fifteen minutes I’m
coming in.”

It was as if the house was rotting from the inside. The smell was foul, like sweet rotting fruit. The kitchen reeked of beer and the stairs of old metal. I placed my palm on top of the bloody one I made yesterday. It couldn’t have been mine, none of this could. I took a single step and the front door slammed behind me. “Father?” I quickly turned around in a confused mixture of relief and dread. It was only the wind.

I lost track of how long I’d been standing in front of my room. The closed door was full of dents from pounding fists.

My hand shook as I grabbed for the knob. It took my other hand to stabilize myself before finally opening it.

How could you disobey me like that?!

Tick. Tick. Tick.

You need to be taught a lesson!

I opened the door, my nose haunted with the smell of yesterday's festivities. His blood turned to the color of dirt. A small dry puddle where the trophy fell was right ahead of me and I stared down at it, eyes unblinking. I almost heard father's grunts.

"How could I have felt like that?"

Yet it felt so good to hit papa, didn't it?

It did.

"No… No, no. I need to hurry." I came to my dresser, pulling out the drawer so hard that one side of the back end stuck out, making the whole thing fall to the floor. I grabbed what I could and shoved it into my suitcase that I dragged from the closet. I wasn't sure what I took, but I didn't want to be in that room any longer or feel the experience continue to carousel in my mind.

Would you do it again?

I propped the luggage near the wall and fingered for the key in my pocket. My body tensed as I took a step in. I kept the lights off, letting the open door give light to the two marbles that rolled in my direction. They blinked. There he was, a broken down old man that could no longer fend for himself. Blood stained the lacy gauge around his wrists and one of the knots had come undone. He seemed skinnier. I guess that happened when one barely had any blood left in their system.

"W-W-Waer…" The old man groaned. "Wa-ater…"

Now that, that was comical! I almost laughed! After all those years of my life, serving and opening and cleaning up all those beer bottles. And now he wants water!

"Now you're thirsty?"

"Ne-need waer."

"I guess this means you're still able to talk."

By the desk where all the jewelry hung was a small glass. Barely half full, but enough to serve his fill.

"Fine father." I took the glass and the picture frame before coming back to him. The cup came close to his lips coated in white paste. My hands shook when I eyed the gash in his head. I let out a deep breath and kept focused on his eyes. "Here's your water, only if you answer me some questions."

"Whh… The hell am I doin here?"

"That's what I also want to know. What is this room? I thought this was meant for your addiction."

"She is m-my addiction."

She?

"You don deserve to be in here."

"No, I do! Just as I have a right to know who this woman is!" I pushed the frame close to father and his eyes went crossed.

"Give eh back! Take your hands off that!"

"Or what? You're going to hit me?"

It didn't matter if he was tied down. I still flinched as his body arched up, fists curling to the ceiling and wrists going purple from the restraints. Father's face grew purple as ribbons of veins pumped across his temples.

"I told her not to have you! And you got rid of her! Now you're going to fucking kill me! Well do it, do it! I dare you to fucking do it! Do it! DO IT!"

My grip tightened around the glass and a ghostly shiver traced a nail across my collar bone. This was too dangerous. Professor might have heard all of this. I needed to go back.

I pulled away a decorative cloth from a nearby nightstand and balled it up into his mouth. The delicate jewelry that was on top scattered on the floor. Before leaving, I let the cup of water pour over his face, letting the cloth soak it up. "There's your water."

Professor was already opening the door as I flew down the stairs, the luggage clunked behind me.

"Hey, are you alright? I thought I heard something, and you were taking a little long."

"It's just me." I gulped down the need to pant and pushed my way between him and the front door, closing the destruction behind us. "The neighbors can get loud sometimes so you probably heard them. I have everything and I'm ready to leave."

"You sure you're alright? You're breaking into a cold sweat."

I didn't hear his words as I looked at the closed windows at the highest part of my house. I waited for them to be pulled down from my father, his fists breaking the glass and screaming out into the world.

"You might be right. I think I am getting a little sick."

With the luggage in professor's car and I in the passenger seat, father's fate was safe for the meantime. My phone quietly buzzed in my pocket and I reached to get it. Before pulling out the phone, professor picked up my hand.

"Did you cut yourself?"

I followed his eyes to a small bit of blood on my fingers and pulled back.

"Sorry, did I hurt you?"

"It's only a small cut. Probably poked it on a hanger while hurrying." I tucked my hand under me.

"Well, I have band aids back home if you need it. While waiting, I also decided that you shouldn't be on the couch with how bad the draft can be. Considering that you are coming down with something. I do have a spare room you could use for now. Give me a little time to clean it and it'll be yours."

I hadn't thought about that. How long would I be there until I became a burden? A day? One month? Two? Eventually I had to find a way to live and stand up on my own.

"Thank you, professor,... You really didn't have to."

"Malory, you know it's alright if you just call me Andre, right?" Professor's keys rattled as he drew them from his pocket, his car rumbling to a start.

"I've called you professor for so long that I guess it just stuck with me."

After the drive, professor helped me with my luggage, and I took off my shoes. We passed to the end of the living room where two room doors rested side by side. Between them was a bathroom of marble and fake greenery hanging over sink lights.

"It's not much but I'm hoping it'll be better than on that couch." Professor opened the room to the left. "Haven't used it in a very long time so mind the dust. You don't remember this room, do you?" He wore a shy smile as he opened the door.

The walls were covered in a thick grey foam that I wasn't sure what the wall color was underneath. The floor was wooden and shined, yet had a few scuff marks on it. It creaked under me as I walked in. To the left was a small bed with white framing. The skirt of the bed was a lace of white. There was no sunlight here which gave me the nervous feeling of being back in my own practice room at home.

"Sorry about not having any windows. But there are lights installed in this room."

"No, this is perfect. Thank you."

"I'll get to cleaning it right away so you can use it tonight."

"That's alright. I don't mind cleaning. It'll get my mind off some things."

To the right was a Steinway, brown and flaking with age. It drew me closer, feeling the dusty wooden cover. I traced a single yellow key, then all the rest until they were all black. No, they weren't keys. It was hair and my hand was tangled in it. I pulled away, clutching onto my wrist as I made contact with the hollow eyes of a shrunken human sitting on the bench. She fixed her gaze on me, wide and bug-like. The little human's legs swung back and forth. Her cheek was swollen and knuckles raw.

Again. Again. Again. Again. Don't you hear papa's command? Do it again!

Professor's phone buzzed to life and I jumped.

"Ah. I have to make a few calls to my conductor but shout if you need anything. I don't mind helping you clean afterward."

"Maybe just give me some cleaning supplies? The rest I'll be fine with." Professor nodded and left me. The bench was empty when I looked back.

I dusted the walls and tucked a fresh sheet into my mattress. With a simple sponge and bucket of soapy water, I scrubbed the floors over and over again. I kept my eyes down, fearing I'd see the small feet of that girl sitting on the bench. I gritted my teeth as a song of strings from nowhere hummed in my ears. It must have been three or four times I cleaned the floor. Each time I turned my back, red blooms started bleeding into the wood. I dunked my sponge into the bucket and scrubbed them harder. The suds had turned red and the sponge was frothing in bubbles. My hands weren't able to catch up and soon the entire floor was smeared in dark red brush strokes. I took the bucket and threw the sponge in one last time, squeezing out any red left in it. It left the water black and thick like tar. The sponge pulsed against my hand and when I pulled it out, father's brain stared back at me.

"You're really working on that floor." The soft clink of ice on glass shimmered in my professor's hand. "Care for a little break?"

I wiped my brow and looked down at my work. The floor shimmered beneath me. My wet sweats clung heavily around my legs and I stretched my arms out. "I think that's a good idea."

After changing, I relaxed on the couch while professor filled the kitchen with savory aromas. The lemon water was refreshing, and I took another sip. Ice cubes slipped towards my lips and I suckled one. He hummed quietly to himself, a simple towel draped over his shoulder.

"And done!" He pulled two plates out and filled them to the top. A fantastic lunch of stewed beef. The greens stuck out vibrantly against the black plate. I went to the kitchen and seated myself, relieved to feel the pang of hunger in me. My phone buzzed in my pocket and I picked it out. Elizabeth's name shone brightly at me. I quickly turned the phone over before any feelings of dissociation took over.

"I remember always eating this during my childhood." He took a bite before looking at me again.

"You never did tell me much about your childhood."

"Yeah well. There wasn't much to say."

I looked with eagerness and scooped the spoon into a potato.

"Fine, fine. Back when I lived in Astrakhan, this would usually be a main food in my household. We were a poor family you see. So discarded things like meat and potatoes were something easy to come by."

"Really? I always had this idea that you were born into a wealthy family."

"It's funny how I get that comment a lot, but I do see what you mean. I guess drowning myself in this lifestyle helps me to forget how things used to be. If that makes any sense. I try not to associate myself with that past life. Too many things I don't want to remember."

Father's image slouched on the chair beside us. The trophy was still gouged in his head. "I get that. I'm trying to do that too."

"To new beginnings?" Professor lifted his glass of water.

I lifted mine and clicked it with his. "To new beginnings."

As evening came, professor was busy locked away in his room. I heard his countless conversations as I unpacked my clothes. All of them had to do with preparing for some concert and a conductor that was always 'caught up in his ways.' It was a nice distraction as the time rolled by. When night came, it was no better than the last. In fact, somehow worse. The foamy walls were creeping in, and the bed kept expanding under me. Two times, three times, so much larger in size until it sucked inside itself and tucked me under with it. The floors moaned under me in slow creeks and the piano sent tangled wires into my ears. I feared that if I looked at the bedroom door, I might've seen the girl again. Or the tearing scalp of my dying father. Just when I thought being haunted by one ghoul was enough, my phone became my savior. I nearly pulled the charging cord out of its wall socket when grabbing it. I clicked on Elizabeth's text.

Hey, how are you? The urge was coming back to me. Not the happy and joyous exhilaration of something deep in my brain, but a worry that tugged the strings on my fingers to type with their own mind.

"I'm at my professor's home right now."

I didn't have to wait long for her reply.

"Don't you think that's a little late to be having a lesson?"

"I'm not. I'm staying at his place for... I'm not sure how long."

"Why?"

"My father. The two of us had a fight and he had too much to drink. I had nowhere else to go. I didn't want to be there anymore."

She didn't reply for a moment which brought a buzzing itch to my shoulders.

Did I maybe say too much? We are still getting to know each other, and I've just told her that my father is a raging alcoholic. What if she is too scared to talk to me? Will she think I'm dangerous?

She didn't type back. Instead, she called me, the ringing bringing me so off guard that I nearly bumped my head on the metal headboard.

"Oh god, Malory I'm so sorry. I had no idea your father was like that. Since when was the fight?"

I rubbed my eyes in an attempt to remove the fog coming to me. "Just the other night."

"S-shit. You know you could have told me, right?"

"I didn't want you to know that about me." I swallowed hard, feeling my tongue grow heavy and my knees locking where I laid. "Besides, you are having a rough time at home..."

"We are friends. You need to tell me if something bad happens to you. I worry..."

My ears trailed off… What was that word she muttered? Why did it ring so strongly in my ears? The word chanted in my brain as I found myself trapped behind my eyes again. How strange a thought, that I was actually getting used to this… This switching.

"I'm sorry… You're right. Everything went so fast and I panicked. It almost feels like he's haunting me." He was haunting me. The light under the door was moved by a stretch of shadow leaking into the room.

"Hey… Come over to my house tomorrow. I think my dad might be able to help you."

I really don't want to be a bother was what I wanted to say. "R-really? I'd love that. I know Andre has been helping a lot, but it'll be nice to be around you-you guys again.

"Exactly. Props to him but you need your friends too. Come talk with me and my brother."

Just friends?

"Malory? You still there?"

Somehow hearing my name managed to bring me back and the *voice* shrunk away. I guess I was seeing the Walker's again. I didn't have any money. Father was the one in control of it. I could've asked professor to take me and I'm sure he wouldn't have minded. But to be a burden…

Father…My money…Bag! My Bag!

I tossed my feet off the bed and went over to the piano bench, tugging around in my luggage until I found the brown envelope. The piles of clothes I meticulously folded toppled over. I ignored it and sat back on the bed.

"A-alright. Thanks, I'll come over then. Does morning or afternoon sound alright with you?"

"Of course! You're welcome anytime."

With that, our conversation ended and I laid back down with the phone close to my ear. I wanted to believe that I was becoming more accepting. And I was. What once brought me such terror was beginning to feel as natural as playing on keys. This nameless *voice* had helped me and almost… protected me when I needed to be. Even if I hadn't realized that in the moment. It also didn't feel like a *voice* any longer. Something closer to a human, with feelings and thoughts… wants and needs. If I'd let it take over while father was hitting me, would things have turned out differently?

CHAPTER NINETEEN

MALORY

THINGS WERE A LITTLE BETTER THIS MORNING. Maybe it was being able to hear Elizabeth's voice, a calm escape from the shadow that continued to watch over me. The fact that she called me that made it seem like she really did care. Or maybe, she cared for the other part of me that wasn't me. It wouldn't have bothered me if that was the case. I was sure the *voice* had caring intentions, like it did for me. Then why had it felt so distant inside of me? Since I escaped father's house, its presence dimmed down, as if avoiding me.

It took a lot of persuasion to leave the house. Professor told me how worried he was for me going out alone. In a few ways he was right. The first time some part of me tried to leave, I nearly crashed. The last time I left the house, I was running away from my bludgeoned father.

"Have you ever taken a bus before? It can be confusing."

"I won't need one. I can take a taxi."

"You don't plan on going back to your house, do you?"

"Of course not." I brought my bag closer to me. I'll be with the Walkers for a little then back here."

He scratched at the back of his neck. His hand was slow, speeding up before coming to a decrescendo. "I guess it'll be fine. I also have a lot of adjustments to make in this house that I've been meaning to do. Just be back before it's dark. Please."

The streets were moist from the early March sun. Although I was in the car of a stranger, I truly didn't feel alone. A thick puff of cigarette smoke fogged the inside of the taxi; all I smelled was fresh air. Time was a fleeting image as I counted the trees and breaths of freedom I could finally take. I flew with the birds that were in the sky, finally feeling the mounds of the hill tops that somehow seemed closer. Elizabeth was there for me, professor… And the *voice*. By the time my eyes saw nothing but the warm hum of sky tickling my lashes, we-I arrived. The car moaned to a halt while melting the air with its black fog. With a scouring face and turban wrapped around his head, the driver pointed to his palm and I gave him his fee.

The house seemed different than the last time. Less intimidating, not as big. The morning sun shone on the walls; the grass was decorated with crystal flakes. Before I reached my second knock, the door swung open and two hands flung around me.

"Dear! Elizabeth told me everything! We had no idea!" Mrs. Walker's head bent down so both our cheeks touched. It took me a moment to recognize her. Her skin's color wasn't tinkering with that light youthfulness. Darke hues circled round her eyes and she had more visible moles than I remembered. Two with the resemblance of a spider's bite on her right cheek, and one right below her eye. It wasn't only her face. She looked more… ordinary. No looped earrings, no fancy blouse that pushed up her chest, but a plain pink one with the collar reaching to her neck.

"I'm sorry for intruding like this again."

"Please, don't speak like that. Come in come in." She hurried me in, like the weather would swallow us whole. The inside wasn't the same either. Yes, there was the perfection of clean white walls and furniture designed in such a way to look like a model home. The air. It didn't smell like burning sage that overwhelmed my nostrils or angry piano notes. But sorrow? It was in Mrs. Walker's eyes and her husband's as he heard us and came down with black silk pants and a white robe. "It's nice to see you again. It's just too bad that it's under these circumstances."

The three of us stood in a triangle, both husband and wife rubbing their arms as if not knowing what to say.

"Hey there…"

The sound of a wheelchair rolling against granite came closer as Elizabeth turned the corner from the kitchen door.

"I'd hug you, but I can't exactly get up."

She really was gorgeous. Through her green shirt and white shorts that hung loose around her figure was feeble skin, capsuling a beating soul that was able to do so much good in a single phone call. With her presence came the other person inside of me again. His words soft and yearning. It was a relief to feel the *voice* close. It sounded crazy, but I was actually beginning to worry about him.

I can see it. I can feel it… I want to see her through these eyes… Tell her how I feel… About this, about everything. Everything.

Mr. Walker poured me a cup of hot dark liquid. The caffeine sparked my eyelids. I would've gone for more, but the taste was too dry and mature. The four of us sat at the dining table, a light above our heads despite how bright the house was lit already. Like they wanted to keep any speck of darkness out. Mr. Walker took a long sip. The way he reacted to the taste made it look like we were drinking two different ones. "Elizabeth told me what happened. I hate myself for not being able to see that side of him."

"Did he hurt you?" Mrs. Walker cupped my shoulder.

And now you're gonna kill me!

"N-no. It was just a big fight."

"Has your dad always been drinking like this?"

"Since I can remember… But it was never out of hand like this." The lies burned my throat.

"Well, I'm glad you're out and safe from there. I can only imagine the stress you've had to go through. The wife and I have been thinking… Elizabeth tells me that you're staying at Petrov's right now, correct?"

"Yeah. He was kind enough to take me in and I really had nowhere else to go."

"By all means!" Mrs. Walker took another sip then placed the cup down on a small knitted coaster. "But you are a grown woman and need your own space, your own privacy. I condone him for that but eventually you're going to need your own place, no?"

"I get what you mean but I don't have enough m…"

Mr. Walker brought a thick finger to the air. "I own an apartment complex not too far from here. And there is a room—well, not exactly a room. But it can function as one."

"I don't understand."

"Now I can't offer you a big room. But I do have a small one you could use. It hasn't been used in a while since the vents have never been able to blow hot or cold air in as it used to be a storage room in the past. But there are outlets… a sink… a window… Oh, and a small bed. And the interior walls do have a nice green wallpaper that isn't too harsh on the eyes." He trailed off like an inspector of a building until Mrs. Walker nudged his elbow. "Sorry, I get caught up in my work sometimes."

It was a very kind offer. Even if I agreed, I had no money, no credit cards, no job. There would've been no way. I gave them the kindest smile I could. "Thank you so much for this offer… But I have no money. My father used it all and I don't have a…

"Don't worry about that right now." I thought he was staring at me, but his eyes were shifted to his daughter. I looked back at Elizabeth, a foot away from my side. The world curved around me like a fishbowl and I rubbed my eyes.

"My parents and I really want to help you." Something warm beneath the table wrapped around my fingers. I looked down and she was holding my hand. Again came the boost of energy raging inside of me like a bottle swimming with fire. She gave a squeeze and a small smile before folding her hands in her lap again.

"Once you're able to get yourself a job and settle a little, then you can start helping. For now, don't worry about it."

"I-I don't know what to say..."

"Just say yes." Mrs. Walker chimed in weakly. Her tired eyes looked back at her daughter, her husband, then back at me. "Or at least think about it."

Mr. Walker had gone back upstairs for his work and I couldn't remember when Elizabeth disappeared. I stood by Mrs. Walker as she cleaned the coffee stains from our cups.

"I haven't seen our daughter worried like that for someone in a long time. But I also haven't seen her smile like that in ages." She squeezed the suds out of a blue sponge. "I don't know what you've done or said to her. Since she met you, she's been coming down to eat with us and talks about her day. Even if it isn't much. As a mother, it almost makes me jealous." Mrs. Walker let out a breath as she placed the final cup down to dry. "I've tried so hard. How did you do it?"

It wasn't me

I held my tongue. As much as I cared for Elizabeth, I didn't own those intimate feelings. How could I explain something I didn't understand?

"Maybe it's her finally being able to talk with someone that's also had it tough." I listened to the *voice* speak. "I know that being in a wheelchair is so much harder and I can only imagine the pain she's been through. She doesn't have a choice in her problems. But I see her as a hurting human being, a girl… That shouldn't be afraid to say how she feels. Not a patient stuck in a hospital like all the rest. I'm not sure if she sees it, but there's a spark in those eyes that I wish she could see one day. Because it really does amaze me how strong she is."

"You really have changed, you know that?" I watched Mrs. Walker wipe her dewing eyes and gave both the *voice* and I quite a surprise when her lips pressed on our forehead. Her breath shook. "I'm so sorry for anything I've said before. I was wrong, all wrong. People change and you've really proved that to me."

Of course. Mrs. Walker was the perfect person. She'd seen every moment with Oliver, seen every aspect of me since I began my practice. I needed to ask. Then I'd go back and ask father. No matter how long it'd take, I'd ask and ask until he budged. Then when I collected everything I could, I'd ask my professor. It felt like a violation to try and pick at my brain, a looming scare that was waiting to happen. I reached forward from the dark space behind my eyes and grabbed for the spotlight.

I'm willing to take that chance.

"How had I acted before?" I felt myself slip back into my body. "It's been so long that I don't remember."

"Well…" Mrs. Walker leaned against the counter, her curls bounced under her. "You weren't the nicest kid. Somehow, Oliver absolutely loved you. He'd follow you to any competition and always tried to grab your attention."

"Not the nicest? Had I hurt him?"

"You were distant, a little snooty. As if you were balancing the entire world on that little upturned nose. Children do go through that phase. I guess for my boy, it happened late. I don't feel this way about you now, but I told Oliver to stop talking with you, that pianists like you would leave him in the dust. But you two got close. Oliver was so happy to be able to finally have a friend. He was such a shy little guy, so I suppose that's the one thing I can thank you for."

"When did we stop talking? Was it long ago?"

"You really don't remember?" Mrs. Walker frowned. "It wasn't long ago… At least to me. You must have been twelve or thirteen. I should have believed my son… But your father was quite the talker back then. I actually punished him for calling Wilton bad names! Can you believe that!"

I grabbed onto the kitchen counter. A strange pressure came into my brain. "Did something happen between Oliver and my father?"

"On the contrary! Oliver got in a big fight with you. He told me how you kept protecting your father even though he knew what was going on. I wasn't sure what he meant by that… I guess in a way I do now. You did give my son a bright red slap to the face and that was the last time you've talked with him or the rest of us. He tried to speak with you after what happened; I'm guessing that never worked out. I wanted to scream at you, it didn't matter if I'd make an embarrassment of myself. But my son and his dad pulled me away before I could."

Me? Hitting him? I thought back to all the times I tried being nice to him, all the little small talks I tried to create. That smile I had, how his eyes wanted to stab me. What kind of disgusting person was I?

"Sometimes it scares me… I can almost see you in my son… He has so much anger like you used to… It's like you two swapped places." Mrs. Walker's hands pressed against her cheeks, years' worth of tears coming down. I wanted to comfort her, say something. Nothing came out and my fingers dug into my arm instead.

"I forgive you for everything and I hope you'll forgive us too." I wondered why she came close to me. When she tucked a finger under my eye, did I realize that I was crying too.

We both stayed in that kitchen for a while and the minutes passed to an hour. Oliver's mother led me back to the front door while dabbing her eyes with tissues. Her smile was tender as I took the first step out. A hand was stopping me by the second step.

"You know… Our son still cares for you. Please try and talk with him again. I've known you since you were young, and I've seen how much you've changed. If you want to find a way to repay us for that room, then please… Please make things right with him."

Some part of me expected to find Elizabeth outside again, on the frosted outskirts of snow and crisp leaves. She wasn't under that camphor tree or smudging snow on her legs. I pulled the picture frame out of my bag and kept it close during the ride back, all the while fiddling with a small tab of skin. I rolled it with my other thumb.

Do I really need to see him? Things are finally starting to look up! Maybe it would be better if I didn't find out. And I've changed.

But you do know. You know very well who was in that picture. We both do.

The soft echo of a little girl's voice licked my earlobe.

No… I-I've never seen that woman in my life.

Well, of course you hadn't. What a silly question.

The radio station snapped on and switched to a channel full of strings playing back and forth, back and forth. I tugged the dry flap of skin off and felt the pain bloom. It came clean off along with a narrow slice of skin.

"S-Sir can you please turn down the radio station!"

The driver looked into the rearview mirror.

"The station! It's too loud!"

"Lady it ain't on!"

How could I hurt Oliver like that and not remember!

Do you really need to pry into things? You don't have to at all, really. Just accept it and play your part.

My part? Everything is my part! This is all me!

If that's true, then why do you feel so frightened? I should be the one scared! After all, you killed papa!

"Ay lady! I said that'll be twenty-five!"

I scrambled for my money as I unbuckled myself and gave him thirty. "Keep the ch-change."

"Well geeee, thanks for your generosity." The man spat a clump of tobacco into his soda can before leaving.

The door was unlocked when I tried for the knob. A light singing kettle murmured inside as I slipped off my shoes. It took me a while to find him as the house looked empty. But there professor was, hunched over on his knees by his room door. It looked like he was picking up scraps of paper. I got closer to him and saw the gloss on all of them. He nearly lost balance when I tapped his shoulder. They drew up tensely as he balled up the polaroids and shut his room.

"Jesus, you gave me a scare! You're back early."

"I actually thought that I came back a little late." I kneeled down beside him. "What are you doing?"

"Just looking through an old album of mine."

"Well, you shouldn't crumple them like that or they'll get ruined." I drew my hand towards them, and he stashed the pictures in his pocket. The edges popped out like a paper bouquet as he got up.

"It's fine, I was going to throw them away anyway. Bad memories… oh! How was your visit? Almost forgot, I want to hear all about it!" Professor turned back to the living room and sat on the piano bench. His movements looked skittish. I followed and sat on the couch. I told all about the kindness the family gave, how welcoming and understanding they were. How I bonded with Mrs. Walker, becoming closer with Elizabeth. Though I wasn't so sure why I held my tongue on the important parts. The apartment, my sweet and sour past with Oliver.

"I've got news of my own!" Professor tousled his hair and gave a deep sigh. "I'm retiring."

"Retiring?" I blinked at him. "But you're still so young!"

"Being almost fifty is hardly young. I can say that music as my career has been quickening my age! So, it's about time to end it. But that doesn't mean ending my job as being your teacher. That's one of the many things that's important to me right now. And you. You can't forget about your music. I know you've been through a lot because of it but I really don't think it's time to give up just yet. You were wanting to go international after all."

I looked down at my hands. I completely forgot about that. "I know… I'm not sure if music is the best thing for me right now. I need to start getting my life back together. A job, a real place to stay. Music wouldn't give me time for that."

Professor lifted himself from the couch and moved back into the kitchen. He poured himself a cup from the red kettle and set a fresh tea bag to soak.

"Malory. Those are common ideas for common people. You aren't one of them. You have a talent and I've seen it the very first moment I saw you. I don't want it to stop growing and I fear that if you put that hard work away, then you might..." Professor grew quiet, his posture looked tense. "Music might have wronged you. I get that, I get that you're mad at your father. But don't forget about all the things it has also done for you."

CHAPTER TWENTY

MALORY

"THIS IS SUCH TERRIBLE TIMING. You're sure you'll be fine here on your own? It'll only be a few hours."

"Don't worry. I promise I'll be fine. It'll be nice to have a house to myself for the first time anyway."

Professor tightened the duffle bag strap on his shoulder. "If you say so. Don't feel bad if you want to contact me. I'm only a call away. I'm not sure what time I'll be back so feel free to eat whatever you want."

I felt bad for lying to him like that after everything he'd done. But I needed to go back. My mind played scrabble on every question I had, or how it would've been to confront my father again. That might've been why I decided to walk rather than take another cab. The cold was a harsh refresher. My thoughts slowed to the timing of fallen snow. I tucked the grey scarf around my neck. The streets had gone slick from the creeping of spring heat and the flakes gave a farewell dance. It wouldn't have taken more than an hour or two to get there and not a breath of tiredness was in me as I quickened pace.

In an almost maternal voice, I heard it again, telling me which streets to take, or to stop myself from running into a passing car while stuck in my thoughts. The *voice* continued with me as the many streets became few, and the passing neighborhoods grew familiar. There were moments when all I felt was my head bobbing up and down, my feet no longer my own. I knew the *voice's* masculine tone like the back of my hands.

His confidence, how strong and persistent he'd always been. Why did it seem so different now?

I looked up to the sky with my roof peeking into heaven's gloom. The house seemed bigger, intimidating. All the moths near the porch light had festered with ants. The door groaned at me like a living thing. The foundation breathed in deep shivers. The tree nearby whipped against the wind like a belt and the piles of empty beers reeked like plaque. The stairs threatened to eat me whole as they spoke secrets into the soles of my feet. I took them quicker.

Bile rolled up from my stomach when I looked down at father's yellowing skin. He was the centerpiece to this pretty room. The underside of him was crusted in feces. Thick coats of drool webbed down his chin and his chest didn't seem to be moving. Neither did his brain now crusted in thick red sheets of mangled hair.

"Father?" I took an inch closer. "Hey… Wake up." I shook his shoulder softly and his head bobbled back and forth. Still nothing.

"I'll give you all the water you want! Just wake up!" I glanced down at his wrists that were now purple and swollen. Rings of red sketched around his wrists and bruised marks of what I could've only explained as teeth were the jewels of those rashes. This time I shook harder and slapped his cheek. His mouth unhinged, leaving a gassy smell of spoiled yogurt. I heard the dryness of his eyes as they rippled open, gunk that looked like maggots in the corners of his eyes.

"Never thought I'd… I'd see you again."

"I was beginning to think that too. It looks like you've done a number on yourself." His gaze threatened to drown me, eyes like glass marbles swimming with ink. Then something changed in them. A softness that was more horrific than comforting. The only kindness I'd ever seen in him… Oh, how I rather would've been beaten. This wasn't how it was supposed to be, how he was supposed to act. He was supposed to hit me, drown me in the sink! Was that a smile on his face? Why wouldn't he scream at me!

"I never meant to do that to our daughter. You understand that, right! But I had no money…"

It was stupid of me not to realize that one of his hands managed to get free. Father took hold of my cheek, his grip tightening around my jaw.

"I was going to lose our home, your special room… Coming here was our dream… Your dream. That's why I brought you here, right? Every time I looked at her, I saw you."

I tried to pull away, only to feel my skin tugged at even more.

"But you were gone, and she was there… I didn't know, I swear I didn't!"

A manic state came to him. Father flew his eyes to the ceiling, pupils dilating like a camera lens. Soon after, his face begin to turn a sickly reddish purple.

"Stop, you're scaring me!"

"And when I did find out… You should've seen her… Aria. I knew I lost her that day, but I couldn't do anything! Only drink and drink and DRINK AWAY!" Laughter polluted the air. I finally managed to pull away at the expense of his nails leaving a warm gash on the cheek. "You know I didn't! How was I supposed to say no to something like that?" Father's hand went to his head, pulling away at his hair. His nails went into the bashed in head, tearing out dry pieces of skull and brain meat. I found myself in the corner of the room as the walls shrank around me, pressing my palms against them with the hopes I wouldn't be crushed. Everything was growing dark and the spotlight was centering on father's madness.

"So much money only a madman would say no! You see that, right!"

"No, I don't! I don't know what you're saying because none of it makes any sense! You're insane!"

"Don't you dare start that up again! I didn't cheat on you! I needed an outlet, your dead self kept speaking! If anything, you're also to blame for my drinking! No! You're to blame for everythinnh!"

His speech was disintegrating into slurs and gasps for air. Fingers locked into a tiger's claw as he fought against the restraints. Four relentless tugs later and he had the first knot coming loose. "Don't you dare think I thuh only bad one in this! Even if you don admiit, I knuh yuaah slept with him behand my baaagh!

The sound of a door closing traveled up the stairs. If it wasn't for father quieting down, I doubt I would've heard it. He was clutching his chest, his body finally seeming to let go of the madness. Two quiet squeaks of the floorboard and I was pressing my right cheek against the wall. This time I knew I closed the door. So, either I was hearing things or someone was inside. Everything in me was telling me not to, but I managed to find the courage to leave the room and peek from the staircase. It was enough to see most of the downstairs and kitchen area if I cranked my neck enough. A shadow of paranoia flickered in the corner of my eyes. By the time I followed in its direction, it already passed the hallway and to the first floor. Father was going insane, I might've been too.

One head throb and I was downstairs. Two blinks later and I was in the middle of the kitchen checking the backyard door. Father had a terrible habit of never locking it. I must have forgotten to lock it too before I left the other day. The only thing inhabiting that space was the square of dirt and a broken beach chair that father called a patio. My breath kept tight for those outstretched minutes before I went back. To put back the knife I didn't know I had in my hand. I stared at the black handle and looked away from the mimicking figure on the blade. Silver smelled just like blood.

I held onto the banister tightly, afraid I'd fall as I listened to father's one-sided conversation. He'd stopped screaming and whimpered like an abused animal.

"Sorray… Imuh susorry." I kept my back from him, afraid, as if knowing what was coming. Father's coos tingled the hairs on my arm.

"I codnt watch you performin knowing wha ah did. Wha ah didn't do for you. Eh was thretning me too. Ah was scared."

I couldn't understand him anymore. A strange pain went into my heart and watered my eyes. A moment's wait was all I needed before turning back around to see his eyes wide and unblinking to the ceiling… So was his breathing, his lips a frozen gasp. I was close to him now, running a hand over his hardened hair. I sucked in my breath but the pain in my chest didn't stop.

"I hate you. I hate you…"

I beat my fist on his chest. I felt the sting of the belt lash on my face. The bruises now long gone hurt more than when they first arrived. Even so… Even so…

This wasn't what I meant when I wanted you to feel my pain.

"I hate you. You hurt me so much. I hate you!"

My body crumpled over his and I screamed into his chest. I cradled his stiffening head and held his purple hand.

"I'm sorry… I didn't mean this."

Why am I apologizing? You do this to me! You're dead, but you keep making me apologize!

"Papa… Don't go."

The screams I heard when I first hit father might've not been mine. But I owned every shrill that came out of me this time. Screaming and screaming, and I kept screaming. I wasn't sure why I was. This was everything I ever wanted. I was free, to do what I pleased and to finally open my wings. Why did it feel like they were clipped shorter? I pressed my head against the floor and pulled my hair over my eyes. All the arrows of judgement were turned to me. All my doing. No voice or blank spaces or experiencing experiences from the back of my eyes. Father was dead, father was right. I killed him. I murdered him.

"Is this what I am?"

The fan light grew darker and my body colder. My feet felt nothing, neither did my ankles. The room which had begun its closure around me took a switch to infinity. An infinity of darkness and white ash that wanted to sink me. Maybe that was alright. If I let it take me down, then maybe I'd wake up to a world where it never happened. Wake up on the cold tiles of the bathroom floor where I simply banged my head and heard father coming in to rescue me. He would've taken me in his arms with breath that smelled clean and brought me to my alive mother. She would've kissed my head and told me it was alright. The Black Beast would've been the only thing dead. A simple piano meant for playing a dead person's song.

I watched that distant... happy mirage of a family. The little girl was hurt, but she was happy. Her father was happy. A soft glow came between father and daughter as I stepped closer.

I want to be her.

If I got close enough, then maybe it would've come true. If I simply closed my eyes to everything, to the past, to the trauma, then maybe one day... it might've actually come true.

If I forget everything... Then maybe everyone else will. And everything could start new.

My pace quickened and soon I was running. The light grew brighter as I stretched out my hand, trying to outrun the static that wanted to eat away every part of me.

That little girl might be gone. But if I can help her forget... Then I can give her the life she deserves. The life I deserve. The life we...

The light grew blinding, so blinding that a thunderous screech bombed from behind it. I shielded my face and slipped onto gravel. I tried to reach out, the image leapt away, replaced by metallic black and the shouts of a young man.

"Are you fucking insane! Get out of the road!"

I couldn't, why should I. Every part of me shook. Not from being sucked out of a distant reality, but from the icy rain that poured down.

"Did you hear what I said?! Get out of the fuc... Malory?" The driver got out. His rustic skin and perfectly combed hair gone slick from the weeping earth. Warm smoke left his lips as he shook my shoulders.

"What the hell are you doing here like this! I nearly killed you!"

And now you're gonna kill me! Just like you killed her!

"No, no, I need to get back. I need to make things right. I was so close."

"Close to dying!" The boy tugged off his grey hoodie and draped it over my head. "Get up before you cause any more accidents."

The downpour wouldn't let me see who it was. Though it was enough to let me get into the stranger's car as he drove a short distance and parked. He opened the glove compartment and wiped water and hair away from my face with a pile of napkins.

"Oliver?... Why are you here?"

"I knew you were weird, but I didn't think you were stupid! What were you doing?"

I stared into the rearview mirror, watching father's body bubble with decay. "I… I was talking to my father…But h-he's…"

"And you decided to go for a jog in the goddamn rain after? Was running yourself over and ending your life on the list?!"

"My father's was…"

"What? Look I already know what kind of crummy person he is even if your dense head can't see it. So, I don't want to hear about him anymore."

"My father's dead."

The emergency light displayed all the blood on my hands. Flash on. Vivid red. Flash off. Darkness. Flash on. Flash off.

"I-I killed him."

Oliver's face turned from panic, to worry? I looked at the phone erect in his pocket.

He's going to call the police on me. And that's okay.

He reached into his pocket and pulled out more napkins. "You scratched up your head from that fall. Damn, your cheeks banged up too."

With the diligent hands of a pianist, Oliver took his time to clear whatever mess he saw. The way he scrunched up his nose made it seem like it was a terrible wound. All I felt though was a continuous heave of loss and a noose that tightened around my neck. The seat was a cliff, my damp legs dangling off the edge. One jump and the noose would've surely done its job.

I kept looking down at the cliff until his hands pulled away. Only then did I realize that his hands were the reason I felt warmth.

"Done. Now, do you want to tell me what actually happened?" Oliver cranked on the heater. He seemed to be shivering too.

"I saw my father again."

I still see him…

"I warned you, I never liked your dad. You know that."

A car glimmered past us, its lights a shimmering gold like his mother's earrings.

"And I talked with your mom before I left. She told me…"

"I know. I was there. In fact, I listened to everything. It's probably just me but what you said to them didn't seem like the complete truth. I still can't believe no one saw the markings when you were younger. Or maybe everyone but me was oblivious to them. Cowards. I mean, how could you not tell that you were covering that up with makeup! That made me the fucking maddest!"

"I still don't remember that. I don't remember him hurting me when I was younger. All I keep seeing is what we could've been."

"Don't you tell me that you're still in denial! You're running from your father in the rain and after all these years you still can't admit that he's been hurting you?! Will it take you to hit me again to realize that?"

Lightning crashed against the rain and struck into my chest. "Your mom told me about that. That I hit you a few years ago."

Oliver looked away from me, his delicate hands turning into a robot in need of oil.

"All you were trying to do was warn and help me and I see it now. Yet I don't understand why I would do something like that to you or forget something like that. It's not right and… I'm sorry about that. I'm sorry it took me this long to apologize."

There was a pause in Oliver's breath. "I never needed to hear an apology from you." He wrapped his hands over his legs. Every ligament, every pulse of those hard working hands. Seeing him just like the day of the competition. His dripping hair hung over his eyes, doing the crying for him. "All I wanted was for you to see what I saw. It made me so mad that you didn't. When you hit me, I wasn't mad. I was mad that it made me care for you more."

Keeping the napkin pressed against my head soothed the pulse that banged my brain.

"You were obsessed… with your father. Always talking about him and how he'd be so proud of you. The only times I'd see him was when he skidded off in his car after picking you up, or talking with other parents. I saw through his lies. And it scared me, you were turning into a reflection of your dad."

Like my father? A disgusting crawl ran over the old rashes of his belt. "Then just like that." Oliver's fingers snapped. "After our fight you came back with a smile I'd never seen before. A dance in your step and a chatter box of a mouth that made me swear you were possessed. I wanted to think that you were finally experiencing a happy life. You took everyone's eyes with you. The only thing was that you left me behind."

I touched a shaking fingertip to my cheek. My knees hesitated against the seat, trying to hide it all in. To hide in apologetic words that kept rushing out of me. Because I didn't deserve it. No, none of this I deserved. Especially the streams of tears that gave more of a relief when I felt his arms around me, and my face buried in his shoulder. He was shaking too, and his grip grew tighter, both of ours did. Not just the two of us. I swore somewhere deep inside, someone else was crying too.

"You're not your father's circus monkey."

The rain brought on harder pours, the wind galloping past the car in whistles that swore to tumble the truck. Dozens of yellow headlights danced like fireflies trying to escape the horrors of the storm. Their lights teased me and tried to make me think back to the visions of a perfect father and longing daughter. I no longer wanted any of it, any of father. Just this single moment. This single moment that made me forget the bloodshed on my floors or the fact that I no longer… or ever had a home. Yet this, two arms folded around each other with rashed faces, was the home I'd always wanted.

I let go of Oliver as he rubbed his tears away. If I wanted, I could have stayed like that forever. But my mind was coming back to reason. The reason why I came. The reasons I'd have to give professor if he didn't see me back at his home.

He's going to be the second person I give a heart attack to if I'm not back before him.

"Well, I didn't expect things to turn out this way." I could've sworn his face had gone a little pink.

"Does this mean we can be friends again?"

"I never stopped wanting to be your friend." His cheeks grew brighter against the red hue of the emergency lights. "I think we kinda established that just now… Crying and all."

For the first time of all the times I've been able to remember, the robot finally disappeared and didn't look to be coming back. His hard cheekbones relaxed, and his lips gave a soft smile. He took my hand and gave it a comforting shake.

Wow, you're amazing! I want to play like you one day!

Well, then you better keep watching me because I'll be the worst competitor you'll ever have. Let's see if you can beat me one day with those tiny robot hands.

Two small silhouettes danced in my head on a sea of parting fog. A slender girl with proud features and a stubby boy with his eyes locked on the world.

We didn't talk as he drove me back; we didn't need to. Being around each other gave a reassuring warmth. Oliver pulled into the driveway and turned down the poorly tuned radio station.

No strings were playing this time, just a rap station. Thank goodness professor wasn't home. I offered his jacket back as I opened the truck's door. He pushed it to me instead. "It's too wet for me to use. Give it back next time."

The steps I took back to the house were slow, my eyes on Oliver. He stuck his head out with a crooked smile and shouted against the rain. "You know... You really seem like a completely different person! But I can get used to that!"

I waved back with upturned lips, ignoring the flight of harsh winds. The warm tingles hadn't left since he drove away. In fact, they increased. I held tightly onto my chest, the booming growing louder. My feet danced a single pirouette and water droplets bubbled away from my hair. My feet spun to the center of the room, a blackness roaming into my view. Dominating the middle of professor's living room was the Black Beast. Since when had it gotten here? I wanted to hate it... So much I wanted to. The music, the competitions, the practice, my future. Father twisted something so pure—a simple series of sounds—into the spawned wires encircling an instrument of torture. Despite the sadism it brought my life, I still found myself drawn to its slender back and perfectly lined teeth, whispering *ride me again.*

The bench was pushed far from the mouth of the piano. I slipped myself between the two, standing in front of the beast. Placing both hands on the keys, the sound of sudden claps came behind me. It roared and the lights in the room grew brighter. I pressed my hands against the phantom dress and turned around to catch the sound of the crowd; my audience. My eyes were met with the silence of looming ghosts.

How long had it been since I'd played?

Not long, but it really feels that way. I hovered my finger over the first note. Not making sounds, but playing at the air above the keys. Then my fingers formed into a chord. Soon, it was both hands crossing that mountain of legato.

I wasn't here anymore. At this moment, there wasn't anything at all but the warm sound of the pedal kneaded by my foot. Its pumping furnace echoed into the air and stretched the notes into an arch that went far into nothingness. I heard them, the hushed voices of those in the distance, wanting to hear more.

Would anyone ever hear more except the phantoms around me?

My hands drew away and hung by my sides. Blood pumped through them, loud and vigorous. The temptation so strong that it might've burst through my skin and crawl up my elbows. It wasn't healthy to be so close to music. This was the last string that connected my father and I. We were both addicts. Being here made me want to play over and over again until my fingers crumbled apart. At the same time, it felt like the rightest thing in this world.

I covered the keys with the fallboard and took the crooked bench, pushing it close to the piano. As I softly tugged it, there was a soft sound of metal clinking. When I stopped, so did the noise. I looked around the bench for the source, and a small gleam of chain popped out the side of the bench. With both hands, I propped the bench open, exposing the contents of random scraps of music papers and a small spray bottle with wood cleaning solution. In the corner of the jumbled mess, the gold chaining led to the small shape of a golden heart. It glided in my hands like a soft current. There was something new about it, making it more of a temptation than a pretty piece. At the left side of the heart was a small latch, barely distinguishable. Before I knew it, both thumbs were on the right side of it and I heard a soft click.

I should have left it alone. The object had overtaken me, consumed me. This small object told me... Commanded me to release those latches. When it opened its sinful lips, I nearly threw it across the room.

I don't understand. Why would this be in here... Why would he have it?

Tick. Tick. Tick.

My Malory, oh my sweet Malory.

I shoved the abomination back in the bench and slammed it shut. Furniture stretching around me, growing bigger and towering over me, then shrinking down below me. The Black Beast had grown in size and the bench shrunk under me, making me trip. A sea of notes burst through professor's doors and threw daggers into my ears. This thing was the heart of pandora's box, and it had the face of my mother.

CHAPTER TWENTY ONE

MALORY

I PACED THE FLOOR IN THE DARK, fumbling professor's number in my phone. He messaged me past five, said he was going to be a little late. It was nearly twelve. Each time I managed to dial the numbers correctly, the thing went straight to voicemail. Eventually I tucked the phone under the couch because it too began teasing me with the hideous sound of strings.

"Make it stop... G-God, make it stop!"

The phone buzzed in my hand, but no number came up. I let it fall to the floor and brought palms into my ears, trying to block the music away. How could it have? If it was coming from inside of me?

"Help me! Make it go away! Take over I don't care!"

I cried for the *voice* to come forward but didn't feel an inch of its presence. I wouldn't have blamed it for not wanting to deal with this. I flipped open the bench again, grabbing for the source of my pain. Her image wanted to steal mine with the quickest glance. Identical in almost every way but age. A single line of hair crossed the side of her cheek. I brushed at my face, removing the hair that wasn't there. The door creaking open was my savior. I had clutched the necklace so tightly that it was leaving marks in my palm.

"Why?!" The words leapt out of my throat before professor made it inside. His entire body was soaked, shoes caked with the grime of dark mud. Some of it was on his cheek, swiped upward like he rubbed at it. He stood there for a moment, seeming more shocked at my appearance than I seeing the dirt all over him.

"Oh, you're still awake? Sorry I got back this late. My car stopped in the middle of the freeway and…" Professor's eyes traveled to the necklace wrapped around my fist.

"Why d-do you have a picture of my mother?"

"Malory, where did you find that…"

"Answer me! You lied to me!"

"I never lied to you." Professor took one step forward and I took two steps back.

"Yes, you did! You said this was something for your friend!"

"That's not a lie. She was my friend. Back when both of us lived in Russia. Your mother was an amazing violinist and left with your father before I got to say bye. I kept it as a memory of her."

Three strings plucked in my ears.

Memories, memories, memories! Something everyone but I had!

"You kept something important like this from me! Right in front of my face!"

Muddy prints followed as he took another step and shook his head. "How was I supposed to know what to say? With you barely remembering things, it would have only made things more complicated for you."

"You think you have the right to keep something like this from me?! To decide what or what I shouldn't know?! You're acting like my father!"

I backed against the bench as professor came closer. His face flushed, a hand scratched the back of his neck. "Don't you compare Wilton to me! I've helped him and you more than you'd ever know!"

"You helping my father?! You say you two used to be so close! But you never helped him with his addiction! I had to deal with it all on my own every time he came home from work!"

Professor halted before speaking. He looked down at the floor and took in a breath. "The bastard refused to ever get a job while he had you and came crying to me instead. Even after I helped him get his house back… Paid for it! He hasn't had a job since! Slumming around strip clubs while I took care of you!"

I told you never ta call me during businesss meetin. Can't hear I'ma busy?

Two needles pinned the back of my eyes. I'd been so used to defending my father that I was ready to do it again. I swallowed down the words instead.

"You think he had a job. But I'm sure the only extra money he's had was from you."

The sound came back to me and silenced the strings. The day I called father with loud booming speakers flooding the background. All those people—women shouting around him. The state of his car—the bundled panties I sat next to, the hickies on his neck, the semen that stuck to my hand. I wanted to throw up.

"The bad part of having a friend is knowing their habits. I haven't seen him do it, but I know where he's been and what he's being doing… I'm sure now you can take a hint to why we didn't get along!"

"Why would he do that? All this time he has been lying to me?"

Professor looked down at my hands for a moment. His face looked glazed over. "I think after your mother died, something in him broke. That still gives him no excuse for what he's done.

You killed her! And now you're GONNA KILL ME.

"My mother…Did I kill her? Is it true?"

"Dear god Malory, what are you saying?"

"Before I left, father said that I killed my mother..." I stared at the dirt on the floor, the blood I scuffed around my house. "I'm n-not, a killer I'm not!"

"No, of course not! Nothing near!" Professor came close to me slowly. "You were right for me to hide things from you. So, I'll tell you whatever I can." A drop of sweat trickled into his eye and soaked his nervous smile.

"Just let go of that and we can talk about anything you want, alright?"

I squeezed the necklace tighter. How dare he ask for it back! My mother was in it, my mother! I switched my eyes back and forth from his, to the necklace in my left hand. Now it was clear that he wasn't looking at it. Rather at my right hand that felt something smooth and cold. It was long and slender, not the feeling of chain links dangling from my fingers. In my curled left hand was the petite necklace. In the other was a jade-colored letter opener, its blade a vivid silver. I looked back at him. His temple gleamed against the yellow in the room and his chest moved in and out at an irregular speed. The blade was pointed right at him and his face had turned into a color I didn't realize people were capable of. I dropped it, making the item spin on the floor. After a few seconds, professor got closer to it, locking eyes with mine as he picked it up.

"Where did you find this?"

"I-I'm not sure. I didn't know I was holding it!"

He passed me, nearing a small desk by the window. Professor opened the drawer just enough for the thin item to slip through, then closed it again. I was still next to the piano, my rear collapsed onto the bench.

"Professor... I-I'm scared. I don't know what's happening to me or what's wrong with me. I keep seeing things and hearing things and ending up in places I don't remember!" I buried my head into the hand holding the necklace. "And now I find out that this woman is my mother. And my father says I killed her, and I find this in your house...

"Malory... No one killed Aria—your mother. She died a long time ago when you were very small."

The necklace turned hot in my hands and I pressed that heat into my head.

"You were around four or five at the time. Aria was always struggling with her health. Since she had given birth to you, her immune system started declining. Then one day, she began getting really sick. Soon she couldn't leave the house by herself. I used to visit her often. Your mother and I were close friends because of music. Your father didn't like that and wouldn't let me visit her anymore. He wouldn't let me visit her during the funeral... But I did. And when I finally saw you..."

Turning his head from me, professor put a hand over his mouth.

"Malory... You were staring at her. Like you didn't know who she was... You weren't crying. But I could tell how hurt you were inside. If I was, it must have been a tenfold on you. I never realized shock could do a child harm like that. When you started taking lessons with me, you never mentioned her, only your father. I tried to tell you that it was alright and that your mother was at peace. You looked at me and asked who I was talking about. I didn't want to think it, but my guesses of you blocking it out seemed to be true. Not just her... So many things you forgot. I guess in a lot of ways it's for the best..."

I found my hands opening the pendant again. I traced a finger over every visible feature of hers. My tips almost felt the thick strands of her hair and the voice that once spoke to me. Alive and well.

Malory, my dear sweet daughter.

I knew what he said was true. From the harshness the strings brought me just moments ago, they also showed me something again as my professor spoke. A little girl, myself. I stood beside her, wanting to hold her hand but couldn't. And she wanted to hold the hand of her father. I felt what she could, the emptiness, the blankness which constantly consumed my past. But somewhere I knew that the emptiness didn't begin there. Something before this moment had led up to this point. The color of pink baby's breath started spreading. My father threw bouquets of flowers from my mother's coffin to the floor, revealing a violin laced in her hands. I know he wanted to break that too. The little girl tried to stop him. Her father pushed her back, fell over on her tiny black heels. I reached to help her up, but she fell through my fingers. All I could do was watch from the blackness behind her eyes and shake at the jail bars of her eyelashes. Would she have heard me? Would she ever? Someone else helped her. A tall man, young with a head weaved with dark locks and two blue glossy eyes. The ocean in them felt like a current wanting to turn into a storm.

"Malory, I'm so sorry… I didn't know you've been suffering with all of this for so long." Professor sat on what little bench room there was beside me. "Is there anything else you can't seem to remember?"

Of course there was. So much. So much that I felt it all build up behind my eyes and pour out to the world, falling onto my lap. I pressed the golden heart against the one I felt I'd lost. "What happened to all those lost years?" Was what I begged to ask. And yet, for some reason, an invisible finger tucked back my tongue. The *voice* spoke to me, his tone finally calming.

You can't trust anyone, anymore.

"I figured since you were little that there was something wrong with your memory."

"Since when?"

"Oh, I'm not sure… Sometime between twelve or thirteen? Though I'm sure it might have spanned out earlier before that." His soaked clothes spread puddles on the bench. "You wouldn't remember things, important things and one day came for a lesson acting completely different. You nearly scared me from how different you were."

"I've heard that I wasn't the greatest person before."

"Maybe to others. But I liked that spark in you, just like your mother. You stood up for yourself, even if it meant having a bit of a mouth. Both of you always had a fire that could never be put out and I was alright with fueling it. Eventually I was hoping it would make you realize what type of father you were idolizing. After though… Doing whatever your dear father wanted. I feel as if it's partly my fault… Since then, all I wanted was to help you get it back. But you don't have to listen to him anymore now, do you?"

I looked at my hands and fingers, finally being able to move and play and do whatever I wanted with them. The sound of bees swarmed into my ears.

"No… I guess not."

The bench croaked as Professor stood up. "Then maybe it's time for me to finally help you fuel that fire again."

CHAPTER TWENTY TWO

BEN

IT WOULD'VE FELT BETTER TO STAY AWAY AND out of control. It was all I'd been doing anyway, right? A protector? What a joke. What she did to Wilton, or at least what I was able to see… I leaned against the wall. My head was drunk and seeing things in flashes made my gut squirm. It was all I'd been able to think about since she fell asleep. Not only that…

I shoved a pillow to my face to stop the world from rocking. "What kind of reaction was that?" Even now I still felt the blade in my hand.

Who knows!

I was freaking out as much as she was. How could I have forgotten Malory's mother like that? Our mother! Such a huge piece of memory thrown in the shitter. That poor puppet wasn't the only one surprised when I pointed the blade. At that moment it was the only thing that felt right to do. During this moment, it still felt right.

Each time I blinked, I saw Andre's comforting eyes, reassuring eyes. Convincing eyes.

I could have spent another eternity in this room tracing around its little world till I went mad. The smell of food already took that job.

Breakfast at night?

Then again, with there being no windows, who knew what time of day it really was. Bubbling grease and popping meat kept knocking at the door to my stomach. A body sharing more than one person really made one hungry. Not in this outfit though. I shut my eyes while taking off the nightgown and strapped on the baggiest jeans and shirt I had.

I stepped out and felt the flash of morning pin my eyes. Guess I ended up spending the entire night awake. This body was definitely going to feel that later. I followed the scent and came into the kitchen. From a textbook standpoint, there was nothing particularly wrong with how Andre was acting. Nothing in the slightest. Pan in hand, towel rested on shoulder, grin labeled on his teeth. He called for me with his maternal tone. His footsteps paced from stove, to cupboard, and back.

Give that to me first. Alright?

The scrambled eggs bounced in the pan as he rolled them onto a pair of plates. Fat leaked from bacon to paper towel. Must've not realized I wasn't watching him, or maybe he did. While in the kitchen, there wasn't a moment of him without upturned lips. In fact, since the talk of Malory's mother, things flipped back like a switch, as if nothing had ever happened. There was always this warm presence I felt when she hung around him. Right now, it was a furnace making my pits sweat.

We ate in silence. One being how starved I was, the other how all his words slipped away from my ears. However, I did watch how Andre sectioned his food. Didn't realize people cut bacon. He sliced the fatty white away to the far side of the plate. The rest of it he stared patiently at like a surgeon and slipped the knife along the meaty lines. Juice leaked on the plate and I could have sworn the dead thing squealed. Thought he would have eaten it after, or at least mixed it in with his eggs. Nope. He rolled it up slowly and stabbed it with a fork, proceeding to mate it with a penny sized-egg. He finally went for the bite and the bacon crackled like grinding bones.

"Makes it easier that way, right?"

I reeled my head up, still horribly mystified by his eating habits. "Easier to what?"

I thought he was going to throw the fat away. Instead, he swirled it like pasta and sucked it into his mouth. "To clean up. That way nothing is left behind."

I handed him the dishes from the table as he turned on the sink. After, I wiped the table clean. His side was completely spotless while mine was dusted in bacon crumbs.

"Here's the last one." I handed him a cup branded in dark coffee rings. His eyes smiled at me; his lips unmoved from their arch. It felt like a staring competition as Andre scrubbed the plate while watching me. The steel scrubbing pad sounded like a fork against the plate, the water from the faucet sounded ready to drown me again.

"You look worried. Is something wrong?"

"Not at all. "I was the first to turn away.

What was there to do in this house but music? I stared down at the keys, Andre being close to my side. We had been like this for over ten minutes until he decided to break the silence.

"You really don't remember?"

"It's just not coming to me right now." I shook my head. All the damn keys looked the same. How were both of them able to play this monster? It was intimidating. The shining keys made me wonder if I had anything unique other than being witness to Wilton's murder.

"Now that won't do. Come. Try anything."

My eyes squinted at the lines and dots that looked more like a Rorschach Inkblot Test than sheet music. Not knowing made me feel exposed, on edge. My feet jittered nervously on the floor while Andre waited patiently. Sitting here any longer would've made me sick. I didn't know how I knew, but I would have thrown up right there if I stayed for another minute or two.

"Your hands should at least look like this. See?"

Being so wrapped up in my empty thoughts, I hadn't realized that Andre was now sitting next to me, one of his hands arching on top of mine. I pulled myself away and stepped back from the piano.

None of this feels right.

"I think I'll try again later."

I hate my fucking voice.

"You have some stuff to get ready for anyway, right? Don't you see that conductor again soon?"

"I actually forgot about that. Good thing you reminded me. It's a shame though. I was really looking forward to having one of our lessons again."

"Same here. We could hold it off for now. I'm still not feeling too well."

"You take your time getting better." Andre adjusted himself on the bench and pulled out his sheet music from a small pile on the floor. His eyes still smiled. "We have all the time in the world."

Andre was busy plowing away at the piano while I counted the tiles above my head to calm my breathing. It was either going back into that room or jittering my knee to a song made by some deaf dude in the seventeenth something century. Malory's phone ringed from the kitchen countertop. I was already thinking of her name before I picked it up. It felt like magic, seeing her name blink on screen.

"Hey, Elizabeth! What's up?" As always, I was startled by the girlish voice that came out.

"I should be asking you that. How you doing over there?"

Something that felt like a finger, tapped the lower center of my back and slipped up my shirt. I turned. No one was there but the continuation of keys.

"I'm... Great."

"Well, that's great. I'm also great because I bought two tickets to this ballet. I was planning on going by myself at first... But in that kind of place, I doubt I could." Elizabeth's voice went soft for a moment; I pressed the phone closer to my cheek." You know, wheelchair stuff."

"Your brother didn't want to help you out?"

Stupid. You obviously know why she's bringing this up.

The heat of hope for her invite was intoxicating.

"You and I both know that piano for him comes before anyone else. Family or not. And taking my wheelchair in there. I don't really feel like being handled by strange workers. Want to come with me? I think it'll be fun!"

"Of c-course I would!" My words railroaded over hers. "I've never been to one before and Andre seems to be busy with his music, so I'm all empty hands here."

"Who?"

"You know, M-m-my teacher."

"Oh, of course! Sorry! I'm so used to you calling him your teacher that I forgot the guy had a name! I'll swing by around two. It's not until past three, but I like being early."

I checked the clock's hand nearing twelve.

"Sounds fine by me." What a joke to try sounding cool and calm. My leg was twitching restlessly. "I'll see you soon."

"Alrighty! Bye!"

I hung up and downed my cup of herbs from the tabletop. I already hated tea, but cold tea was a new ring of hell.

Chocolate milk would have been so much better.

I went to the cupboard and fished for a porcelain jar covered with chickens. Grabbing the spoon inside, I dunked two mounds of sugar in the tea, then one more to be safe. I let the microwave do its job for a minute or two.

"You sure sounded."

Two steps back and I would have hit into Andre. He reached under his curls and dabbed his beading forehead with a small blue napkin.

"Just Elizabeth. She was asking if I wanted to go to a ballet with her."

"A ballet, huh? What about her brother Oliver? Is he going?" He went over to his metal trash can, popping the lid open and letting the napkin fall.

Makes it easier that way, right?

"No. Only us two. He's busy with music I think."

Andre hummed while stretching his arm past my shoulder. The hooks of his curls brushed across my cheekbones as he grabbed something from behind.

"Ah, I get that." His breath was like baby gnats flying near my forehead. His voice was sappy and sunk heavily in the air. "Are you actually going to go?"

"Why wouldn't I?" I stared at him, this time I wouldn't turn away first. He gave me a simple glance and looked past me to whatever he was grabbing.

With the same expression he had all morning, he pulled back with a lemon porcelain cup in hand. "Well, after everything that's been going on with you, shouldn't you rest a little? Going out so suddenly like this might make one reckless."

"I think I'm way old enough to decide that for myself."

Andre burst with laughter. "I guess being your teacher for so long is getting the best of me. You're right. I can control your music, but I certainly can't control your actions. What time is it at?"

"Little over three. She wants to come by at two, so we aren't late."

"That's perfect then. The earlier the better."

Tick. Tick. Tick. Tick.

Andre watched the clock near the side of us, resting up on the kitchen wall.

"Well, you better get ready then. Time flies fast when excitement takes over."

Monochromatic colors were something Malory always wore to performances. She was never a colorful child. But her tiny shadow always intimidated people, myself included. Sometimes it would be blacks, dark blues, or sometimes a grey with the intentions of the piano and her becoming one. I wasn't her and she wasn't me. I watched the girl staring back at me, copying my movements in the brightness of the bathroom. The silhouettes of devil's ivy hanging over the lamps made thousands of hands crawl around me. I slapped my neck, could have sworn I felt a gnat nearby.

It had gotten easier to look this body in the face, though I wasn't sure if I fully accepted it yet. Maybe I never would've. I shut off the lights and took off my clothes. All I was able to find in the luggage were bright yellow button-ups and black slacks. Might've looked like a bumble bee, but it was better than wearing anything too girly.

"Well, that wasn't as bad as I thought it'd be." It wasn't comical-looking like I'd pictured. I rolled the sleeves to my elbows and tied my hair in such a way that it almost looked short. I splashed water on my face and slicked back my hair. Maybe these colors were too bright, maybe they were comical. Maybe she'd laugh, but it was all I had. Taking in a deep breath, I observed myself one last time. If I had to go out there looking like a bee, then I'd make sure to be the mother fucking king bee.

"Did you find a dress you liked?" Andre asked as he continued to practice in the other room.

"I think so. Though I wouldn't exactly call it a dress."

I neared the piano as he stopped playing. He did smile, it was the ones you'd find in the back of newspapers. Often paired with a wheezing stomach and tingling sides.

"Wait, are you really wearing that to a ballet?" His voice hitched a small hiccup, his grin stretched.

"Well, I was thinking since I never wear anything colorful, that I might try this on."

Really, that's your excuse?

"Oh, my dear sweet Malory!" His hair tousled as he shook his head. A warm hand cupping my chin and I jolted. "Your eyes are already so full of color. And ballets are no different than your performances. Wearing something like that... Might not exactly be proper or humble." His hand slipped from my chin and fell onto the sleeve, rubbing it between his fingers. "Have you forgotten it's still cold out? Even with a jacket on, this thing won't do anything for you. Unless you were meaning to catch stares." Professor lifted himself off the bench, folding the music book closed and heading towards his shelf. "What about your performance dresses? Got any of those?" He tucked the book back into its empty slot.

My face grew warm as I looked down at all the yellow. "Yeah... I have one or two with me. But I'm not really feeling like dresses right now."

"Well, if you try one on, maybe you'll change your mind. You still have time."

The warmth turned into a burn rising up my cheeks. "No. I think I'm good."

Andre's back was still against my redness. His voice seemed restrained. "Now why are you being like this?"

"Being like what? I just don't feel like wearing a dress. No biggie dude."

"It isn't the fact of you wearing a dress. It seems like you have more conflicting matters with me. Why is that?" His tongue clicked the top of his mouth three times.

"Confli… what really? Look. I'm not arguing with you or anything like that. This is something I feel more comfortable in right now and if you ask me, a dress won't protect more than what this thing can."

"Really now?" Andre gave a slow turn and sat back on the bench. Both his legs tightly crossed as he rolled up his prune sleeves. If anything, his colors were no better than mine! The guy was a fucking grape. "Did you wake up on the wrong side of the bed that I fixed for you? Not feeling comfortable? Maybe from the breakfast I made you? Your tone is really something else and you… your friend's earlier than expected."

Right as he finished speaking, two loud beeps came from outside. Andre went over to the window and peeked out. "Was she coming in a cab?"

Being caught off guard by whatever that was took me a while to respond. What was he spewing? He motioned his hand for me to come closer. I stayed right here. In fact, I went the opposite direction to grab my bag and slipped past him to the front door. "Look, I don't know what I made you so upset about, but I have a show to go to."

He didn't say anything back but turned away to return to his music.

I rushed past the cobbled stone path leading to the cab. On the last step was a soft crunch. I peeled the bottom up to look for a small pebble wedged inside. A small crushed bee had half its body looking like cream cheese. Some of its legs kicked up and I smudged my foot down, feeling nauseous after realizing that none of them were attached to its body.

There she was inside. The sun had turned Elizabeth's hair into an auburn color. I opened the door and her eyes smiled at me from her seat to the left. The soft color of a plump succulent hung around her body. Its ends reached close to her knees and the top traced the outline of her breasts. Elizabeth's braids were jeweled with tiny flowers and her wrists dangled with hoops of silver. If I truly was a bee, I would have fallen madly in love.

The car hummed as it began to move forward, coughing out puffs of grey.

"Loving the outfit! Very sunny!" She blinked at me with full lashes.

"I, I also lo-like yours." I cleared my throat. "You won't be cold from wearing that?" I asked, my eyes glued to the color, onto the fabric that clung around her waist.

"Of course not! I have this." Elizabeth showed me her white jacket made of soft fur. "Even if I did, we won't be out long and only half of me can feel it!" Her laughter increased with that last bit.

"Heading to the Koch Theater, right? By Lincoln Center Plaza?" The driver spoke in a dry voice, a smoker's cough coming up.

"Yup, that's right!"

I had the urge to look out the window. Through Andre's drawn back curtains, I saw the silhouette of a shadow.

"Oh, and you can take your time getting there. We are both pretty early for the show!" The man grumbled something under his breath. Elizabeth didn't seem to notice. She smiled once more at the driver, then at me. "You don't have a curfew, do you?"

"Course not, how old do you think I am?"

It didn't take long to reach our destination. Elizabeth seemed less patient than I. She'd occasionally look out the window. Not to see the scenery or buildings that rose like elastic bands to the sky. She turned her head quickly to the rear window, watching a car speed past us. Other times she would clench her fists and rub a thumb in her palm if the driver was coming to a fast stop near a red light.

"Are you feeling alright?"

No answer. Only the pinkening skin of her hands and the white mountain peaks coming from her muscles. Like sister, like brother?

The man was kind enough to offer Elizabeth help into her chair. She responded with a tip instead, saying she was thankful but liked doing things on her own. I unfolded the chair for her and gave her a steady hand as she dropped in the seat. She seemed light, but the chair gave such a loud crack I was scared she broke it in two. After he left, Elizabeth stared at the fortress before us. We both did. Its vibrant yellow glow through the glass walls seemed to outshine the sun, just as Carnegie Hall outshined the moon at night. Four slender chandeliers hung at the entrance, and a water fountain in the middle to guard the building. Black marble encircled it like a fire pit, the lapping of spouting water acting as ravenous flames.

As a tall shot of water made its way back into the pit, a figure passed close to me, then another, pulling my eyes to follow it.

A wash of lavender, a spark of pink, a tide of blue.

I turned to my left.

Orange, lemon peach, lustful red, sapphire earrings, exposed knees.

Oh, my sweet Malory

"Nice place, right?" I looked at Elizabeth as she rolled her chair close to my side. Her smile was smaller.

"Yeah… It's very… Colorful."

Wearing something like that… Might not exactly be proper or humble.

I blended in perfectly. If I listened to him, I would have stuck out like a sore and bleeding thumb.

The inside was as pleasant as its exterior. The glow grew brighter once we went inside. It must have been the walls magnifying the sun's brilliance through the glass. At each end of the outstretched area were two stone statues. Their long hair was made of marble balls reaching down to the nape of their necks. Both figures were caricatures, having deformed bodies that one might've called art.

I came close to one of the women behind the counter. The wood was decorated with a tiny bell that was only meant to be rung for assistance. Not for children who'd be dragged along by eager parents. Despite it all, I was eager to slam it ten or twenty times to see how loud it'd echo in here.

"Hi. I have reserved seating for two."

The woman gave me a synthetic grin of pearly whites. "And where is the rest of your party?"

I looked beside me. Elizabeth was still near the entrance of the building, her baby green drowning in the sea of color dressed as people.

"Give me a minute. I'll be right back."

The woman politely nodded, and I went back to Elizabeth. Her head hung like a wilting flower, her hands moist and trembled in the crumples of fabric in her fists.

Tick. Tick. Tick.

Somewhere in the distance, I heard the breathing of a clock, the shaking of an ankle on the floor, the gestures of a robot having a malfunction. The impatient fingers tapping on music books. "Hey, are you alright? The ballets going to start soon and that lady at the counter wants to see our ticket."

"I can't do this." Her voice sounded like it'd been knocked out of her. "I-I thought I could, but this is all too much!" Elizabeth brought her hands back onto the cold metal. In two swift movements, she turned herself towards the door and sped out.

"Elizabeth! Hey! Come back!"

She swerved, nearly running into a couple before going through the door.

I felt myself running after her. My lungs should've gone into overdrive, but they continued to pump like a furnace through the forest of colors. What a strange feeling, to feel the possession instead. I smelled wood furnishing coming from nowhere and a cold that wanted to restrict my legs, yet powered them instead. That puppet cared for Elizabeth too. With her helping me run, and my worry for Elizabeth, we both caught up to her near the fountain. The feeling of her got into my arms, and I found myself wrapping my hands around her speeding wheelchair. It screeched to a stop and she turned at me, us. Sticky spikes for hair clung around her chin. She battered her head back and forth. I feared in those moments that she would have hit one of the metal beams of her chair.

"Let me go! Let me leave! I can't do this!" Her eyes screamed at me as a ring of pink closed in on her pupils.

"We can! We can leave anytime you want! Just tell me what's wrong!"

A throb came from the lower part of my cheek. Maybe she didn't mean to hit me. It could have been the thing that made her quieter. Because the moment the slap came, her voice grew soft and her eyebrows raised in surprise.

"I'm sorry… I didn't mean to. I just can't do it." She wailed and grabbed onto her hand like she was the one that had been struck.

"If you don't feel comfortable being here, I'll find a taxi and we will leave right away. You don't have to tell me what's wrong. But if you do, I might be able to understand you a little better." I took her hand in mine.

For a moment, it seemed as if she was possessed too, her body less tense, more open to vulnerability. She nodded and wiped both eyes with the back of her wrist. As I waited for her to speak, I felt myself take full control again.

"It's been so long… Since I've been to a place like this." She shook her head and clutched onto the thick jacket enveloping her body. "Do you know why I'm always so bitter and stupid to my parents and brother?" She pulled out the pair of tickets from her pocket. She kept her eyes glued on them, tearing up all over again.

"Tell me. I'm all ears." I sat beside her on the cold ground, our hands still together.

"I blamed my mother and father for the longest time. You see… I used to dance. Not just for fun or some hobby. Like you and your music, I was obsessed with ballet. It was my everything. But my parents never supported it. 'You're too tall.' My mom would say. 'Your skin is too dark.' It's the last thing anyone let alone a child expects to hear from their parents. But my mom loved my brother's playing. And she set her future on that. With her teaching and support, he became the fucking star of the stage. Competition after competition."

Elizabeth's grip crumpled the tickets.

"I didn't let my damn mother convince me. NOOO!" Her laugh was hysterical, and it made my chest hurt. "My amateur self got better. Something I thought would never happen actually happened! It happened! I got into so many ballets. By then my height didn't matter, neither did my skin. Maybe my parents saw a little of my potential too. There were times when they would take me to my performances and watch. But one day Oliver's competition bumped in with mine. Of course, they took him and told me that I could reschedule it. I'm sure you and I both know that's not how it works. I know my mother's not stupid and she knew this. So, I took matters into my own hands."

Elizabeth had stopped crying. Her eyes pointed at me, but she didn't seem like she was looking at me. She was looking at something else past the blacks in my eyes, trying to peel away every layer of me.

"I called a cab to take me there. I never made it. The driver was r-reckless. Driving too fast on the freeway during winter. You know what's funny? He got away with only having a concussion! A CONCUSSION! But me, I lost the only thing that made me feel worth something."

The most painful thing was that I was unable to shed a single tear, all of them locked behind my eyes. I feared that if I didn't keep those tears under control, it might've burst my eyes open. I felt the pressure of them bulging up, reddening. I felt the girl inside too. A turmoil from artist to artist that I wouldn't ever understand. What could I have said to her to make her feel better? Well… Nothing. I don't think she wanted me to.

Nothing would've ever replaced what she lost. She just wanted to share her pain with someone, and I felt every inch of it.

Elizabeth's hand hung lifeless like a bag of wet sand. She looked at me with doe eyes, cheeks rashed from her sobs. In this moment, I cared for her more than I ever had. I got up and rested her head on my chest. She squeezed my thin waist with her weak arms. It was enough to let three tears fall from my cheek and a waterfall from hers. She kept shaking for those minutes. I looked down at Elizabeth, her skin goose-bumped.

"Come on." I said. "Let's go back inside where it's warm, okay?"

Elizabeth finished collecting herself. By then, the colors had disappeared, exposing a naked marble floor. I led Elizabeth back to the counter and tried to flatten the ripple of mountains that had grown on the tickets.

"Are we too late?" Elizabeth asked the woman.

"Of course not. If you hurry in now, you'll make it before the curtains open." The woman pointed gingerly to the door across the hall. "Just head for those big twin doors on your right."

"Thank you." We both said.

The woman handed me two programs. Both of them had the name of the ballet printed in thick white lettering and a black background. To the side was a realistic drawing of a swan in slumber. Swan Lake.

"Will you two be needing assistance?" She referred to both of us, though I knew she was only looking at the silver cage surrounding Elizabeth's thin legs.

Elizabeth looked almost embarrassed to answer and blinked at me instead.

"No. It's alright. She has quite a way of moving around on her own."

Besides the audience, everything was a complete red. From the walls, to the ceiling, the floors and chairs. Stretched across the walls like a ring of bracelets, were gold trimmings that outlined the box seats planted around the perimeter. I had feared while walking in, that our seating would have been somewhere difficult for Elizabeth to sit. Thank god our seating was at the edge of the middle row. Elizabeth managed to wedge herself between her wheelchair and the auditorium's chair, sliding down onto the cushioned seat.

I folded up the wheelchair and sat beside her. The lights dimmed around us.

"Thank you again." Elizabeth spoke in whispers. "For coming to watch with me. And listening to me. That's all I ever wanted from someone and you gave it to me."

A single instrument began and soon the rest followed, tuning themselves into the same pitch.

"Of course. I'll always be here for you."

Both curtains drew back, revealing a scene of what looked to be painted trees, seasoned with the color of autumn. I almost felt its warmth. It collected in my left hand. Elizabeth had taken it in hers, squeezing tightly. A small row of what looked like crystals formed around her eyes. Her voice was breaking into quiet fragments. My body pulsated to the beat of my heart. I took her head in my hand, lowering it onto the crook of my shoulder. Elizabeth squeezed her eyes shut, as if the beautiful ballerinas were dancing goblins. Her body, shaking at first, finally slowed down into hiccup motions. I knew that I would've never been able to understand the pain Elizabeth had inside. But I did know that seeing someone you loved so much in pain, became the most painful emotion you'd ever experience.

The ballerina continued to leap, her surroundings now eclipsing with the synthetic moon. Soon she was alone. The strings played a mournful tune. She spun in a white dress, faster and faster. Small white feathers flew down onto the stage and blew across the surface. She was turning into a girl, her curse of being a swan lifted for a single night. Through a trance of fixed eyes and Elizabeth by my side, I wondered.

Would I ever stop being the swan and finally become a full human?

CHAPTER TWENTY THREE

BEN

HER TEARS PUDDLED INTO MY LAP, her shoulders twitched from each cry she tried to hold in. My cheek had been resting on her bed of hair, the smell of coconut product and fruity mist coming from every brown wave.

It was near the end of the ballet that she finally straightened herself up. Elizabeth raised her head, slipping her hand away from mine and rubbing her dewy eyelashes with both hands. She gave me a final glance before moving her attention to the stage. I would've wiped every tear for her, if it meant that she'd still hold onto my hand.

When the standing ovation came, all the dancers lined up and bowed their heads like dominoes. Everyone rose and applauded. She and I remained sitting. By the end, I wasn't really sure what the two of us had been watching. A girl turning into a swan. A swan wanting to turn into a girl. My mind had been somewhere else, focused on a dream that scattered apart—and formed into a new one by each side glance she gave me and each drop of dew that fell from her chin. Each one that rolled down had their own story. Our first encounter at the hospital and the flames I saw in her eyes. The other was the dimly lit cafe. How my body filled with such adrenaline that the world never felt more real. The last was the memory of the present, this very moment. I held my own hand, wishing for hers. Wishing for my existence to be something more than a protector of this body. To be hers, so she would no longer feel like a swan stuck to swim in her silver lake.

"How did you like the ballet?"

I blinked twice into reality, feeling the sudden cold hardening in my lungs and my jacket hanging loosely on me. Icy droplets of a nearby fountain flew past me. "I gotta say, I never expected boys to dance like that." I let out a raspy cough, as if that would have changed the tune of my voice.

"Well, ballet isn't only for young girls! It's for both genders! It's hard stuff to dance like that!" She flexed her arm like some bodybuilder.

"Today really proved that to me. But I'm not so sure how I feel about ballets yet. I think you'd have to take me to another one." I grinned at the proposal while trying to keep a strange awkwardness away. It'd been in the air since we left the building. Being side by side with the threatening silence only made the thing grow. Did she feel this way too or was it just me?

Cars and taxis alike passed by us. A bus halted nearby, unloading its passengers before going off with the sound of compressed air spouting from the rear. The fountain continued to curl as the weather dried my throat.

"Do we really have to let this day end yet?"

No, I don't. Ever.

"Don't ask me. You're the one that probably has curfew now, not me." I blew the frost away from my fingertips and pocketed them in my jacket.

"It's just… I don't want to stop hanging out with you yet. We barely talked since all we did was watch." Were her cheeks turning pink? She flicked her head away before I could look more.

"I mean, it has been a while since I've traveled the city." I gazed up at the skyscrapers. Their glowing eyes looked down at me.

Don't you mean never?

"Are you asking me to be your escort?" Elizabeth raised a lovely eyebrow.

"Maybe… If you're up to it."

"Well, then of course my lady." She curtsied in the chair and my cheeks grew warm. I stared at her and what a smile she gave me. We both broke into laughter.

There was never an area filled without people. That's New York for you. A new face with an entire life's story every time you pass, never to be seen again. Elizabeth's face was something I didn't want to be new and forgotten but something that aged with time.

Despite the occasional smell of old soda and grime from nearby trash cans and homeless folk, New York could've been seen as beautiful. A beautiful chaos of bulletin boards and strips of light that burned all three layers of my eyes. The golden glow of Carnegie Hall cast a sharp shadow against the setting sun. Her wheels turned white with snow as I led her chair from behind.

"Ah yes, there!" Elizabeth plowed away with a sudden force and rolled into a green and white striped shop. I was blasted with the smells of garlic and over-matured cheese. People bent over tiny tables haggling at pizza wedges larger than their heads. A chubby man with a thin mustache spun stretched dough behind the counter. I didn't know Hitler made pizza.

"When's the last time you had a slice?"

"Never actually."

"Really?! No way! Funny how it's the food everyone talks about when visiting. Yet here you are never having any and me not having one in centuries." Elizabeth shouted to Hitler the obese chief as he placed the dough down. "Two please! Just cheese."

Hitler grinned at her and cut two slices with a rolling blade. Cheese strung up from the sides in a delicious mess. He handed her the food on a flimsy plate and she handed him the money. We went back into the streets since all the tables were taken. Elizabeth folded her pizza into a burrito and chomped down. Steam spewed from her nose like a dragon. I let the weather blow on it for me before trying a bite. My taste buds sizzled with salty cheese and sweet tomatoes. Elizabeth must have seen how my eyes lit up because she giggled while taking another bite.

"A show and dinner? Hmmm… Wouldn't people call this a date?" Her lips parted as she licked a dab of sauce from the crook of her mouth. There was a strange calmness to her eyes that seemed almost seductive. Then again, anything she did was like that for me.

I choked on the last bite and kicked a fist to my chest. My ears steamed. "A-A what?"

Whatever flickered in her eyes was gone and she threw the crust away. "Alrighty! Let's go onward!" Of course, she was joking, I was being delusional. At the same time…

She didn't deny it.

The one thing I wasn't delusional about was the time. I saw it in her eyes too. The bulletin boards and lights from small shops became the new sun. It didn't matter how much light was in the city. Both of us knew that being out late would only bring danger. This place did have interesting characters at night. A grown man trapped in a woman's body and a girl stuck in a wheelchair wouldn't exactly have the upper hand.

She spoke before I could as I threw my plate into a nearby bin.

"Hey, we should head back soon. It's getting late." There was a kind of

sadness to her voice, but her face didn't show it. "First let me ask you, did you at least have a little fun?"

Did I have fun? I had so much more than that.

"Y-yes. Yes! I'm glad we didn't leave after the show. And I didn't realize pizza was this good."

"I'm so glad!" She let out a sigh of relief. Her eyes didn't look it. She peered down at her fingers and played with them.

A stretch of awkwardness turned into a heavy blanket and I knew she felt it too. What else did she want me to say? What else did I want to say?

My heart beat painfully in my chest and I twisted my shirt in my hand. My palms sweated like a mad man and my mouth was sucked dry of life. Elizabeth looked at me and I gazed away.

Stop hiding like you always do.

"Guess it's time to get us a ride back. Before it gets too late, you know." Elizabeth's hand slowly raised up.

You might never get this chance again. Ever.

My knee twitched to the sounds of my throbbing heart. My breath grew hot, but I still didn't look back at her. I closed my eyes. I saw nothing, and I'd continue to see nothing if I never did anything. All I'd ever be able to see was this moment, and how much I could've said something. The rest of my life would've become a series of could haves and memories of possibilities that I shot down before they even had a chance to stand.

Fucking say it.

Or I could've cherished just this. This was the best I never thought I'd have and it'd be enough. Friendship was enough.

No, it wasn't.

It would've been enough. How would things have gone otherwise? Complicated messes that she'd never understand because no sure didn't. Something like me shouldn't exist. Yet here I was, breathing with lungs I struggled to call my own. Thinking with this shattered and split up brain and seeing with eyes that were only meant to look at a damn ceiling. I'd never be able to claim life as my own. I'd never have a body in the form I wanted. But… If I said it… This moment could be my own. Something I could finally call mine rather than Malory's.

If you don't say this, I swear you're going to regret it!

JUST FUCKING SAY IT BEN…

"I want to dance with you."

I'm sorry, I what?!

Her mouth simply stayed open in shock, horror… maybe she'd slap me again. I'd slap myself harder, what the fuck was I saying? It sounded better in my head! Elizabeth's hand froze in the air before lowering. A taxi slowed down in front of us. She waved it off and it left.

"I'm sorry, but have you forgotten that I'm a cripple? The hell?"

My hands wouldn't stop shaking and the wind against my skin felt like punches to the chest. "No, you're not." I reached my hand out to her and did the best manly bow I could. "You're Elizabeth, and you're a beautiful dancer." I waited for her to hit me. Her face was beaming red. She looked smaller in her chair; both her hands tightly squeezed together. I swallowed once before going through with this crazy, stupid proposal.

"I want to help you dance one last time. Will you let me?"

It felt like ages before she took my hand. So light, it was barely there, so cold that I wanted to embrace her forever. "Put your arms around me." She did. Then I lifted her carefully from the silver cage and into my arms, the imaginary stage. Her feet dangled off my arm like a doll and I kept her back supported with my palm. I never wanted her to fall again.

I heard it, the echoing fall from the hospital and the way her eyes were enough to burn the entire world. I turned slowly, and swayed us back and forth. A car's radio in the distance became our waltz and the batting of a crow's swings became her audience's applause. Now as I held her in my arms and danced in the streets of New York, I felt the fire too.

"Do you feel the stage?"

Her hand softly clutched the front of my shirt. "Yes. I do."

"Do you hear the cheers of your audience?" A murder of crows now appeared. She gave them a soft wave as I spinned her twice. Then her hand met the other and she created a graceful circle with her arms. I saw the delicacy that was lacking in her brother as she moved her hands from position to position. Her neck leaned back in my arms and in this moment, she truly did look like she was dancing. She closed her eyes and smiled. "Yes, I hear them."

Snowflakes fell around us, like dandelions in the wind. "Catch the bouquets. These are all for you. It's all for you." A crow flew away, and the radio music shut off. She cupped her hand around a snowflake. She watched it melt in her hands. The snow was now a puddle of water, but she kept staring closely. Elizabeth bit the corner of her shaking lip. Curling into my arms, she began to weep. As if she was in physical pain, as if she was dying. As if she was feeling the fire behind her eyes. I'd stopped moving by this point and hugged her tightly. I was crying too, and I couldn't seem to stop. It wasn't for the same reasons as her. This very moment was the first time in my life that this heart beating inside of me felt like my own. That as I held her under the flickering lights, I truly felt like a man. The reflections off the buildings showed it, my arms as I carried her felt it. The weight of this hair was no longer holding down the me that lived on the other side of the mirror. She mumbled under her breath, her shoulders hitched from each tear blooming on my chest.

"Do you see me?"

Is this what it means to be human?

Her eyes were clouded in a fog of tears and I pulled back a few strands of hair from her ear. "Of course I do."

"There's also… Another thing I want to tell you. It'd been bothering me for a while. All these feelings that you gave me, I've never experienced any of this before."

"What do you mean?" She wiped her eyes on her jacket's sleeve.

"Meeting you in the hospital has been the best thing that ever happened to me."

"I screamed at you."

"No. You had a light in your eyes that made me want to learn everything I could about life and try things I'd never done before. I've always been stuck in my room, staring at a wall. You made me want to try a go at life rather than let it pass." I brought her closer to me, as close as our faces could meet. "And now I have a feeling in my chest that makes me want to learn everything about you."

A small white flake dusted the top of her nose. Her face glowed in a luminance of colors. Most of them a rosy red.

"I think, no. I have feelings for you. More than the friendship kind."

A yellow lantern buzzed on. She wasn't saying anything, wasn't doing anything. Would I have expected her to? Even a turn down would've been better than the stretch of silence.

"Elizabeth?"

"You didn't think I noticed?" She rested her head into my chest, and I felt the warmth of her breath. "All your stuttering and the way you jitter when I look at you. It hasn't only been once that I'd seen you blush. You think I wouldn't notice all those signs? So… Did you notice me as well?" Her voice softened as the wind and her eyes danced from building to building.

"I'm a little lost in what you mean."

"You think I'd be in anyone's arms like this? Course not." Elizabeth looked back at me, in all her beauty. "I've got something to tell you too. Come here." She motioned for me to come closer.

I bent my head down a little and looked down at her.

"Ugh closer! Make i-it a little easier on me!" Elizabeth grabbed my shirt and pulled hard. It came untucked in an ugly way. The backside slipped out and beat against the wind. "It's not nice to tease someone like me." Her breath pirouetted in the spiral of my ear and once it hit the center, I shivered. The way her eyes flickered before they shut, the sheen of sparkled white that dusted her cheeks. The beating of my heart disappeared into the gallops of rising wind. No, it wasn't the wind, but her voice that gave a quiet murmur over sweet breaths. I kept staring as the snowflakes on her cheeks became stars, my emotions twisting with the galaxies, and our two lips coming to the center of our universe.

I wasn't sure who pulled away first. My stomach felt the heat that'd lowered from my cheeks and I slowly pulled away. My hand remained tangled in her hair. Elizabeth, more feeble-looking than ever, whipped a finger near the corner of her mouth. I still tasted her on me.

"It really is getting late." Was all I managed to say.

"So, a little dark scares you?" Her eyes flickered again. Her lips raised at one side to give a hint of mischief. "It's always so busy out here. People moving back and forth, always in a rush. What about going somewhere, where there aren't any people at all?"

"Somewhere more peaceful you have in
mind?" My fingertips played with her hair.

"Well, I wouldn't exactly say peaceful.
But I think you'll like it."

"Alright, I'm all for it. Where are you
gonna take me?"

"That's a surprise."

I should have stopped after the kiss, that I know for a fact. But my hunger and unbearable need to touch her kept closing in on me, intoxicating me. One touch was all it took to turn the key. She called a cab and we rode to who knew where. She told the street address to the driver, her voice but a whisper to his right ear. I wasn't sure how long it took to get there. Elizabeth sat with a shy hand in mine. Time chiseled away so quickly as I caught a glimpse or two of her eyes staring at a stain on the seat.

I could barely breathe by how tight my chest had gotten. My body tingled and I could've sworn I was about to have a heart attack. I looked up to a glowing billboard with flickering letters. It simply said: **MOTEL**.

Motel?

It was a simple one you'd see as a quick pit stop for truck drivers rather than exotic ones for overnight stays. "What are we doing here?" was what I was going to ask. But I knew, and knowing it locked my knees in place until she nudged me forward with one of her wheels. The rooms stacked side by side, an eerie similarity to where I first met Elizabeth. We came to what I assumed was the check-in room. A large woman was crammed at the other side of the counter like a suffocating sardine. To her right was a small sign for a no smoke zone. Her ashtray was more of a bowl, toppled with dead cigarettes. She looked to be in her late fifties, smelling of peppermint gum over a freshly lit cigar. I wouldn't have been surprised if smoking aged her twice as much.

"How long?" The woman croaked.

That hit me on a personal level. How long? I… obviously didn't have one. My hands stuffed themselves deep into my pockets to make sure there really wasn't anything there. Nope, only lady parts.

"Just for tonight."

The smoke addict slapped a key with a thick piece of plastic on the end onto the counter. "Yuh room's six. Jus to yuh right. Don worry. Yuh won't need tah take any stairs."

It was standard. A dark colored carpet with intricate patterns to easily hide stains. A bed the color of coffee and cabin wallpaper. The ceiling was as pale as my exposed shoulder. Elizabeth's hands scissored around my buttons till the shirt was inches from slipping off. The tips of my ears burned and something down between my legs throbbed. A ghost. She then laced her arms around my neck, and I carried her out of the chair. It stung to see my reflection when I placed her on the bed.

"Please, don't embarrass me with that look." Light glowed off her shoulders as the fabric slipped and her zipper lowered. "Lights o-off?"

"Yes please."

One hand on her back and the other in the bends of her knees. Compared to the hospital visit so long ago, she had grown heavier, I was so glad she had. The first time I saw her, she barely weighed anything. Now she was filled with more life. Life in her arms, life in her cheeks, life in her eyes. Her legs though, they remained the same. Their weakness showed through as her thin feet pointed towards each other.

"Don't look there." She took my chin into her palm, bringing my eyes back to her face. "I don't like myself down there…"

"Well, I think your legs are one of your strongest aspects."

The bed creaked when I helped her onto her back. Her hair spread out; her side exposed from the zipper. Although the room wasn't cold, small goosebumps rose on her skin. Her arms rested lazily over her head and for a moment, I wondered if she'd done something like this before.

I kissed her and felt the kick of energy back in my chest. Two curious hands traveled to my back, pushing away the hideously long strands of hair to the side. Elizabeth was fumbling with something under my shirt and I flinched. There was the sound of metal on metal. No, I didn't want her to undo me. Not looking like this.

Tick. Tick. Tick.

"I rather keep it on. I'm not very comfortable with my chest showing."

Elizabeth's finger sealed my mouth shut. "And you think I'm not? Just close your eyes and relax. You're not the only nervous one here."

Her journey began at the top of my forehead. I would have been fine with her staying there. I would have been fine with staying in the city after the kiss. A shadowed tongue left her mouth and swirled around her lips. A single kiss on the cheek, a row on my neck, a strong one planted on my shoulder that almost felt like a bite. She traveled down the two mountains and at once I stiffened. My illusion of feeling like a man was dying.

No, not yet, Not yet!

I pulled myself closer, flattening my chest against hers and trapping her hand before she could grab anything. I wouldn't lose this fight with myself. Not when I'd finally been able to be with her this close. Elizbeth didn't give up either. She found a gap by the underside of our bellies and brushed her hand there. One of my hands was tied under her head, and she grasped onto that arm. My lips were no longer moving at this point as she continued to travel. My tongue had turned into a sour sponge in my mouth. Hers entered like a serpent and licked along the sides of my dried up rose bud garden. I felt the rigidness. As much as I wanted to pull back and grind my teeth, I couldn't. She would have lost her tongue. Instead, I was lost in this freezing moment and a terrifying feeling of nostalgia.

Elizabeth ducked her head close to my ear. She let out a breathy word. I couldn't hear it at first, her sighs louder than her voice. The mysterious word kept growing louder, a chant of some kind that coiled in my stomach.

"M…M…Ma…"

She somehow managed to tumble herself on top of me. Her lifeless legs dragged behind her like a tail as she neared my face. Nearby was the rattle of her bracelets. Elizabeth's hair blinded the room, trapping me in her lowering gaze. Two moons in her sky in the midst of an eclipse. How did someone with such little strength hold me down like that? The only explanation was that my energy and will was stolen by her lips pressing up against the center of my chest. The warm touch struck a painful chill up my spine.

"M...M...Ma..."

No. Don't. Don't say it. Please...

A tear formed as I felt the lower part of me split in half. A parasite, a stinger, had made its way inside, pinching, pruning somewhere that was never supposed to be open. Then it split into two, spreading apart, going deeper and deeper, moving up and down. It wasn't humiliation or physical pain. That disappeared the instant she twisted her fingers inside of me. It was instead a hurtful idea that became the painful truth.

"M...Malory..."

There it was.

I looked into her eyes, but she had never looked back at mine. Not since the day I'd met her. Elizabeth stared at her. Her. I... I had fallen in love with someone who never knew I existed.

CHAPTER TWENTY FOUR

BEN

EVERYTHING HAD GONE NUMB DOWN THERE. I couldn't tell if her fingers were still in… there. The little weight she had sunk into every part of my chest, filling it with concrete. Elizabeth's eyes were closed, probably rolled to the back of her head, imagining the curves of this body rather than me.

"P-Please get o-off of me." My voice was brittle, choking.

Her lips continued to suck on the cancerous mound on my chest. She bit on a fleshy marble.

"G-get o-off of me."

"Hmmm?" Her lips hummed the tune of a mosquito as she finally rolled her eyes back into place.

How did emotions have the ability to change so easily? Once a burning desire for nothing but that person. The warmness of being close. It didn't matter if it was in the cold, or in the wrath of summer. You would endure it for them. How you'd learn to understand, to be patient with them. To hold their hand as they told you their greatest fears, hoping you wouldn't think they were crazy. Now it was the desire to push them off in hopes for them to crawl away in a corner, never to be seen again.

"I said get off of me!"

Elizabeth pulled away, a soft squeak as her lips broke free. Her grip loosened, and I took that as my escape. I wanted to hate her so much, to toss her off the bed with such force that she would've never wanted to see me again. I hated myself for feeling that way. Instead, I laid there crossing my arms over my eyes. The beating in my heart blasted in my ears. I had to block it out, I wanted to go away and let her see the Malory she moaned out to.

It took a while, but her weight finally rolled off me and she laid nearby.

"I'm sorry… Did I hurt you?"

"Yes—no. It's not your fault. I know you didn't mean it, but I couldn't t-take it."

"Tell me. If I made you uncomfortable or went too far in anyway. I figured that this was something you wanted to do…"

"It is, it was." I sat up, all my weight had gone to my head and hair. This body's damn hair!

I want it all gone.

"Why did you have to call her name?"

"Who?"

"Why couldn't you keep her name to yourself?"

"Her name…Who's name?"

"You said… Malory."

I felt the flickering of confusion in her. It didn't matter how dark it was.

"Yeah. Your name. I said your name. Look if that made you feel awkward, I get it and I won't say it again." She pushed a pillow under her head to get a better look at me. Her cheeks were still glowing from sweat in the darkness.

She's never going to understand. Once you tell her the truth, she'll think you're crazy and never want to see you again.

The bed was painful to sit on and the fire in me kept growing. I slid off and clicked on the lights. I cringed when Malory's hair tickled my back, my chest, my shoulders. She was teasing me! Playing with my emotions! "I remember everything. When I first met you at the hospital and told you my name. Ben. That's me. The reason why I couldn't remember when I first went to your house wasn't because I couldn't remember. But because that person you were talking to wasn't me. It was… the other girl. That damn puppet."

"Okay, now you're really not making sense."

I ignored her and pulled the hair away with my coiled fist, letting Elizabeth see every part of me that wasn't me. "This isn't me. This skin you see, this hair! Every damn bone in this body and every lump of fat under this skin isn't mine!"

Tick. Tick. Tick.

"Malory, please calm down. I'm not understanding what…"

"My name isn't Malory! It's never been Malory!" I caught a glimpse of a small child in the mirror. Wide-eyed, bruised chin. She was wearing an oversized white dress. My purpose in life was meant to be her protector. Now she became something I loathed. The ghost child jumped off the bed beside Elizabeth and skipped to the shadow that stretched below a lamp. She looked at me for far too long, as if she were still here. The little Malory took a bow, her eyes deprived of life. Her foot disappeared when she stepped onto the lamp's shadow, and soon did the rest of her body sinking into it. I blinked the illusion away. "That ch-child has been gone for years! And I still don't know why the fuck she's gone! I don't think I ever will! Because that girl is trying to make a life that's a lie! Everything she believes is one big fucked up lie!" I pointed at the disappeared apparition, then looked back into the mirror. The reflection made it look like I'd been pointing at myself.

It was painful to watch. How her eyebrows lowered, her lips growing smaller. She followed the direction of where I saw the small Malory. Elizabeth looked back at me, waiting for me to give answers to all the crazy I'd been saying. She opened her mouth to say something. Nothing came out.

Good. Maybe it was better this way. I replied to her by throwing on my coat and going through the front door.

"Malor… Ben… Just wait! Wait!"

I was out onto the parking lot when I heard her. I slowed to turn around but felt her fingers snaking inside me and decided to keep moving forward. Did I know where I was going? No. Did I know Elizabeth was heading to a hotel for something more than a simple sleepover? Of course. I also knew that I would have been fine with just that kiss. That made me happy enough. It did make me happy. Now I was hurrying out, tightening the jacket around me. I felt like a prostitute trading themselves for scraps of paper. The buyer calling the name of a lost lover while using the slut's body as a real life ex-girlfriend simulator.

Luckily there had been a cab nearby, a man with silver hair smoking near it.

"Ay lass, sorry but I'm done for the day." The man flicked the rolling switch of his lighter.

"You can take one more ride." I came to the door beside him, going for the handle before his hand pressed against the door's frame.

"Listen to a man when he's talking."

"Listen to me when I'm talking. I need to get back home. "

I glanced back at the hotel, then at the man. He stood straight with legs apart, his striped clothes looking like a mobster. The driver had quite the chiseled face with a firm jaw sticking out like a hammer. Maybe he saw it in my eyes, or the stains on my cheeks. Because that sturdy jaw loosened a little. He massaged what little hair he had left and picked up his coffee fedora from the hood of the car. He took two puffs of his cigarette and let out a small groan.

"Rough night, huh? Someone gone and broke your lil heart? Or are ya here for business matters?"

M... M... Ma... Malory.

"They called out the wrong name."

I massaged my chest as my heart calmed. Clouds rested in the sky like floating moss and the man hummed softly to the tune of a classical radio station. Not that I would' known any of those songs. The first one was a piano piece that could have starred in a depressing commercial for animal abuse.

Why do people bother listening to this?

"Could you roll down the window please?"

The fedora on his head nodded and cold blazed into the car. The man cranked on the heater for himself as I let the cold numb all the aches in my abdomen. It still felt like there were fingers inside of me. When the piece finished, the man stopped humming and tilted his head to me. "Listen kid. I know that heartbreak hurts like a bitch. I learned that after my third wife. Mind my French. But trust me when I say that there are other, better men out there for ya. You just gotta keep looking around rather than sticking to just one of em."

"Girl."

"Eh?"

"It wasn't a man. It was a woman."

"Well shit." The man grew quiet as if in thought, then let out a hearty laugh. "Now that's somethin I don't hear every day."

The city was left behind and the neighborhood streets started coming through. Fedora man hummed to music again and another song came on. I was surprised that he was able to sing a pitch that high. A violin's voice began strongly and bellowed back and forth with a set of thick piano chords. The violin stepped higher on its imaginary steps and the piano scattered after it with eager fingers to pluck its strings. The violin teased the piano with its magical voice and swam around with it in this playful, childlike melody. Then the stringed instrument began to slow into a calm whistle and was soon drowned out by the piano. What seemed like a duet turned to a battle between instruments. I never realized music had the ability to sound so fearful. The piano was chasing the poor thing and it was barely able to keep its voice going. The violin was no longer singing. It was screaming. The noise drilled into my brain and I wanted to cry out too.

Make him stop, Ben. Why didn't you make him stop? Can't you see he's hurting me?

"Hey, can you turn that off?"

The man kept humming and the piano muffled my voice.

Why are you hiding? Aren't you supposed to be helping me?

Malory's voice screamed inside of me; the piano violated my ears.

"Excuse me!"

"Eh?"

The violin shrieked from the violation.

BEN IT HURTS!

"Turn that off!"

"Jesus alright!" Fedora man awoke from his humming trance and clicked it off. "What boot got up your ass?"

But the music wasn't off. It was playing louder than ever and the bristling of wind felt like millions of gnats crawling over me. Static ruptured from the corners of my eyes and the car smelt like varnished wood.

I need to leave.

I reached over to my side to grab the wallet from Malory's bag. The bag wasn't there. Neither was my phone. It was still back in the hotel with Elizabeth. I glanced back over at the driver and he didn't seem to notice my panic. We were only a few streets down from Andre's house and the man was slowing towards a stop sign. New York was a big place and neither of us would've ever seen each other again. The dude actually seemed like a good guy. I took my chances and ran out, leaving the door flapped open.

"AY YOU BITCH, GET BACK HERE!" The car screeched behind me, but I kept forward. It was a good thing I brought a jacket, or I'd be a vivid target. I beelined through the trees with the sound of a car's motor a distance away. As the driver came closer, I pressed up against a fence. He zoomed past me, his classical music and mobster voice disappearing.

I kept close to the fence, its shadow eating me. The mud froze my toes as I tugged the jacket tighter onto me. I spent a few minutes more in hiding before leaving. It was a relief to have my thoughts at a halt. But when my feet started treading, so did those memories of the hotel. I passed a tree that reminded me so much of the one at Elizabeth's home. I snapped off a fresh twig and hoped it felt some of my pain. Instead, it angered the sky and the wind began to pick up. I pulled the jacket closer to me and wished to see only ceilings again.

Andre's porch light flickered on. My attention focused on his keys. I was a lucky bastard to find them in my pocket. I tried my best to ignore the girlish shadow stretching beside me. The shadow shook nervously, and two moths flew alongside to coax its fear. They came too close and got roasted in the lamplight. My hand didn't want to open the door. It wanted to stay outside and go somewhere far. Far where? I'd die in the snow or be gang banged in the streets. The shadow took my hand and led me inside. It echoed my movements, its head slumped to the side as I scuffed my feet on the floor. They were packed with mud and grass, and smelled of shit. When had these ever been my feet? Or this dark being for instance. I'd never claim its silhouette, or the breath I bottled up in these lungs. My feet, its feet, her feet, seemed to know where it was going before I did. On the wooden walls of Andre's home, the shadow multiplied and bent, stretched, and shrank with each curvature. They trailed past the slick couch, a subtle moonbeam bouncing off its sticky surface. The piano moaned as I passed it. It wanted Malory, craved Malory. It wanted her to place her chapped skin on him, for her breathing to pump him full of life. Just like Elizabeth.

A bright light clapped on in the bathroom; Malory's figure dawned back at me. Leaves in her hair, puffy red eyes, tiny dry lips. I dug into the drawers, searching and searching for something through soggy breaths. The hands finally found what they were looking for and I gripped it. The object's twin wings circled around my fingers which lead to a connected set of blades. If I closed my hands the wings would shut. When I stretched my fingers apart, they would glide back open. Continuing this movement made it look like it was flying. Would I've been free to fly with it?

The mirror had freckles of dried water marks. Malory's reflection toyed with me, neutering my hate. At this point, I might've as well cut her body up, scoop off her flesh mounds on the chest and throw them away.

"I want to be free..." The scissor's edge left a dragging scratch across the bare chest. "I want to be free..." I brought it up, tracing it across my cheek then between her breasts being a host to my soul.

Maybe that wasn't mine either.

Was it my hands that shook in fear, or was it her? Just like that day long ago. That was one of the few things I remembered from the past. The last room Malory was in wasn't so different. A tiled bathroom taken over by her tired pink eyes. Malory would have ended it all, ended me. But something was watching over her while I cowered away. It made her stop hurting herself; stopped her from feeling the pain of the past. Eventually, it helped her disappear.

"I want… to feel like me."

The girl in the mirror cried at me. I loosened the aim and strangled my fingers with hair. I yanked my hand away from my scalp. A few strands broke away in clean stinging snaps.

I'd never be able to change this body. It would have been enough to simply imagine. In the end, her face would always be staring back at me. The helpless sunken eyes of a child that never managed to age since that day. What pained me more was the fact that I didn't protect her when she needed it the most. I cowered and let her suffer the things none of us wanted to remember. The memories that were blocked away in order to let us live day by day.

The first snip was all it took. What a euphoric feeling it was to feel the weight fall off! Malory's reflection scorned me with hate. Good. That made the second snip easier. It all went to the floor.

"You're a coward." The girl on the other side said.

The third snip was close to leaving a slice in my neck.

"You'll always be one!"

I shut my fogging eyes to make her go away.

"Closing your eyes won't get rid of me!"

I felt my finger pricked by the blade but kept going.

"You're a coward that isn't even real! YOU'LL NEVER BE REAL!"

"GO AWAY!"

"I'M ALREADY GONE!"

I stood in the masses of hair around me. It itched under my feet and sweat stung my eyes. In the reflection was a slender body with visible collar bones. I traced the blade along the bone. The remaining locks tickled down to the fatty ends of my ears. A simple act of cutting hair had a way of reshaping the face. It was true; I still had the same face and the same body, but I looked more of a young boy. I should have felt happiness with this new body, the body I was finally starting to get! Then why did this moment of freedom die so quickly? It felt like I put her in harm's way. Betrayed her. Flayed her up.

Her eyes stared back at me. Pupils large and fearful. So black that they almost shone purple.

"I'm sorry… I'm just so confused. I don't know what I'm supposed to be doing anymore or how I should feel! I thought I knew at first. But now I feel so weak that I can't even protect my own heart. Now I've gone and done this to yo…

Tick. Tack. Craaaack.

Short strands of hair dusted my shoulders as I turned towards the noise. It could have been the house moaning and stretching from the cold. Maybe the floorboards were finally beginning to warp. I gripped the scissors tight and prayed it was one of those as the sound grew louder. The noise stopped right outside the bathroom door. How could the sounds of wind and creaking floors have a shadow from

under the door? Simple answer. They didn't.

CHAPTER TWENTY FIVE

MALORY

I KNEW HE CARED ABOUT HER. The feelings Ben had towards Elizabeth were far stronger than the ones I had. She was an acquaintance to me. No, a good friend. We were but sad parallels, she and I. Two girls striving for the things we loved. The only difference was that I still had that ability. She… would've never be able to touch a stage again.

"So that's the *voice's* name. Ben."

The name should have hurt me. How much it reminded me of father's middle name. Benjamin.

I stepped onto the bathroom floor greased with water. "Ben…"

A little girl sat wedged between the bathtub and toilet. Her hair was as black as a crow dipped in diesel. Her skin looked moments from turning into a ghost. She might have become one, if I didn't do what I did. Heavy fog misted the bathroom mirrors and floated around like clouds that refused to cry. I felt the steam seep into my bones, growing weary, growing tired of trying. That was how she felt that day. I kneeled beside her thinned body; white dress dampened against her skin. A red blotch rested in the fabric. Two glassy eyes looked up to the ceiling. She wasn't dead. Just fading. If Ben had helped her, then maybe things would have gone differently. He would have been the strength she needed.

Nothing in those eyes wanted to live anymore. It seemed to be that way for a very long time. This frail little thing that looked like me was young, perhaps twelve or thirteen. I blinked at the foggy clouds and knew I could never be this girl. I brushed the locks away from her face, only for my hand to go right through her.

"What is that?"

Her lap was covered in blonde hair. By her feet was a thin wooden thing with a small piece of metal on one end. A violin bow. It only made sense for her to want to go this way.

That child has been gone for years!

Seeing the red stripes around her neck was enough to know what she was doing. Her hands came up again on each side of her neck with the strings tight across the knuckles. Those empty eyes ran tears as she wrapped the homemade nose around her neck. The girl stifled a cough and gave a small whimper. Not from the pain, but a call for someone to come. To stop her before it was too late. Her father was probably off at the bar banging prostitutes while crying out his wife's name, and her dear professor stopped having the eyes of a teacher long ago. If no one was going to come for her, then who would? Ben didn't feel close at all, and I don't blame him. I don't blame any of us. This hadn't been the first time she'd hurt herself just for the marks. At first there were bruises around the wrists. It seemed only natural since all anyone did was look at a pianist's hands. That was what pianists were, nothing but a pair of hands. Once she realized that didn't work, she raised the bruises to her arms. Not even her friend looked at them. The little boy with copper skin. That only made the anger in her grow. Soon the pain wasn't a signal to ask for help, but turned into a twisted pleasure and reminder that this part of her was what she had in control. It was as if she was trying to prove a point. Soon that point would've become a dagger and she really would've been gone.

The day Oliver noticed it under the makeup was the day she was about to break. It was the morning before this moment. She hated Oliver for how long it took him to notice the wounds. By that time, she had become so obsessed with gaining her father's recognition that the bruise was something she felt she deserved. By the time Oliver saw her again, she was gone. It was also during those moments that I could see more, feel more, ready to become something more than a spectator. A *voice.*

The girl banged her feet against the floor while trying to strangle herself with violin hairs. Maybe she thought it would have led her to her mother.

I put a hand on my neck. Something was burning in my throat and made my eyes sore. The mirror was still thickly fogged over so I swiped a palm over it. Wrapped around my neck were red burn marks, tightening like a viper. Stumbling back made me fall right beside the girl. We were both gasping, dying. Then again, when had she really lived a day? This moment seemed to be the most life she ever breathed.

"You need to stop before it's too late!" I dug my nails into my neck in desperation to find the strings strangling me.

I don't want to be here anymore. I don't want to feel anything anymore!

"Then let me! You won't have to worry about any of this!"

The girl kicked at the floor and the strings went tighter. I coughed onto my hand and swore the next one would show blood.

What if he finds me?

"I'll tuck you away and make sure no one ever finds you again!"

And papa? Who will help bring papa back to normal again?

"I will! I promise!" I brushed a hand through her hair and though my hand went through, she smiled like she felt it. Her grip grew looser and I struggled a breath in.

You'll love him?

"I will. I swear I will."

Even if he screams at you?

"I'll take in all of it."

The girl looked at the nothingness I called myself. Veins took the color of poison and spiraled up her face like veins.

One more thing. You have to make my papa proud.

"I'll be all the things he wants us to be. I promise you that. Just let go of the strings!"

I felt her dissociating as my vision began to flicker. The aching sounds of violins were finally starting to disappear and her hands grew limp. Her head rolled against the wall and my eyes were just about to lose all sight. One moment I was simple voice, like Ben. An independent thought that lived inside her head. A companion when she thought she had none. Now I had gone inside of her, put her body on like a glove. But not her mind. Her mind had gone somewhere deep. And with that depth, the memories of any trauma began to sink. I felt her take the past from up to this point and hide it away. Along with the memories, the people that hurt her, and the fire in her personality that made so many fear and love her. With what remained, what did one get? A system. A way of protecting one's self from trauma. With that means an alter by the name of Ben that watched over the body at night. And by day, a perfect alteration of a girl… Not even. A puppet that loved her father and all those around her. Even if he screamed at her till the one note was played right. A person who'd shoulder all the pain till it couldn't be felt no more. There would be someone with no more trauma, as if born new. You would have me. Malory's alter.

I peeled the strings away, feeling myself for who I really was. Many of them had folded under my skin and left bloody creases. I moved her hands—my hands—the world still bending and burning around my throat. The strings slit through my knuckles and left them bloody. With her gone, she took the noise of the strings too. I kept still to catch my breath. The fog in the bathroom was going into my brain. I felt all the memories begin to fade. Soon, I wouldn't remember why I was in here.

Under the bathroom door, darkness loomed. It stretched across the floor and made the door swell. One hand around my throat and the other to help me up, I tread closer to the darkness. The door didn't lead me back to Malory's living room. Rather, to a place tangled with ropes and cables, etched in darkness with a frame of velvet curtains. I grabbed the door, my head still swarming with bees and took a step out. I paced myself, fearing I'd fall over the snaking ropes. I peered behind. Though I had taken only a few steps, the door I came from was gone. All that was left was to go forward.

The wooden floor groaned under me and brought me to the lights of a stage. An orchestra looked to be getting ready, strangely there were only stringed instruments. Someone sat in the middle of the stage, the spotlight shining so brightly on their body that it was hard to distinguish who. The floor stopped moaning under me and grew ghastly cold. Whatever darkness was behind me had caught up and pulled me into its clasp. I reached outward but it was too late, I was back in the bathroom again. Not the one in Malory's house with blood on her mother's violin strings. Itchy hairs pricked my cheeks and golden scissors laid across my legs. My finger looped around a small dark lock beside my ear. My other hand plummeted into the corners of my eyes, kicking out the hard debris of nighttime tears. I rubbed my neck and felt no pain. Just a dry throat.

That's right...

I saw it all last night and the horrors Ben felt. He felt so in control, yet so lost while holding the scissors. So alone. Soon after must have been when I fogged out. I rubbed my swollen eyes and lifted myself from the floor. My hands, my legs, the scattering of hairs, none of this was mine. It never was. The past was never my own, only the fragments of this present I tried to make good. That and the horrific content I found in hitting Malory's father.

Who was I really then? If my purpose were to forget and be what was needed to survive, then now? What would I've become once all the memories came back? I didn't feel the same. My body felt hot, like fire boiling in fire. A shiver scratched down my spine. My breath heaved deeply. I felt my pupils stretching, darting back and forth as the feeling of paranoia came over me. I felt angry.

At least I had my professor—Malory's professor—through the bad and the good, he had always been there. Through every performance, through the moments of me lying on the floor... From almost drowning in the sink by my own father's hands. He was always there; he had always been good. Always.

My head stung and my heart thudded like soldiers of war. Looking back at my reflection, I traced the jagged cuts of thick hair. Ben never had that support. He had always been here with us, somewhere in the brain. In the beginning, looking up was his only job. Staring up at the ceiling at night even if it exhausted the body just so he knew we wouldn't get...

Wouldn't get what?

"Malory?"

Needles stabbed into my skin. My lungs rather than expanding for air, felt like they were sucking inward and crumpling. It wanted to squeeze me, crush me, kill me. I swallowed the thick saliva down. There were three knocks and I stared at my chest. What was this alien reaction? My ribcage wanted to burst out of me, and I pressed my hands against my chest in hopes for it to stop. The beating of rushed blood pumped into my ears and flooded my eyes with static. I almost heard the strings calling me. All this time, they had been warning me.

"Are you going to be done anytime soon? I only have one bathroom you know. Also, why is there dirt all over my floor? Are you doing alright?"

I sucked in my breath and reached for the knob.

Don't do it!

Andre was on the other side, scratching his neck. I heard the skin follicles building up under his nails. He looked up from the knob with his baby blue eyes.

Doesn't have the eyes of a teacher.

"About time. Do you realize how long I was wait…" He paused. At first his mouth drew a straight line. Then it opened wide as if on the verge of a panic attack.

"What did you do there?" Andre's voice had a strange highness.

I stayed put, my hand still pressed to my chest.

"You cut your hair."

"I'll clean up the mess. I-I just felt like doing something new." I pulled the jacket around me, feeling like the strings were still around my neck. Where did the rest of my clothes go?

Go. Go. Go.

"Something new? Is that what all this is? Is that all it's been?" Andre stepped into the bathroom and grabbed a bundle of hair off the floor. "Is that why you were also late last night? Doing something new? Who told you that you could do this?" His nose twitched and looked down at my grime-covered feet.

Tick. Tock. Tick. Tock. Tick. Tock.

"I went to a ballet, remember? That's all it was. And I chose to do this myself. Do I have to ask permission to cut my own hair?" A sense of defense rolled onto my knuckles.

"So that's how it is now. You also gave yourself permission to track mud through my house?" He shook his head and let the pieces of hair fall through his fingers. Andre's neck twitched in a strange way, as if swatting away a bee. "You've been lying to my face. I feel like you don't respect me anymore!"

I was still inside the bathroom. If I closed the door now, I might've been safe inside. But there were no windows to escape.

"I thought I taught you well! I thought you were finally changing! And I thought you would have told me! Not a single thank you!"

Run. Run. Run. RUN!

Too late. Andre was in the bathroom now. Since when had he grown so tall? His slender figure bent over me like a tree's shadow. His blue eyes grew brighter.

The defensiveness grew stronger and I soon knew it to be Ben. It was only a fleeting moment, but he came forward. "What I did with Elizabeth is none of your business."

"Well, how curious! I didn't take you for that type of girl." Andre stepped out of the bathroom, one hand disappearing into his hair. There was the twitch of his neck again. "I'm not talking about last night. I'm talking about Wilton."

Wilton's image flashed in my view, his decrepit body laying over a smear of blood and feces. "You know how he acts. That's why I came here in the first place." I heard the sizzle of Wilton's brain bubbling.

"Enough with that. Let's get real and honest. You in your dress and your perfect—well once perfect hair. Sooo sweeet! To everyone you meet! God, I could eat you!" Andre pivoted on his heels and placed a hand behind my neck. I gritted my teeth, one of his fingers tickled at the baby hairs. "I know the dirt inside of you. The grim you leave behind for others to pick up. What you really are. I knew that spark would one day return and I'm already seeing it now. But I'd never thought you'd be against me. I taught you so well to obey me after all! We were finally getting along!" His nose hovered in between my eyes and I tasted his breath. "Fess up. You can't stay innocent forever. I know you better than you know yourself! I've seen it all!"

Go grab the scissors puppet.

I kept my place. His hand was still on me and he would have reached me before I reached the scissors.

"You won't say it? Oh, fine then!" A wide grin sliced through his face. His fingers played the back of my neck like keys. "A dead man doesn't disappear you know."

A vigorous knocking came at the front door. It rested for a moment before pounding again. Louder, more violent. "For heaven's sake. Who is it now?" Andre let out a breath of annoyance with haste in his step and disappeared into the living room.

My arms locked and so did my legs. Mental roots planted me on the floor. I couldn't find the first step to get free.

A dead man doesn't disappear.

My mind zigzagged to the moment I heard father's last breaths of insanity. His bulging eyes, his screams, my ear pressed against the door, and the noise I thought I heard downstairs.

"Well, speak of the devil." Andre's voice left a chill down my back.

"Where is she? I know she's here!" The other voice said.

"Calm down with that tone of yours."

Quietly stepping away from the bathroom, I went to the entrance of the living room, hiding behind the bend of the wall.

The figure was blocked by Andre's back, his lean body creating a shadowed path in the morning sun.

"I want to see her."

"Well, I'm sorry but she's busy right now."

"As if! She's right there!" A tanned hand revealed itself from Andre's side.

"Oliver?" I came close to both of them. He wore a grey sweater with oil stains around the neck. "What are you doing here?"

"You tell me that!" He stepped closer to me, his hand ready to push Andre if he didn't step to the side. "You've got some explaining to do."

I kept still as I looked at Oliver. He wasn't looking at me but at Andre. "Alone. I wanna talk alone."

"She doesn't need to speak with you. Do you realize how rude you are? It's barely morning and you're here in my home shouting at me and..."

"What are ya her father?" Oliver grabbed my hand and pulled me past Andre. Andre let out a quiet laugh and looked at us. "I doubt I look anything like Wilton right now." Then he gave a simple smile and squeezed my shoulder. "Don't be long."

Oliver let go of my hand and went through the door. Before I followed, Andre's hand tightened. "For your sake."

I couldn't hear half of what Oliver was saying. Most of it started with how things were my fault or how I never really changed. I wanted to cradle my head in my hands as its weight grew. The floor creased underneath my feet from the weight. The cold already started numbing my hands and it was trying to numb my mind too.

"Aren't I right? You went out with her last night, right?"

"I did." I focused on the bag he slipped off his shoulder.

"Well, when I saw her, she was bawling her damn eyes out. Why is it that the only person I could think of doing that was you? Since it was just you two. What makes me the most pissed off was how she was in a rundown hotel by herself late at night. Why is that?" Oliver put a hand to his mouth and looked at the blushing baby's breath garden. "She was naked! Before she told me anything, I swore she was raped."

And now you're gonna kill me!

Dead men don't disappear.

M…M…Malory.

I know the dirt inside of you.

"I-I didn't mean to leave her." Ben's voice rolled up my throat. "It was something she wanted. I thought I did too but…"

"Something she wanted to do?" Oliver took a step back. His foot crunching on the ice sounded like broken glass. "So, you did…You guys? You guys did do…It?"

My eyes grew blurry with Ben's tears and the taste of iron came when he bit down on our tongue. "I'm sorry. I know I'm a coward… You know I'd never hurt Elizabeth. You're right. It was a selfish thing to do… Especially how much I knew Malory cared for you. But I can promise you, it'll never happen again. If she doesn't want to see me anymore, I won't blame her for a second. Even if I wanted to, I doubt it… Especially with what's happening…"

"You what?"

Ben disappeared, leaving the sting of his regret for me to bear. Oliver's hand spread out and raised in the air. I didn't squint, or back away as the air of the slap beat the air. Oliver's hand was an inch from my cheek and froze there. He blinked away the moisture from his eyes. "I should hit you for what you did to her…"

"I deserve it. She shouldn't be mixed up in all my mess and I didn't mean to drag either of you into it." I managed to step forward and his hand flinched beside my cheek. "Oliver, you know I'd never try to hurt her, especially you. I've done so much damage already and I'm finally understanding everything." Andre's image smeared into my mind. This was my only chance.

"If you really want to redeem yourself in any way, you'll stay away from us." Oliver turned to leave but I grabbed his shoulder. He jerked back, I kept my hold. They were shaking with mine. I might've never been able to make up what I've done to Oliver or his sister. But once I go back inside, I don't know what would happen, or if I'd ever come out again.

"I know you're the last person who'd want to help me. But I'm begging you, tell your father that I'm taking his offer. I won't have to interact with any of you, I'll stay out of your life. Tell me the address and I'll drive there myself. And I'll pay for everythi…"

Oliver's hand slapped mine off, his lips recoiled in disgust. "Are you fucking serious? After the shit you did and now you're asking my family for help?"

My muscles pumped in nervous spasms against the cool air. "There's something wrong… If I stay here any longer, I know I'll be in danger."

"In danger of what?" Oliver's eyes lifted from me and froze while looking up.

"It doesn't feel right to be in this house anymore. I'm remembering things I wasn't supposed to. Andre isn't how I thought he used to be. I- I just need you to tell your dad and I need you to call the pol…"

A tight grip bunched up the fabric on my shoulder. I traced the arm and it came behind me. Black curls, that playful uplifting grin.

"Care to continue this inside? It's getting cold out and we can't have you jeopardizing your hands, can we?"

"Oliver please..."

"No, I'm good... I was just about to leave." Oliver turned his back on us and went down the pebbled steps. Before he got to his car, he turned and kept his eyes on me. I pleaded in silence. Finally, he gave a small nod. "Wait for my call. Alright? I'll see you later, Andre."

"What a shame!" Andre shouted. "Oliver it was real nice to see you and I'm so glad you and Malory made up. Tell your mother I said hi."

Andre's grip hadn't left me but traveled to the crook of my neck once Oliver left. We were back inside, and he locked the door behind us. He arched an eyebrow. "What were you talking about with him? You mentioned something about Samuel, his father."

"I was telling him that I wasn't going to take his offer. Of taking the apartment he offered me. It was too much to afford."

"You made the right decision." Andre released me and walked with quiet footsteps. "Because if you left, then you'd be paying more than just money."

"Why did you say that about my father?" The words fell out of my mouth.

"Continuing that conversation? Fine then." He looked out the window before shutting the curtain and turned to me. "When I saw you at my doorsteps asking to stay the night, I knew you chose me over him. I knew you felt the same way as I did! Later I got suspicious. I knew you were lying to me, so

I followed you. At first, I felt so bad for you wandering in the snow alone! You made me so angry when I saw you going back to your house that I was going to take you then and there. And I was! It was so easy to get in! Wilton always leaves the backdoor open. Oh! But when I saw the blood. I thought he hurt you. I do admit I wasn't in the right mind. But that didn't matter to me. I was going to save you! Once I heard you open the room door, I knew there was more to it. If it weren't for this cold, I wonder how long it would have been before someone smelled something." Andre carefully took off his shoes and placed them beside the door. I moved to keep my distance from him.

"Don't be like that… It makes me seem like I'm some horrible monster! I'm always doing the best for you." He sat down on the wooden stool and cocked his head. "You do know that I'm clearly your only real companion in this. You weren't exactly having the sanest mind either. I almost gagged seeing Wilton's dent in head. Not even I would do something like that."

I swallowed the acid rising out of my throat. It stung my gums and singed the tip of my tongue. "You are a monster."

"You're the one that enjoyed killing him." Andre gave me a thoughtful expression. "With how his condition was, no one would have called that self-defense. Especially the police. How careless could you be for leaving him there? What if someone found him?"

I backed away into the living room and found myself pressed against the back of the couch. The Black Beast roared silently beside me. "You're going to report me, aren't you?"

"Oh, not at all! That fucker had what was coming for him!" Andre let out a laugh. "I was so scared of you wanting to go international. I couldn't stand the idea of being away from you. But you really are good at convincing me. The day I found you on the floor soaked was the day I was going to take things into my own hands! He left the door wide open while you were just there! Thank god you didn't look into my duffle bag or I wouldn't know how to explain all that!" Andre stared at the fans while I backed away into the kitchen.

I felt inside the drawer but there was nothing of use. Spoons, forks, no knives.

"What are your little hands grabbing for now? Something dangerous?" Andre got up and paced towards me like a hunter trying to corner a rabbit.

"Stay back!" I ran to the next drawer and was met with the same result.

"You think I'd leave knives around after you pointed a letter opener at me? This is for both our safety; I can assure you."

He came close and I jabbed a fork into his thigh. He didn't do anything at first, just stared in shock. Rather than letting out a scream, he wrapped his arms around me. His embrace was soft, then a violent jolt as he tried to pull me away from the kitchen.

"Let me go!"

"Why must you be so fussy! "Whether you like it or not we are in this together from now on."

I kicked my feet, but no blow could hit since my back was to his chest.

"No more kicking from you. The last one you gave me really ruined my neck!"

A hand clasped over me before I could scream. Andre's hand was too tight for me to bite. "Can't you make this easier on me? Everything I've done is for you! I thought you started seeing that these past years, but I'll make you see it again if I have to! Have you also forgotten that I don't like it when you don't listen!"

The kitchen shrank away and I was pulled into the hallway. The Black Beast grinned at me before disappearing from my view. Twice I almost got free, only for him to grab hold again.

My view had already gone faulty before he tied me up. During the struggle, I twisted to get free and hit my head hard on the doorframe. My body slumped after that as he tied me to a piano's thick limb. I wasn't sure what he tied me with. It was cold and spiraled in clumps like wire. The knots he made felt thick and pinched against the skin of my wrists. I winced from the pain and Andre came close, folding my hair behind my ear. His fingertips were clammy as he hushed softly in my ear. "Hush now. I do admit I was… A little grabby when you were younger. You're so much like her. I promised to be nice if you listened, didn't I? You were so good until now!"

A fire hurled in my lips and I felt Ben grab hold, spitting on Andre's face. I turned my face away to prepare for the hit. He only smiled at me. One of his thumbs wiped the saliva, the other hand went into his pocket and pulled out a small fabric tissue. He spread the spit in the middle and folded it neatly. "Once we're on the same page, then I'll untie you. Until then, think of what you've done."

"Let me go! You can't keep me forever! Someone will hear me!"

"I doubt anyone will hear you. These foam panels did their job before so I'm sure it'll be no different now. And I'm not keeping you here forever! That would be crazy talk! Just until you calm down and we can talk."

He went back to the door and closed it behind him. Before it closed completely, he popped his head out into the dim, his teeth shining at me.

"Where are you going?! Untie me! Andre!"

"Remember how you begged me to go international? Well, now you're having it. I'm packing for our trip to Russia tomorrow. I can't wait to start a new life with you and leave all this behind us. You'll see soon and when you do, you'll thank me. Who knows, maybe you'll do a little thankful gesture for me."

"I'd never go with you! Ever! I'd rather die!" Andre was already gone, and the door gave a hard click.

The breaths started slowly. I tried with everything I had to keep calm, somehow. The room was shrinking and the restraints around me felt like they were getting tighter. The thought of my hands turning blue and falling off began the first set of hitches. A ghost of Andre's hand around my body kept the pace of my heart going faster. Seeing Malory choking herself all those years ago brought me to hysteria. I struggled to breath, as if the wires were now around my neck and I kicked at the floor. Over and over again my eyes went out of focus, readying to plummet down into the abyss.

I can't let us die here like this!

And yet I was. Memories of being pulled in here began to flicker, any closer and they might've as well disappeared. Trauma. Trauma. Trauma. Our mind didn't want to take it and already all the panicked thoughts were sinking away. I'd be damned if I let us smile at that bastard like nothing ever happened. I'd be damned if I let everything slip away again.

Too late, I was already falling away. My last breaths drank up a taste of darkness. I managed to struggle out any strength I had left into a scream. An orchestra already started playing in my head, so I let my hands take the lead and pressed hard against the strings.

CHAPTER TWENTY SIX

PUPPET

SCREAMS RECOILED FROM THE WALLS. I used my wrists as a saw against the wires. My hands were drenched in either sweat or blood, it didn't matter which. What did bother me was the song that had been going on a loop for the past two hours. The sound of a violin crying, the Black Beast pressing against it with malicious intent to drown out its screams. Static played along too but not from my brain. Soft mumbles of what sounded like a pin on an old vinyl. The piano's leg swore to break my back after each blow I gave. The keys echoed from each push. To no avail. On a nearby shelf, a small metronome ticked back and forth. The thing was like water torture that buzzed the center of my forehead. The song grew faster, and I quickened my speed to catch up with the strings.

I grit my teeth tight to stop the screams from scorching my throat. My hands relaxed behind me and I let whatever liquid was on it drip down my fingers. How heavy my head had gotten, I let it slump to the side. I was out of breath, out of stamina, and out of ideas if I had any at all. Instead, I bit my gum and let out a silent cry. The darkness stung my eyes like the sun.

The record player stopped and a door from somewhere opened and closed. A shuffling of feet, a humming, the door unlocking.

"Quiet now?" Andre slithered his head through the door. He closed it behind him and held a small bag in his hand. "You promise to not make any more sounds?"

My head stayed slumped; my energy was nonexistent except from an internal pounding.

"Good." He came close and kneeled. His face filled with dread. "What have you done to your hands!" He placed his on top of mine and I coughed up a cry. "How can you play like this now? You need to take better care of yourself, don't I always tell you that?"

He placed the bag down and touched a finger to my wrist. When he brought his finger back, a smear of blood was on it. I barely felt anything, the pain transformed into a cold numbness. "No more hurting. If I really were terrible then I'd leave you just like that. You poor thing. Give me a moment and I'll be right back." Andre left through the open door. So close to escape, it was maddening.

A minute later and he was back with cotton swabs, a brown bottle of peroxide, and bandage cloth. He closed the door behind him and stared back. "Don't try anything you'll regret. All I'm trying to do is help." The pain was sharp while he unclipped the wires. I winced at each one he broke, as if it were a part of me. Two lightning bolts struck up my arms and to my elbow. I hissed when he dribbled the liquid over my wrists and turned away. I got a glimpse of torn up skin, ragged like a stretched towel.

"Let me go and I won't tell anyone. I swear."

Andre looked confused and cut the bandage with golden scissors. "What do you mean? I did nothing wrong. Who was it that murdered your father? I certainly don't remember doing that. You beat me to it."

"I didn't murder him!"

He tightened the bandages around me and tucked the end into one of its coils. "I don't care what you did with him. All that matters is that you're safe here with me. I'm taking care of you like I always have! I cleaned up all your beautiful hair and mopped the floors. Be patient with me like I am with you." The medical supplies were tucked behind him and he brought forward the bag he brought in earlier. It looked like something to be given to a child for their birthday. Pink tissue spoofed from the top and the brownness of the bag made it seem like some vintage item.

"I'll open it for you so you don't strain your hands." Andre tossed out ruffles of tissue paper and pulled out white silk. He spread it out with his hands. For a moment, I saw Malory's mother. Her beautiful dark hair and porcelain skin. The skies were colored with spring and around her was greenery. An ache filled my bones while I traced the memory of her white dress.

"This didn't fit you well when you were younger. But I know it'll fit perfectly now."

Soft frills on the bottom were crimped with age and the shoulders were dusted in grey. The lace shivered as he swayed it back and forth. So did I. "You'll try it on for me, right?"

Something discolored loomed through the whiteness.

"Right? I'll let you go if you do. Think of this as a pact for trust."

I looked back at the door then at him. "I-I need to change in the bathroom then."

"Shy? Oh, don't worry I won't look. I've watched you grow for so long I'm surprised it still brings you discomfort. Though… I can't help but feel proud of what I shaped. The most perfect student." The dress was left on the bench and Andre turned around.

Damn it.

It took me a while to take the dress, but he didn't mind the wait. A whistle loomed from his lips while tapping his foot. It was the same song as ever, the one that matched the tune in my brain. I finally grabbed the dress to make him stop and he did.

"I really wasn't going to help your father. Why should I for taking your mother away from me? Could you believe it? If she stayed with me then you would have been my daughter." His eyes flickered at me before turning away. "You were there hunched in my garden. So small that the flowers were nearly smuggling you. When you looked at me, I nearly lost my voice. I could tell that you were going to grow up to look like Aria one day. Only with my help of course. Wilton was going to destroy you."

My clothes were already off and the dampness in the room gave me raised hairs. In the back of the dress was a spot of light brown just below the crotch. I gasped, letting it fall to the floor and Andre's face wrinkled. "Do you know how careful I've been to preserve this?" I pulled back as he took it from the floor and dusted it off. Nude and all, but the predator kept his eyes on mine. It felt like the most vulnerable spot on my body and I wanted to shut them tight and hide.

"Don't drop it again."

The dress was on and Andre turned back around. His face filled with a disgusting delight. "I knew it would fit. If only you didn't ruin your hair. I'm sure a wig will do."

Nausea tempted me but I kept my balance.

"I don't see any use tying you up again. Once your hands heal, I can teach you like old times! You're going to love it."

There was nothing in the room to defend myself with. If I had any strength. Andre took the scissors and peroxide that could've easily burned out his eyes. The bench was empty too, only piles of scrap paper that I'm sure wouldn't have left more than an invisible slice in his skin. He took my clothes and folded them into the brown bag. Then he took out a phone that buzzed in his hand. I covered whatever I could with my arms and tucked my head close.

This is the end for me. He's going to hurt me or who knows what if I make him mad...

Tears clouded my vision and I raised a finger to them. But there were no tears. The filmy view covered me up completely.

I won't let this happen again.

Static lingered in my toes and left aches in my knees.

"Ben? Is that you?" I whispered.

I can't keep hiding and doing nothing.

The static was in my ears when it was too late. I barely saw him, just a shadow person that shoved me to the floor. Only the blues in his eyes showed. So close that I felt their tides curl into me.

"I thought we were on good terms." A square light stretched into view. My vision doubled. "What did you actually tell Oliver?"

I winced at the pressure on my wrists. A nimble finger wedged itself in the bandage folds and pressed into me.

"Tell me!" A heavy throb came to the back of my head. Sleepiness rolled over me as my head shoved into the floor again. Andre's palm pressed against my eyes; his grip wanted to crack my skull. "The good thing about being older is that you'll be harder to break this time. I've done so much and yet you don't stop! Seeing things like this leaves me no choice."

How small my body grew under him. After he pulled the screen away was when I began to hyperventilate. Nostalgia, nostalgia, the worst kind of déjà vu. The room twisted and I felt myself being sucked into the floor; a fly smeared against a trap. His knee wedged between my legs. My brain crackled; her body ached. Then everything stopped.

Tick. Tick. Tick.

He never had the eyes of a teacher.

My eyes rolled to the ceiling and the internal orchestra grew. The numbness so welcoming, devouring. I couldn't move my body; I didn't want to. This was all too much, we needed to forget right? Wasn't that my job? Better than to be taken by him. The silver of Andre's button down was coming loose, and my body was being jolted back and forth, one leg up, head pressed firmly down. I sank deeper into the floor, the jaws of night creeping into my memories and smuggling them. I didn't want to forget. Andre would never change. Nothing would... ever change.

Now behind my eyes I fell, hands of darkness pulling me deeper than I'd ever gone. My body that I left slumped began to move. It wasn't fear I felt near, or anger. It was courage.

CHAPTER TWENTY SEVEN

BEN

"NO ONE SEES YOU LIKE I DO. They treat you like you don't exist." Andre's hand rested tight against my eyes. His breath slick like poison. "But I have seen every part of you." Andre stood me up, grip still tight, and slammed me against the piano. I felt nauseous from how hard it was to force myself forward. Once I did it, I felt it. The fear was gone.

"You don't know who I am." I brought one hand behind me. The cool of the piano made me shudder. I kept my mouth tightly closed. Why did I taste mint on my lips?

"Of course, I do." The bastard pressed himself against me and cupped my chin. His other hand rested on the rim of the piano. The phone still glowed in his pocket. I kept breathing in his breath. His words were going to my head.

"I can't trust you. So, for now I'm going to tie you back." He wasn't going to tie us back. I saw it in his eyes and felt it up my leg as his hand disappeared under the dress.

You're a coward.

"No, I'm not!" I slipped my hand onto the piano's lid prop and pulled it down. All the weight fell on Andre's hand and he screamed. I ran to the door and juggled with the knob. It wasn't locked but my sweat refused me to get a proper grip. Blood leaked through the bandages and left the knob feeling like oil. I looked back to Andre as he crumpled against the piano. He kept hissing through his teeth and wrenched his head at me.

"THAT'S IT! I'm done being nice to you!" He wedged his hand out. The joints were peeled backwards, and his fingers pointed towards the ceiling. Purple rose on his knuckles and blood squirted from one lost nail. I had my grip on the knob and closed it behind me. Seconds later, Andre's banging and letting out muffles were drowned out by the foam in the room.

"I'm counting to three! Let me out now!" The thumping continued and I swallowed down my heart as I ran for the door. Each time my bare knees grinded against each other sent dysphoria through me. I didn't dare look at the feminine parts of me.

"One!"

The knob was worse than the last and sweat beaded across my forehead. Puddles of it leaked through the dress.

"Two!"

The voice sounded so much closer.

"When had it been like this?" I pulled at the knob, but it only justified my horror. The locks were inside the house.

"Three."

Andre's knocking stopped as my heart did.

Tick. Tock. Twrack.

A sharp pain came on my neck and my knees hit the floor. My mind was carbonation and seconds from fading. A blurry triangular box rested in Andre's blurry hand. The object kept ticking. It had to be my mind playing tricks. No one's smile ever cut from ear to ear.

Twick. Tack. Tick.

The metronome dropped to the floor and red stained the back of it. My body felt a tug and my hands dragged beside me. Either I was going to pass out or it was darker than night. The grip on my ankle was weak but consistent. The softness of carpet tickled for a moment before being dragged along the cool wood again.

"I'm going to teach you a lesson… Look at what you did to my hand!" Mangled flesh jingled in the corner of my eye. The meat was in shreds and a plump muscle pulsed near the thumb.

Not again, not again.

So sleepy. If I closed my eyes now, I'd never want to wake up. The comfort kept coming to me and my eyes fluttered. My legs still had strength somehow. I curled my toes in his hand and shot them forward. I hit some part of his face. Andre grunted and let go of my left leg. I pushed it into his fucked up hand and he collapsed, cradling it. The world was a kaleidoscope that threatened to stretch me and tear me into fragments. Andre's house was a heartbeat and everything shuddered.

I refuse to let anything ever rip us apart again.

My knee wobbled as I stood and limped away, nearly hitting my chin on the doorframe as I drew close to it. It came open easily and I locked the door behind me. The other side was quiet though I doubt he passed out. Andre was still groaning but I didn't hear any movement. I slumped against the wall as I let the spinning world slow. My mind felt like cracks in a mirror and I saw so many of myself. Small ones, blurred ones, young ones. Some smiled and the others looked away, not noticing my glare on them. My eyes shut until the spinning past. But the cluster was still there, clearer than ever. Ten, twenty Malory's kept their small bodies huddled all around. Some hovered on walls and others trapped themselves in picture frames. I crawled closer to all of them. Two Malory's stood, their paper bodies surrounded in dry pink flowers. Another rested with a pin jammed into her forehead by a crucified Christ figure on the wall. I wanted to step back but only came closer. A Malory of eight or nine was sleeping on her side beside a Malory bending over piano keys with a Griffin's back. Another rested her head with closed eyes to the side, unaware and uncaring of the picture being taken of her. Bile rose a wave to my throat as I viewed this... fucking altar. One of the Polaroids looked not too long ago... Sleeping in the bed Andre let her have. Who knew how many times he'd been taking pictures of us while we were here? Another one was that poor puppet... Malory's alter scrubbing the floors, suds staining her clothes into a painful transparency. A slender picture, the tallest of them all, defiled the word disturbing. This Malory was older, older than she was now. Small crow's feet deepened the corners of her doe eyes and her hair reached down to her stomach in curtains of black. In her hand was a violin.

A grumble still far away, was heard on the other side. I kept my eyes wandering till I met with a violin propped at the edge of the altar's table. It felt like a ghost in my hands and sent a cold wind through my lungs. The hazel wood looked brand new. Polished to perfection and not touched with age, except for the small initials on the side of its arching bottom.

A.H

The bow rested at a desk by a row of closed blinds. An old looking record player's pin hovered over a glossy vinyl. Near the center were Aria's same initials. My fingers didn't hesitate to place the pin down and soon the record spattered to life. Watching the vinyl spin on and on was hypnotizing so I shifted my gaze to the desk. Not much there other than scattered papers and unique pens that didn't belong to this era. On the desk was a small oil lamp and green tipped match sticks.

Andre came hard on the door and I feared it was about to budge. I looked under the bed. Empty. Most of the drawers were filled with piles of papers, sheet music with cursive lettering on it.

"To my dearest love." My voice hitched.

My dearest Aria. I miss your song, the sound of your voice. I play it every day but nothing amounts to hearing you in person. Please come back to Russia. While together, you hid your pregnancy from me. I always knew you to be full of fire. Never deception. Nonetheless, I don't blame you completely. My once dear friend Wilton has always been one for deception. I can only think of you to be a victim. But I won't stop loving you, I can't. I know this sudden marriage of yours is so you can live in America. If I was the one there, I know you would've picked me. Come back to me and to Russia where you belong. I promise you if you do, I won't care whose child is in you but that I will care for her like she is my own and that alone. My affection will never run dry and I will keep playing your song till you come home. Andre Petrov.

This letter was sent three months apart from the next. The writing by the same person, but the cursive looked more rushed.

I understand you don't want to reply. Have I been bugging you? Don't you see the grief I'm going through? Can you not feel it too? Russia has become so ugly without you and I can no longer bear it. I m taking my things and following after you. My love is still so strong that I know I ll find you in no time. When you see me again, you ll finally be able to see things right.

I tore through the unopened seals, each one silencing the bangs on the door. Aria had sent every one of these back.

If I get this letter back, then I ll know all was in vain. That my love was nothing to you and that the things we ve done are all but dust. I will leave you with this. You won t survive this marriage with your condition. You ve always been weak although your mind is the strongest I ve ever known. Stay with him and that ll be gone too. Would you really want your child living with someone like him? Once Wilton destroys you, she will be next.

The love letters burned my fingertips like acid.

They burn!

I quickly took the betrayals and piled them high over the bed. After, I tore down every picture of Malory hanging on the walls, shredding them in my hands. The banging increased as I walked to the desk and took a match. I dropped it three times before I had a grip on it. The matchbox was bent and wouldn't start the match. Not a single spark. After I got the first flair, it died almost instantly.

"If we are gonna be stuck here…" I struck the match again. Nothing.

On the other side, it sounded like something heavy being dragged.

"Then I'll show you. Andre. What kind of fire we really have."

The match was lit and I dangled it over the scraps of paper. It was horrifying, the paper was burning but the flame was going out.

"No, no, no. You can't go out!"

"I'M COMING IN!" There came a sudden thud on the door. Like a boulder crashing against it. I took the lamp, its contents swishing near my fingers and flung it in the center of the bed. A sparkling blue light erupted and came up in a pillar of fire. A blazing tentacle scorched my brow and a flying piece of exploding glass sliced past my lip. The flames shot to the ceiling and blanketed it for a fleeting moment.

It sounded like a gunfire when the doorknob shot out of place. Andre had made his way in with a sledgehammer.

"This was meant for your father. Not you."

I saw the idea of us dying just like Wilton and backed up.

There is no way in fucking hell that I'm letting us die together.

With luck as my guide, I picked up the violin and held it over the thrashing flames. I kept a straight face but felt that any closer, my arm would have turned to steak. He looked at me like I was holding a weapon. The hammer dropped beside him, nearly crushing his toe and both his arms went up. The ruined one dangled. "Hey there. Let that go right on the desk."

"Move past the door bitch." I narrowed the violin, flames lapped at my arm, but I kept my stance.

"Dear god, you really are insane! Fine, fine. See we can be adults!" His voice wavered with the flames as he gave me a clear path. "I promise I won't hurt you anymore. Just put Aria's violin down."

"You mean her mother's violin?" I shook my head and looked back at the violin. I drew it away and Andre let out a breath.

"I knew you'd come to your senses. Now give it..."

"Everything here can go to hell." I cracked the instrument down the middle with my knee and tossed it into the burning soot. Andre gave a piercing cry that shook the room. He rushed towards me and I braced myself, only for him to pass and dig through the flames. I stared in awe at him. Fire crawled up his arms and scorched his velvet sleeves.

"ARIA! ARIA! ARIA!"

I ran, the heat already beginning to follow. The flames had devoured just about everything in the room and was going to eat the entire place soon. Of course, it was still locked, but I tried the front door out of panic. There wasn't a kitchen door. Only one door in this entire damn house. I tried the windows by the piano and desk in the living room. None of them felt like they were ever meant to be opened. I opened his desk and found a crystal paper weight beside a letter opened. I took both and hit the rock against my reflection. The window warped back like thick plastic. Only a thin scratch that barely stretched two inches. I tried again and again but to no avail. Either these things were made of diamond or this body was too weak. If Andre was still alive, he would've gotten to me before I got out the window.

Shit, shit, where can I hide?!

Stupid, that was what I was. My chances might have been greater if I kept at the window or looked for my phone to call for help. Adrenaline took over and rather than using it to my advantage, I went back into the practice room and shut myself in.

"Fuck." There were no windows in here and smoke already started to smell the place up. If I screamed in here, the fire would've melted me before the foam walls.

"Elizabeth." Tears cooled my cheeks. Why had I called her name?

"Elizabeth!" I remembered the ballet, when she took my hand in hers and we danced in the snow. The simple brownness of her eyes and freckles on her skin. She brought me to life… What I hated the most, was how I'd be okay… I'd be okay if she called me Malory again. Whether we kissed, held hands, looked into each other's eyes as I told her I loved her. I would've begged her to call me by that name.

The tears didn't stop pouring when Andre came in and pinned me to the floor. His arms were blackened like wood beginning to char. If she or the whole world turned me away, at least I would've been at peace with myself and know that I tried to make a difference in Malory's life.

He pulled my dress back and flipped me over. My nose hit the ground first. I kept calling her name.

"Elizabeth…" I winced as the dress came up to my waist, my throat itched from the bloody taste in my teeth. He ripped the underwear off and stuffed it in my mouth. I choked on the fabric, but kept calling and calling for her.

"Why would you do that to me? How dare you touch her things!" Andre slammed his thumb right below my Adam's apple. "His sister, huh? So, you really are that type. Don't worry… I'm not too jealous. Soon you'll be calling my name like old times. This time it'll be until you can't breathe anymore. I'll fix you straight."

The sound of his buckle coming loose brought flashes of Malory's father. His body six feet under. I feared her at that moment, the other alter. I thought she was crazy mad. Now it was time to embrace that part of me too. I gripped the letter opener and stabbed it into something blindly. I turned onto my back and found it barely grazed his neck.

"You bitch!" His hand was against mine as I drew it up again. The friction kept the blade in the air, our eyes locked on one another. The fire roared behind us. Sooner or later, his strength was going to beat mine. Until then, the blade shook with furry three inches from his right eye. The wounds in my wrists were opening up and leaked blood to my elbows. I blinked the fog away as the pain swelled me with a ravenous furry. Two inches from his eye. No longer a coward, no longer letting these moments slip away from my hands. At least now I could say that I didn't back away without a fight.

CHAPTER TWENTY EIGHT

PUPPET

I WAS HOME AGAIN, BACK IN THE BATHROOM of Wilton's house. The violin strings laid in my hands and sweat drenched the back of my neck. I held the strings tightly as a reminder while getting up. The room rippled with each footstep. The sink was stained yellow and my hands were stained with reddening crease marks. The bathroom door was wide open, the other side a sea of black. Music was playing again, my mother's music from the other side. Her mother's music. The mirror above the sink seemed larger than before, contorted. It warped reality like a funhouse mirror, blurring and stretching my body. I met my reflection which wore the same black dress before Malory's father attacked me. I went closer to the mirror, how could've that been right? And yet it made all the sense in the world. I touched my reflection and it tried to touch me back. I felt it all on my side. The nose, the cheekbones, my eyes, the fine hairs above my lip. All the mirror's image touched was a smoothed out porcelain face. Not a single feature there except prominent ears. It didn't have a face. It didn't have an identity. The thing was only a shallow replacement. An imposter. I looked away from the lie and went for the door.

The sound of darkness was that of wood. It clacked like heels under my bare feet. Something slithered under me in its blinding sea, wrapping around my foot and trying to stop me. The invisible rope crawled up and coiled around my head. It fogged my mind and pulled away moments from me. Hitting Wilton after being whipped from behind. The moment of gritting my teeth as I sawed away the wire with my wrists. Finding out how I came into this world, Malory's attempts to kill herself. The first step of independence she would've ever had in her life. My brain wanted to split as I tried to pull it away. But the snake kept whispering pretty fables. There wasn't only one of these memory snatchers. Two or three would try to pull me back. Sometimes a dozen strangling my neck and toppling me to the floor. Their tails rattled like a fast-paced metronome and had hands rather than serpent faces. Malory was down here somewhere, she was safe. If I had let everything consume me, then everything would've gone away.

Maybe it's better this way.

I lessened my hold on the invisible body. It slithered past my wrist and wrapped around my neck.

I should stay here forever. Andre will never find us if we just forget and hide.

Right as the thing slithered to my head, the strings came in screaming voices. They joggled the ground and shook my thoughts back into place.

"It's her. Malory."

Ben's voice came forth too. At first. I thought he was calling to me. He was screaming her name instead.

ELIZABTH!

He was out there by himself, fighting for us. If I'd let this all go, everything would've been wasted. I pulled it away and it snapped off my body like elastic.

The music grew louder. It was the only thing I knew that headed me in the right direction. My ears pressurized as if submerged in water and wanted to pop. A sudden flash blinded me, and I was surrounded in yellow. Stage lights speckled the ceiling and the darkness turned into a stage. Pieces of unknown still lingered as shadows casted a circle around the stage. They had human bodies and propped a violin under their foggy chins.

There were at least fifteen and synchronized the same tune. A white object took the center of the stage. In quietude, it bundled itself together and hung its head low. My vision pulsed when I tried to come closer, and the shadow players' volume went into crescendo. Though they had no eyes, I knew their attention was on me.

What rested in the center was a girl with hands over her ears. A red stain folded between her legs. I touched myself to make sure nothing was there. Her body kept still but her lips quivered under her hair.

"No one ever heard anything." Her voice didn't belong to a little girl. It rasped and gargled, like her lungs were too small to take in any air. The voice belonged to an adult, someone my age. "It hasn't stopped since I came."

I kneeled beside her and fell back when she lifted her face up. "You said it would stop but nothing has changed! I can still see and hear everything!" She blinked through clear pus that trickled out her eye. "I've been suffering here all alone!"

The shadow players strung a screaming string and the girl covered her ears again. Her voice wavered. "This was mommy's favorite. She used to play it all the time on her violin. But you didn't know that, did you? You're not me! You got to live so many years in a fantasy. Did you really think that would have made professor stop hurting me?"

"I'm so sorry. Malory, I thought, I just thought… If I could let this body live without memories of everything… Then it might have become true." I tasted the salt trickle down my lips. To no longer live as my own person. Since when had any of us been able to live since that day? Playing out a fable as puppets tied on the strings of two masters.

"You might've been able to convince me when I was little. Now look at our life! I should have finished the job in the bathroom!"

The violins raged off into absurd heights. The noises were not only strings, a piano's voice sounded like a cat running over keys. The stage floor was being pounded by an invisible fist. It shook everything and the floors began to crack. It felt like I was too.

LET ME IN!

"You're right!" I grabbed her wrists. Before, I passed right through her like she was the ghost. Now, it looked like my hands were the ones fading. I gripped tighter. "You were right! I shouldn't have forgotten! But we were all little back then. weren't we?! We didn't know this would've happened right?"

The girl looked at our hands, her head still low. "I should have been stronger. I could have stopped him…"

"No, you wouldn't have. Because that wasn't your job. You were a kid and still are!" I looked away from my fading hands and put her cheek into my hand.

"M-Maybe he thought I was leading him on. I should have told papa. He would have saved us. You hurt him!"

"You were a victim. And you couldn't take something so terrible. No one blames you for that! Your father wasn't helping you and your mother was gone. I know how much you loved him, but he always knew, you knew that didn't you?"

"Stop that! Papa did nothing wrong!"

"Exactly! He did nothing Malory and because of that you were hurt over and over again by Andre!" Malory's hand sank into mine, her body felt as cold as that last day.

OPEN THE DOOR NOW!

"I know everything now. I'm so sorry you had to suffer here by yourself. But you aren't alone. Ben's out there right now making sure we are all okay."

The girl laughed through her teeth and the shadows looked upon her. "I'm broken."

"Who isn't?" I blinked hard. My view was feeling transparent. Everything was fading into everything and my hands looked like a stencil of what they once were.

"We are going to get out of this. Together. Look at me."

Malory in all her frailness lifted her head. Her eye was bruised badly… The strings still had their marks on her neck, and Andre's fingerprints were pressed into her shoulders. She saw through my eyes and I saw through hers. "Okay. Let's leave."

The last string played and the floor dropped down like sagging paper. We both fell through and kept holding onto each other. I brought her closer to me as the kaleidoscope of memories stretched around us. Lights shined on us and flickered rainbows in her eyes. The brightness shot sabers through my hands, through my chest. I blinked at the unbearable aura and watched as my hands completely disappeared. Though I couldn't see them, I still felt my hold on her. Panic rose to my throat with the thought of disappearing. I was close to letting her go and freeing myself. Freeing myself for what? For the house I was trapped in? For the man that betrayed and molested a young girl? For the life that literally tore her mind apart? I pulled myself closer to Malory, our bodies flying downward, headfirst into the light. My vision was lost for a moment. I opened my eyes and looked down at the red mark flapping against my legs, our legs. Trauma was the thing that tore her apart. Now it was the thing bringing us back together.

The fall continued but the lights began to die down. A shroud of white surrounded our bodies protectively. At first I thought it was the wind, but the hum was too comforting. The woman's skin bloomed a soft pink around her lips. She looked younger; her hair not yet brittle from age.

"Malory… My sweet Malory." The mother rocked the child back and forth, her face glistening with sweat. Each breath Aria gave, her lungs crackled up into her throat. A young man was beside her. He wore a brown coat that looked unused, unsoiled by addiction.

"Look at her hands! Look how wide she stretches them!" The man cupped the child's fingers in his. "Our baby girl! You're going to be something great someday."

The mother laughed sweetly, and the memory went away. A soft pink and blue blurred around us. Time was slowing, or at least it felt like it was. These scenes I saw, lasted but a second. I felt inside of them, as if these memories that were once hers alone, were now mine. The warm spring breeze danced across Malory's cheeks. Her seven year old hands were occupied with the flowers that swept Andre's house like cancer. She looked at her father while he pleaded to Andre. She wasn't sure what it was, only hearing of money and promises. Malory came up to the two right as her father was about to leave. It looked like his addiction hadn't started yet. A water bottle was crumpled in his hand. Malory followed her father and looked back at the house. Back then, it reminded her of a fairy cottage, and the man looking back at her resembled an elf. Since when had he stopped looking at her with the eyes of a teacher? Perhaps never. Maybe he already knew what he was going to do the moment he saw her. The moment he smiled and made a deal with her father.

"I'll pay for the house. All I want is to see your daughter again. You'll drop her off to me every week. Do we have a deal?"

"What are you going to do?" Wilton's hand held onto Malory's.

"Just piano lessons. What would it matter to you anyway? Unless it does. Does it?"

"You'll pay all the loans."

"Yes. All of it." Andre smiled kindly at the child.

Wilton squeezed onto Malory's hand for a moment. "Then… Nothing else matters."

"Papa, is he your friend?"

"Yes, we are great friends. Best friends. I knew your mommy very well." Andre scooped her up in his arms.

"Mister you know about my mama? What was she like?" The girl asked excitedly.

"You don't remember? Well! She looked like you."

Wilton stood from behind, too much of a coward to take back his word.

"How come?" The girl smiled but looked back at her father.

"I see it in your eyes. I know you're capable of that fire your mommy once had. With my help, I'll make that grow so you're just like her one day. Wouldn't that be great, Wilton?"

The memory shattered away as I felt us being dragged into another one. My eyes, how tired I was getting. How scary the thought was… That I was feeling less and less of myself. Malory seemed so happy when given the dress. Andre had always given her flowers even after the day he took hers from her. As if it was a reminder. Red blood on the back of the dress. He played her mother's soundtrack to block out the screams. The strings grew louder, her muffles softer. Her face bumped against the wall over and over again. The piano bench was rocking with Andre's body while hers was being squeezed under him. He was calling a woman's name, not the girls. There must have been a time when the headboard knocked her out. The next moment she was in her teacher's arms, being carried back to Wilton. He was holding a bottle now and rather than asking what happened to his daughter he said, "Does that cover the first house payment?"

Once the memory faded, the crash came hard. The bed felt like cement and my wrists were coiled with rope. My body was cracking into two from the pressure in my stomach. I cried, I screamed, we thrashed our heads around.

Tick. Tock. Tick. Tock. Tick.

"Keep looking. Keep looking until you have the tempo memorized. Only then will I let you go." Andre's voice was retched. Two and fro went to the blade in front of me. From one side of the triangle to the other. "You feel the tempo in your body too, don't you? Do you feel the tempo moving inside of you?"

My stomach felt like it was going to burst. I wanted to cross my legs to stop the urge to urinate on the bed sheets.

"You played too fast last night. I can't accept my student playing so rushed." I bit my lip and he let out a breath. He kept invading me, even after turning off the metronome. "Say it. Let me hear the tempo. fifty-four exactly."

The small heartbeat rang so loud in this child's body. So loud… it was all she thought about and all I heard. She counted her blessings and sang to the beat of her heart.

"Tick. T-Tick. Tick. Tick. Tick. Tick. Tick." I felt her voice waver and wait for someone to protect her. Ben was always near her since the trauma began. Sometimes he'd talk to her or come out at night when she thought the shadows were going to get her. He was unable to face the tortures and hid instead.

It was intoxicating, how much rage was one girl able to hold? Her body surged with it and blood boiled in my ears. On the stage she was small, feeble-looking. Malory's hands were behind her, clutched so tightly that her nails were bloody. I feared her anger and how much it reminded me of hurting Wilton. Rather than forgetting, she took it all in and kept replaying those memories over and over again—a permanent mark that would've never left her mind—no matter how much I tried to block it all away. Even now, I felt it swarm into me, every part of her, everything that made her who she was now. Any aspect of what I was or who I thought I was, kept melting, diluting; her everything now beginning to feel like my everything.

In that moment, the ropes were gone, the pain had ceased. Andre left our body and I took that chance to turn around on my back. Reality came back as a glimmer of silver in my hand, her hand. Blood waterfalled when Andre's eye was struck. It didn't pop, but folded into itself like lips. The blade was pulled back and Andre fell hard onto his broken hand.

"I'm back."

Malory brought a knee into him and more blood oozed out of his eye. Her body felt hot as she got up. Her mother's dress was beginning to catch fire. She cocked her head in bewilderment then let a smile pass her lips. She tore the fabric away and balled it into her hands. Fire scorched her fingertips. She didn't seem to feel the pain. I didn't either. In fact, if things kept going as they were, I wouldn't be able to feel anything anymore. I was okay with that. For the price of me becoming one with her, for the price of having the same goal, we could now destroy the beast.

Malory took a handful of Andre's lovely hair and lifted his head off the ground. Was he crying? No, it was only puss. She forced the flaming cloth into his mouth and used another hand to keep his jaw shut.

"Do you like it?! You always loved this dress and how I wore it!" Malory cackled and I couldn't help but laugh along with her. "You craved it. Now you can EAT IT!"

Andre coughed and gargled; sparks flew from his mouth.

"Hell was never down there. It's always been here. Now you can live in it forever!" Malory dropped his head and it slumped onto the floor. The fire lashed at us and she took a step back. The foams on the walls looked like melting faces. She treaded through the flames, the wood hot on her toes. The hallway had turned to soot, and parts of the ceiling were beginning to fall apart. We coughed on the smoke and ducked under a wooden beam. Andre left the hammer there, flames seconds from touching it. Malory took it and dragged it behind her. The Black Beast crackled as its legs charred red. In the background, her mother's recording was warping from the heat. She came close to the piano, how small it looked to us. It was no longer a beast, just a warping piano. I lifted the hammer along with her and swung it into the piano's side. Fire was sleeping in its body and a flash of bright red and yellow blasted out from it. The heat came too close to our face. It felt welcoming. We lifted the scorching bench and threw it against the wall of flames. We smashed the piano again and again until it was only her will swinging the hammer. I blinked away from the fog and tried to take control of one of her hands. All I managed was the twitch of a pinky. A moment later and I couldn't do that. I was back to being a spectator. Soon, not even that.

"*I don't want to disappear yet.*"

"I can feel you. More stronger than ever. More together than ever." Malory's voice was a calm echo in the chaos. She put a hand over her heart and closed her eyes. "You aren't going to disappear. You coming together with me, isn't that what you wanted? Isn't that why you took my hand to save me?"

"*You're right.*" I felt the darkness sinking into me, felt myself sinking into her. Malory let out a deep breath, it felt like a part of me had done it too.

"You feel that? See? You're always going to be here with me just as you always have."

From the fire, something slugged out the hallway. The man dragged himself on his legs, a smile on his face. No, it wasn't a smile. The skin had melted off his cheeks, exposing bone. Fire left their marks on his legs. He didn't seem to notice. Maybe he was already dead. Malory looked down at the man and we felt no pity. He grabbed her ankle, his grip like air. Malory was right. How much we have grown from this, and how much more once I was one with him.

Andre gargled through his teeth, the fabric still in his mouth. His eye was crusted over and swollen.

"Together?"

Together.

I lifted the hammer up and brought it on his back. Puffs of black smoke left his lips. The hammer dropped from my hands and laid askew on his back. He stopped moving and so did I. Malory fell on her back and sat up. Her breath was dry and labored from the thick air. It was during these last moments that I saw Malory turn her head up to the red sky. Flames overlapped the ceiling and boulders began crashing down. There it came up from her lips. A giggle swept out and crackled with the flames. Tears fell from her eyes, beading her lashes with their pearls. The fire laughed with Malory as the last bits of me became one with her.

"Finally… Finally… Do you hear that?" In her soot-soaked dress, her cut up wrists, she laughed and laughed until she could barely breathe and choked on her tears. Her head fell into her hands and her body shook while blue and red flickered out the windows. The single piece of me felt her relief and I shared one last tear with her.

"After all these years of torture…"

After all these years…
"The strings have finally stopped."

EPILOGUE

MALORY

IT ALL BEGAN WITH A SINGLE NOTE, plucking the voice out of my seven year old throat. I took a slow breath in. Synthetic air filled my lungs and lingered down my throat. With closed eyes, I let my ears take control. The shadowy conductor tousled his hands back and forth. My audience rose before I finished. Of course they did. They all loved me! Feeling the pressure of keys sink down under my fingers… Hearing the sound of invisible notes continuing to form and disappear around me. The lights above me struck fire against my skin and I took in their scorching warmth. I danced my fingers on air, the Black Coward bending with each press of the pedal. I could've crushed the thing at any moment if I wanted. As I stood, there he was in all his glory and love.

"Papa." I echoed.

His skin was the color of old milk and his eyes turned up as if looking at heaven. He remained seated as the shadows applauded me. I wiped away the tears quickly. He always taught me to be strong, to never cry… I don't think he would've ever been able to see these tears, even if I wanted him to. That was okay, this all was. Being in this space alone, he was finally able to see me perform. I used to be angry with the other me, hated her even. Now that she was with me, I understood her a little more and she the same with me. At least here… I had papa all to myself.

The clapping erupted near my ears and I blinked my fantasy away. A stupid looking boy clapped his walrus hands at me. Drool dangled off his mouth and one of his slippers were gone. Disgusting. I turned away to something more pretty. I'd never seen trees so vibrant before. Their lime leaves brushed into thick bundles while painted with a slight yellow from the over-saturated sun. Had walls always been this lifeless? The chilled exterior, so bodiless, flat-chested. Yet my fingers couldn't seem to stop touching the little grains across its surface.

"Ben would have loved to stare at this ceiling. How boring it must have been for him all those years." The perfectly painted trees spiraled from the walls above my head. Flat metallic hummingbirds fled in place from a prancing dog. Its teeth were as square and white as a human's.

Was skin always this damp? A single sweep across my cheek and they came back shined with natural oils. It had been so long, too long. The last thing I remembered before coming here all those months ago, was being carried out by men in yellow. My body was laid on a stretcher while being wheeled into the ambulance. On the way to the hospital, somebody was holding my hand. It felt like my father's, but it was much too veiny for that. The young man kept calling my name and asking so many questions.

Tick. Tick. Tick.

Despite it all, how I loved my stay. Except for the young boy who wandered the halls, tapping his fingers on his teeth. If only his tapping was louder. That much more to break his teeth and quiet him for good. I would have rather listened to the clock than him. Its metronomic clink reminded me of my teacher. That older girl with torn off calluses might have swallowed the batteries again, letting her guts boil and melt. The nurses had to remove all of them.

"I wonder if hell made his burnt skin any darker."

There was no such thing as time here. The same as the place I hid away in. Only a railway of memories on the stage. Each shadowed violinist butchering the song my mama used to play, the one that used to muffle my screams. I would have been fine at first after cutting my arms open with a blade and strangling myself with her violin hairs. Now I was glad that the *voice* saved me. Did she really back then? It took my anger to rise up in her… Trying to call her with my symphony of strings just so she would've had the guts to shank that child molester.

I didn't seem to feel anything at first when I arrived here. The damage done to my body made me swear I was going to die. The room with nothing but cotton walls and itchy straps across my arms. Now that was something so terribly boring. There were no windows there just like there were none when I was taught to ride him and see how long I could've held my breath while he strangled me. One, two, three, he would say! I thrashed in that room for hours, until a nurse put a strange shot in me. During those days, weeks, however long, I was left to wander in my mind and replay flashes of the house on fire. No strange children to look at. No reporters, no police with disturbed faces. Or nurses that pretended to give a crap about us. About me. It felt so good to be able to say that word again. Me. Just me. Oh, and an occasional depressed wave of Ben. I saw his dreams sometimes which made me sick! Why would he keep dreaming of the girl that raped him?

They don't let me hide pills in this place. I thought I was clever enough to hide them in my cheek or at the cliff of my throat. Boy did they sure check! I couldn't understand the effort. Most certainly they were filled with sugar and baking soda.

I continued to stare at the battered fingered girl. Already she had chosen a freshly healed pinky for the taking. Then I looked at the boy, a dry wound in the middle of his forehead. Observing everyone for the many sun rises I had been here, they all seemed much more sane in the beginning. The girl's skin picking was a small habit and she often talked with me. Perhaps it really was the pills? Or the fact that you could only talk to the walls in your room for passing hours of the day. It really was quite depressing. Lucky for me! I cheated the system.

"Ben? Can you hear me?" I smiled. He hadn't shown up much after we were rescued from Andre's home. Occasionally he took over the body at night. Once he realized there was nothing left to protect, he kind of stayed back behind.

The police never found papa's body. I never told them what I did to Andre and no one ever found the collection of photographs he took of me. Ben burned all of those and Andre's body was almost indistinguishable. If the fire ate him whole, then maybe I could have escaped this place. They did find his back though cracked in two. Maybe it wasn't whether they found his body or not, but my rambling of nonsense and telling about people that lived inside of me. I guess that was better than them thinking I was a tiny bipolar bludgeoner. I looked down at my stomach. Speaking of tiny, when was the last time I ate?

A visitor was coming through the barricaded glass door. Visitors were allowed here, though I wasn't sure why. Wouldn't they fear getting their necks ripped out because we were apparently so crazy? The crank of metal gears was enough to bump my body up from its straight posture I was taught to do. The nurse in plain white clothes let the visitor in. She had short curly hair, plump hazel cheeks, a curvy body with a contrasting pair of skinny useless legs. Her simple nails rested in her lap as a boy pushed her from behind. My cheeks grew hot and my stomach got queasy.

Oliver! Oliver! How I missed Oliver! How long had it been since I'd seen him in his large shoes and small chubby body? Once a child, now much more than a man. Since I was allowed visits, they came to visit me weekly, giving Ben the only reason to come forth. I didn't restrain him, and I'd never felt a stronger happiness emitted from him. Somehow, it was something greater than my love for papa. Still though, it was strange how he wanted to talk with someone who hurt him so badly. They did make up… In the beginning, Oliver's sister looked afraid to speak with Ben, like he was some monster. Asking for him is the first thing she does now.

Oliver brought time with him in the form of his shorter hair, bigger form, and two hooked creases around his lips. He looked so tired. I squeezed my hands together nervously. In the end, I was sorry for what I said to him last. But how long I tried to make him notice me and everything Andre and papa did to me. Sometimes it made me laugh, how contradicting I'd be. I'd never betray father, yet how desperate I became. His scoldings were becoming too much for me to bear. Sometimes I hated myself for still loving him.

"Hey there!" Elizabeth waved. I kept my eyes on Oliver. They came close to the table I always sat at, the seat that felt the closest to a piano bench.

"It's nice to see you again." I placed my hands on my lap, as if ready to begin my performance that would've only happened in my head. If I did have the chance again, my wrists were far too damaged and weak. I stared down at Elizabeth's legs and looked back at my hands.

Huh.

Oliver sat beside me. A couple of weeks ago, he wouldn't come close. I tried not to linger on that thought for too long, or I might've felt ashamed. Although he was close, he looked into my eyes like a stranger. The witch doctors let him in on the juicy details of my 'mental illness' and he hasn't looked at me the same since we were little. It hurt, but it would've hurt more if I never got to see him again.

"Hi uh… um…" Elizabeth fumbled with her hands. She looked awkward. It usually was in the beginning, not knowing who was in front. I wasn't sure what made distinguishing Ben and I so difficult. He loved her, I clearly didn't. Elizabeth also seemed to adjust more than Oliver so I'll give her that.

"Is Ben here? Oh sorry. Did that sound rude?"

"Nope." I laughed. Ben was usually out by now, but I restrained myself. He and Oliver's sister would get so into talking that I'd be too ashamed to intervene. Since I got here, I never had the chance to speak out with Oliver.

"Oh… How is Ben then?" Oliver's sister looked at me with her cute eyes, and I caught my eyes traveling to her lips. I shuddered. Boy, did Ben sure know how to jump in my skin. I felt him wanting to speak and take her in his arms. His energy throbbed in between my legs and blurred my vision. I could've let him see her. I know it wouldn't have happened, but feeling someone take control again gave me fear that the latch to my door would close again. I deserved to speak to Oliver. I deserved it! I didn't mean to be cruel to Ben, but it had been far too long. I closed my eyes for a moment.

Is it okay if I could talk with Oliver this time? I know you want to see Elizabeth but…

I-I'm sorry. I always get so excited to see her. What about if I give her a quick hi and bye? After that I'll be out of your hair. I get to go out next week though, alright? Deal?

My knee jiggled up and down…

Fine. Deal. Also… Thank you for fending off Andre. It was really brave of you.

Hey, that's why I'm here. I hate it but this is my body too. And it wasn't just me. She helped a lot too. Do you think she can at least still see? Or maybe hear us?

I'm not really sure. The last moments I heard from her made it feel like she was disappearing. At the same time, it felt like she became one with me.

I feel bad for calling her those names. She was only trying to do the best for us.

I've said some nasty things to her too. But I think we are all past that drama now, right? I mean look at us. Sure, we are here, but we made it, didn't we?

I let myself sink back and saw a flash of Ben as he stepped forward. He was such a handsome man. His smile was kind and I felt the hurt in his eyes as I realized that Elizabeth would never be able to see him like this.

Yeah. I guess so. I'll just take the spotlight for a few minutes. I won't be long.

Take your time.

I let myself relax in the darkness of my mind and listened. That was all I'd be able to do until I could go back out again.

"Hey, it's me." Ben spoke.

"Ben! It's been awhile! How are you?" Elizabeth's eyes lit up and she cupped his hands in hers. She let go after glancing at her brother. I couldn't tell Oliver's expression. He turned away too fast.

"It's only been a week and I won't be spending a lot of time out right now. I've been too selfish with time these past few weeks so Malory will be out in a bit. I just wanted to say hi."

"I want to take you out again soon. Will they let you?" Elizabeth's focused on a passing nurse.

"Eventually. Probably. I can't make any guarantees though. The way they found me gives me a hunch that I won't be getting out just yet."

"He had everything that was coming to him. I don't get why the victim has to be here. It makes no sense to me…"

"Is it weird?"

"What is?"

"Knowing that I'm like this… Aren't you embarrassed? Scared? Especially knowing what you know."

"I'm glad I know and I'm not ashamed. You shouldn't be either. If I didn't, I really would have kept wondering about our time at the hotel. You really put up with a lot because of me. I'm sorry for not being more understanding sooner."

Ben looked around our home, these new living conditions and the people that would've continued to become more mad around us. I wished to never see any new faces. No one deserved to live out a cruel life, only for this to be their next destination.

"No more apologizing. I'll let you know the moment they let me have more freedom." Ben sounded rushed and looked at Oliver. Why was I feeling these emotions of his? Guilt? Shame? Wasn't he happy to see Elizabeth?

"You're a good brother you know that? You always seem to put your sister first. She really wants to talk with you so I'm gonna go for now. I'll see you soon Elizabeth."

Before Elizabeth could speak, I felt an almost forceful shove as I was brought forth again. My ears buzzed and I felt dizzy from the burst of reality. Ben didn't bother to stay close. He went really far away, as if running away. A second or two later and I couldn't detect him anymore.

"He just left." I rubbed my forehead. "He isn't wrong though. I have been wanting to speak with Oliver. I guess he is finally giving me that chance. Is it okay if I speak with him alone though?"

"S-sure…" Elizabeth put on a big smile. I knew it was fake, I saw the disappointment in her eyes. "I'll wait in the hall okay?" She turned to her brother and squeezed my shoulder softly. She was looking at Ben not me. "Bye Ben. It's nice to see you again, Same to you Malory. I'll see you later."

"It's so nice to finally meet you." I smiled at her, and she gave a genuine one back. "I'll see you next week. Bye!"

Minutes passed, the clock grew louder and that girl biting her nails shuffled in the background. Oliver hadn't turned back to look at me and I kept my eyes on the painted trees. He watched his sister leave. Maybe he wanted to go too… I kept shivering; it took everything in me not to cry. If father was never in debt, if Andre treated me like his student, if I never broke apart, if I never put on my mother's dress, I might've been kissing this boy under a real blooming tree right now. I could've been holding his hand or playing a duet with him. I could've been out of this place having lunch with his family. I would've been showing off my skills to his mother. If I could've gone back in time, I would have put out the fire in me long ago and told him how I really felt. That I was the one who admired him before he noticed me.

I finally looked at him, his eyes resting towards the floor. I barely heard my own voice when I spoke. "I'm sorry for slapping you."

I didn't expect him to smile or let out that sad laugh. A knife twisted into my chest when he looked at me and patted my hand. I wanted to hold his in mine but saw the image of Elizabeth and Ben.

"I've forgiven you for that a while ago."

"Then why haven't you talked with me?" The words I withheld forever flooded out of me. "I've been here for months. It hurts you know…"

"I felt like I didn't have the right to speak with you. I saw all the red flags. Yet my stupid stubborn self didn't want to help you. I felt like you deserved it. Now look at you… If only I did something sooner." He peered at me; his eyes glossy. The way he arched his eyebrows low… I felt their sting.

"What do you mean? I'm perfectly fine! Well, except for my crappy hands. I know you were the one that called the police. I'm glad she asked you for help." I leaned closer to him.

"Is she… Gone? That other girl or whoever…"

"Oh no! She's kind of becoming a part of me. Her thoughts are mine and mine are hers."

"I see." He clearly didn't but that was okay.

"Why? Do you miss her?"

That question seemed to catch him off guard. I watched his cheeks carefully, waiting for them to change color. "She was kind to me… But she never did seem like you. I can finally see that now. No one I know has spunk like you…"

I hope he didn't hear my deep sigh. I let the tension slip from my shoulders and rested my head on a propped arm.

"So, it really is you right now?"

"That apology wasn't enough to know?" Well that hurt, but I didn't blame him for being confused.

"I'm sorry. I'm tryin to get used to this illness. Multiple personality dis… no that's not it. Dissociative identity or whatever the nurse said it w…"

"This isn't an illness. Ben isn't a disease, she isn't either." I pulled myself away. "We are all just trying to survive, even if it means splitting apart to feel more together in this mad world."

"Sorry that's not how I-I meant it to sound."

"It's fine. I get it." I waved my hand, not wanting to get deeper into it. My eyes looked to Oliver for confirmation. Judging by how he bowed his head in what looked like shame, his fingers pattering invisible keys on his thighs…

"Trauma does crazy stuff, sometimes it makes the people it hurts crazier. It's stupid and unfair."

Oliver took my hand into his. I should've felt flushed, embarrassed silly. He didn't look into my eyes, trying to search for something or someone. At this moment, I knew he was looking at me, only me. I felt all the years backpedal, rewinding to a place where terrible things and terrible people never existed. All I saw was he and I, two grownup kids living in an unfucked up world.

"Do you finally recognize me now?" I fought a smile through the tears, and he held my hands tighter. He leaned his forehead on mine and I finally shed a tear for something that wasn't pain. I never thought I'd see my best friend again.

"Yeah… Malory, it's been a while."

ACKNOWLEDGEMENTS

I never expected to feel this much love towards my book and I'm grateful to have so many people I want to thank.

The editing process seemed scary at first until I met Johanna Petronella. Her enthusiasm and love towards my novel really gave comfort when experiencing the stress of self publishing for the first time. Close to the time I found her, I had the luck of finding Dragan Bilic. His formatting skills really were the elements my book needed to feel more whole. His kindness and patience in answering all my jumbled questions will always be remembered with much thanks. Since I am also an artist, it was such a nerve wracking thing to be thinking about my book's cover. Anamaria Stefan managed to get rid of the stress and brought my vision to life with her wonderful creativity.

And oh goodness. When I created my little donation page, I didn't expect to receive much or anything at all. Seeing the love and support from all of you donating really was astounding. I wish I could meet every single one of you someday and shake your hand. Now that would be an honor.

My beautiful betas, it has been such an exciting experience to share my book with you. You guys continued to ask for each new chapter and read at a devilish speed. The support and hype you have shown towards this little baby of mine is more than I would have ever asked.

I also want to thank my beloved boyfriend. For many years, my days and emotions felt like blank slates. You got rid of the robot side of me and taught me that it was okay to be vulnerable and to have feelings rather than stashing them away into the void. You helped me become human and for that, I will never stop loving you.

I can imagine how nervous my parents must've felt when I decided to do writing as my career. Once I began showing you that my book really was going to be out into the word, you cheered me on with this new path and expressed how proud you were with our relatives. Can't help but feel a little special for that.

Once again, thank you everyone. Now it's time for me to hop onto my next book!